Falling Girl

R. Allen Chappell

Dedication

Falling Girl, the tenth book in the Navajo Nation Mystery series is dedicated to those readers who have so faithfully supported this series from the beginning. Their comments and suggestions provided the inspiration for this book.

And dedicated to those *Diné* who follow the Beauty Way. While their numbers may be fewer each year, they remain the well from which these stories flow. There is no reckoning how many are left who understand the old ways or cling to the ancient traditions, but to them I say, *A-hah-la'nih.*

Acknowledgments

Again, many sincere thanks to those Navajo friends and classmates who still provide "grist for the mill." Their insight into Navajo thought and reservation life helped fuel a lifelong interest in the culture, one I once only observed from the other side of the fence.

Author's Note

In the back pages, you will find a small glossary of Navajo words and terms used in this story, the spelling of which may vary somewhat, depending on which expert opinion is referenced.

Table of Contents

1

Missing

Charlie Yazzie looked up from a stack of reports to see Thomas Begay slouched in the doorway and knew instantly his friend was in a foul mood. The man had somehow managed to circumvent the receptionist making his way unchallenged to Charlie's office. While this wasn't the first time, the Investigator never ceased to be amazed at the man's audacity. Putting down his pen, he sighed and fixed Thomas with a speculative gaze.

"What? There wasn't anyone on duty at the front desk?"

Thomas let his eyes wander toward the ceiling as he considered the question. "On duty? No… but there *was* someone sitting there."

Charlie ignored this droll attempt at humor, saying, "So, I guess you don't recall our talk about how we're tightening security, and *everyone* is supposed to check in at the desk?"

"Everyone here knows me, Charlie." Thomas eased his lanky frame into the nearest chair and hooked a thumb at the new title on the door. "Director of Legal

Services now, huh?" He smiled. "I wouldn't let that get away with you, *Hastiin*… if you know what I mean."

Charlie sighed, pointing through the glass at the outer office, he said. "You may not have noticed, but that's a new girl on the desk. She may have been involved in her work when you sneaked by her." He cleared his throat and sniffed, then continued his contrived defense of the girl. "Arlene, on the other hand, who *does* know you, happens to be on vacation this week."

Thomas snorted, "That girl out there was involved in her work all right. That's a romance magazine she has hidden in that folder. And I don't sneak."

Charlie frowned through the side window to the outer office and focused on the obviously preoccupied young woman, "You still could have announced yourself, Thomas, maybe saved the girl from getting fired." He knew he was dramatizing the consequences involved, but still… Thomas was good at drawing him into these untenable positions and he wasn't going to let it happen again. It was now a matter of principle.

Following the direction of the Investigator's gaze Thomas leaned forward to study the girl, then shrugged as he declared, "I doubt you'd fire her, Charlie. You know she's Councilman Ben Benally's daughter, don't you?" He gave the investigator a lopsided grin. "Big Ben might not like that, you know."

Thomas's wife…better known to her constituency as Lucy Tallwoman…had recently been elected to the Tribal Council, and this despite being married to Thomas Begay. She was now one of only two women serving on the Council. Forced to attend a good many political gatherings in his wife's bid for the seat, Thomas was now on a first-name basis with most of the local politicians and becoming familiar with Tribal power structure.

Charlie glowered as he narrowed an eye at the sly young receptionist. He'd figured her for a slacker from the start. He knew she was Big Ben's daughter all right—that's how she got the job—he hadn't liked it then, and he didn't like it now. Nepotism, even after all these years, was still a stain on reservation politics. But that didn't excuse Thomas Begay. Turning to lock eyes with the tall Navajo he growled, "What can I do for you my man? As you can see, I'm a little busy this morning."

Thomas rose slightly, leaned across the desk and poked the Investigator in the chest with a bony forefinger, his voice a sinister whisper, "Where is Harley Ponyboy?"

The Investigator, a little taken aback, thought it an odd question. If anyone should know the whereabouts of Harley Ponyboy it would be Thomas Begay—the two were nearly inseparable.

"What? Is he missing?" he joked.

"It damn sure looks that way…no one's seen or heard from the man in days now. That's not like him you know?"

Charlie leaned back out of range. "Well, now that you mention it, I haven't seen him either. So, what makes you think that's a problem?"

"He was supposed to meet me at George Custer's office yesterday morning to get lined out on a new dig the Doc's starting next week. He didn't show up."

"Maybe he forgot."

"Harley don't forget…when he's sober."

"You think he's drinking…?"

"He hasn't had a drink in nearly a year."

"He could be sick."

"He don't get sick, unless he's drunk."

Charlie cracked a smile for the first time, "So, maybe he could be drinking?"

"Naa… If he was drinking, I would have heard by now." Thomas's tone turned a shade darker, "The Doc and I took a run out to his place this morning. He wasn't home and it looked to me like he hadn't been there for a while."

Charlie waited to hear what conclusion Thomas might have drawn from all this.

"Sheila Badinni lives just down the road from him. When we stopped by there, she said he came to her place wanting to borrow a few bucks on his spare tire. Harley told her he needed enough gas to get to Farmington. He mentioned he might be coming into some money soon and when he did, he would come for the tire." Thomas threw up his hands. "I doubt those people had more than five dollars between them, but they let Harley have it …along with a five-gallon can of gas. They didn't keep his tire neither, made him take it with him." He chewed at his lower lip for a moment. "With a truck like his, I guess they figured he might need it." Thomas grinned as he shook his head in disbelief. "I don't know what it is about Harley—people just seem to like the guy for some reason."

"I guess so..."

Thomas slapped a hand on the desk and his voice carried more of an edge when he said, "What business would Harley Ponyboy have in Farmington that he couldn't tell us about? That's what I'd like to know. You and I are about the only family he's got left."

Charlie showed little emotion at this, hoping not to encourage the man. "Sounds to me like he's just broke; maybe went into town to see about a job."

"You're not listening, *Hastiin*! He's got a job waiting for him with the Professor. He could get a draw on his wages if he needed money."

"Well, then, maybe he got himself put in jail. Maybe he's sitting in a cell in Farmington, right now."

"Maybe. But I'm getting a bad feeling about this. Harley Ponyboy has just not been himself lately"

"So, what are *you* thinking we should do?"

"You're the Investigator, for Hell's sake, I figured you might at least know where to start."

Charlie sighed, clicking his pen in and out a few times before answering, "I guess we could call your nephew, Billy Red Clay, over at Tribal, see if he's heard anything? I hate to bother him with this though, busy as he's been lately…"

"I already talked to Billy this morning; he told me they don't have Harley locked up. He said he would ask around and maybe check with his friend that works down at the jail in Farmington. You know, see if they have him up there."

Charlie could see the man was working himself into a tizzy, and nothing good ever came of that.

"Before we get too excited here, *Hastiin*, let's just wait and see what Billy comes up with."

Thomas sliced the air with the edge of his hand sending a paper flying off the desk. "I'll tell you what it is... Harley's been spending too much time alone out there in that trailer house. That's what I think. I was hoping once the Professor put us back to work...the little bastard would get his mind right. This isn't just about money; something else has gotten into him lately."

Thomas was getting worked up and Charlie could see now that nothing would appease him, short of a significant show of effort on his part.

"Go home, Thomas, and cool off. I'll call around and let you know what I hear by this afternoon. We'll go from there."

Thomas rose, pulling his hat down low over his eyes as he moved to the door. "I'll be back..." he replied without turning around, making it sound as ominous as possible.

The Investigator watched as his friend marched himself past the workstations and up to the receptionist's desk—saw him take off his hat to the girl and hang his head slightly.

Well, that's more like it; he's apologizing. Then, just as Charlie was congratulating himself on this minor victory, he saw Thomas draw himself to his full height and point back at Charlie's office, saying something to the girl that turned her face livid. Cramming his hat back on his head, the man then turned on his heel, and with a malicious grin, headed for the door. The girl, left speechless, watched him go, then slowly curled her lip mouthing something Charlie was glad he couldn't hear. Several nearby staff members could hear it, however, and turned as one to frown back at Charlie's office.

~~~~~~~

After lunch, the Investigator reluctantly picked up the phone and dialed Tribal Policeman Billy Red Clay. He knew the young officer had plenty on his plate already—being Tribal Liaison Officer to the FBI had been keeping him on the run of late—Charlie doubted he had time for freelancing favors for friends, or relatives.

"Red Clay speaking..."

"Charlie Yazzie here, Billy, I hate to bother you but was wondering if you'd heard anything about Harley Ponyboy? Your Uncle Thomas is worried..."

"I just did hear something, Charlie, about ten minutes ago, he's not in jail...not yet, anyway."

"What do you mean—not yet?"

"I ran his truck through Motor Vehicles to see if it had turned up wrecked or anything, and they said their records show it was sold or traded in yesterday morning. I called the dealership they had listed. The owner of the place said it was basically a cash deal on a nearly new Chevrolet truck. The guy said he could only give Harley two hundred for his old truck, and even that was more or less a gift as far as he was concerned."

There was silence on the other end, making Billy think for a moment that he'd lost the connection.

"Charlie? …Any idea where someone like Harley Ponyboy might come up with that kind of money?"

Charlie didn't have a clue and doubted Billy's Uncle Thomas would have one either. One thing for certain, something wasn't right. Even when Harley and Thomas had been drinking, it was generally Harley Ponyboy who was the stabilizing influence. Thomas himself often admitted it was his friend more often than not, that kept them from spending even more of their life in jail. But that was all in the past; both men had mellowed considerably over the years, Thomas no longer drank, but even with his help, Harley Ponyboy struggled to follow suit.

Billy Red Clay, obviously now pressed for time, coughed politely. "Charlie, I've got someone on hold. You might want to run by that car dealer and have a little face to face. He's a pretty straight shooter from what I gathered. Still, I think he may know more than he was willing to say over the phone." He paused. "It's that first big car lot on the left going into town. I'd do it myself but just can't get loose this morning."

"I know, Billy… I may do just that. Your Uncle Thomas is coming by in a few minutes. I expect he'll want to ride along. He's pretty upset about this for some reason."

~~~~~~

Thomas Begay pointed out the sign well before the cross-over lane. It was a large and somewhat garish sign that could be read from quite a distance.

DAPPER DAN'S
NEARLY NEW AND BARELY USED CARS & TRUCKS.

"There it is!" Thomas bellowed, thinking Charlie was going to miss the fast approaching turnoff. Throwing a hand in that direction, he nearly knocked Charlie's hat off.

The Investigator took a deep breath and gritted his teeth. "Dammit, Thomas, I can see that sign as well as you can." He slid into the turn lane with a jerk of the wheel, and then in a more conciliatory tone, said, "Isn't that where Lucy bought her pickup?"

"Yes, it is… And where I bought my truck, too. A lot of people from the reservation trade there. The man's been in business, in that same spot, for years now. That has to mean something. I know I didn't have any problem dealing with him."

Charlie got lucky and scooted across the busy intersection just ahead of an oncoming string of traffic. As far as this particular dealership went, he'd checked before leaving the office and found, compared to others, they'd had very few complaints over the years. The investigator felt a twinge of uneasiness as they pulled into the lot. As far as he knew, Harley never had more than a few dollars in his pocket his entire life. *I can't imagine the man having enough cash for a new truck...or any truck for that matter, Hell, he could barely keep gas in his old one.*

As he parked in front of the office, Charlie saw someone peeking through the nearly closed Venetian blinds. It had to be close to quitting time and he wondered if the person inside would open up for them.

He and Thomas stepped down from the truck just as the office door opened to reveal a rather impressively dressed older gentleman. And Charlie thought to himself, *I wonder if this is the owner?*

Studying the Tribal emblem on the pickup, the owner, if that's who he was, met them with a practiced smile—pleasant looking man with a bit of a paunch, thinning grey hair and freshly shined wingtips. The shoes went well with the expensive tan slacks he was wearing.

This must be Dapper Dan himself. Charlie couldn't help smiling.

The two Navajo came up the steps to the veranda-like façade exchanging side-glances, Charlie trying to appear as official as possible. The man ushered them in and pointed to chairs as he parked himself in a seat behind a huge mahogany desk.

Dapper Dan obviously wasn't one to dilly-dally with small talk. "I'm Dan Murphy," he said, extending a hand, "What, can I do for you gentlemen from… Legal Services, is it?"

Never knowing what might pop out of Thomas's mouth, Charlie made it a point to take the lead. "Yes, Legal Services, I'm Chief Investigator Yazzie, Charlie Yazzie." He didn't know why he'd said *Chief* which wasn't part of his official title. Something about the other's dress must have triggered it. He rose slightly to offer his hand across the desk.

Murphy took note of the badge on the Investigator's belt but didn't appear worried and shook hands with a firm grip. Before Charlie could turn to introduce Thomas, however, Dan had already extended a hand in his direction.

"I believe we've met before, Mr. Begay." And then as an aside to Charlie, "I sold Thomas's wife a pickup not long ago. The woman drives a hard bargain." Turning back to Thomas he flashed a grin, "I had the feeling, though, that she might have been coached beforehand."

Thomas, surprised, smiled nonetheless, and rose to shake his hand.

Murphy shook hands along with a running commentary, "I understand Mrs. Begay is on the Council now…good for her…be sure you offer the Mrs. my congratulations. Another woman on the Council might be exactly what they need out there." The big man paused. "I believe I once sold you a truck as well, Thomas, some time back, am I correct, a blue Dodge, I believe?"

Thomas could only grin and nod.

Both Navajo were impressed with the man's smooth ways and stylish dress and could see now how this car salesman had become so popular among folks on the reservation.

The big man seemed to know what they were thinking and waved it away with a chuckle. "I grew up in San Juan County—taught school here in Farmington for a while, and later over in Aztec for a time. My Great-grandfather was one of the first whites to move into this country; one of the few who weren't Mormons." He smiled. "The LDS had a strong influence over the Navajo in those days. Still do have, from what I've seen. My Great-grandfather was one of the few *Gentiles*, as they were called back then, to establish trade with the *Diné.*"

Charlie chuckled and considered this for a moment. "Well I wish you'd been one of our teachers over in Aztec. Thomas and I were at the BIA boarding dormitory there. I'm sorry we missed you…not that we didn't have some good teachers, we did…for the most part." All three smiled at this, each having his own opinion on the Great BIA experiment, a program designed to integrate whites and Indians by having student boarding facilities adjacent to previously all-white campuses. One last shot at the Federal Government's fading dream of assimilation for the Navajo. There *were* those, then and now, who found value in the program, remaining staunch believers to this very day. But not everyone. Not Thomas Begay.

Charlie cleared his throat, "What we've come about, Dan, is our friend Harley Ponyboy, who we understand purchased a truck from you recently."

The car dealer, now with a little more concern in his voice, was quick to answer. "He did indeed, red Chevy half-ton, only a couple of months old and with very few miles on the clock. Best vehicle on the lot," he declared. Pulling out a file drawer he extracted a folder which he laid open on the desk for Charlie's inspection. He sounded sincere enough when he said, "I hope there hasn't been an accident, or problem with the unit?"

"No, no, nothing like that. It's just that we can't seem to locate Harley these last few days. Of course, he may have just taken a little vacation without telling us. He hasn't been in touch for a while. Not like him at all I can assure you, but anything's possible with Harley." Here he cast a sideways glance at Thomas Begay. "Certain individuals have begun to worry. It seems our friend may have come into some unexpected money recently and we're afraid that might have complicated things for him. He's not had much experience in financial matters…not of the size we're talking about."

Dan, clearly relieved, didn't hesitate to offer his account of the recent transaction. "When your friend went to pay for the truck and brought out a deposit bag full of cash, I naturally voiced some concern. I had to inform him we are obliged to report to the authorities all cash transactions over ten thousand dollars. Mr. Ponyboy then told me he'd held the winning ticket in one of last week's Lottery games and then produced an official form and bank receipt, verifying the money as such." Dan chuckled, "He said it would be a week or two before he had his new check book and didn't think I would take a counter check for something this big. He went on to tell me this wasn't something that could wait. He said he had need of a dependable truck right now."

Looking over at the sales contract Thomas gave a low whistle and glanced at Charlie. "That's a lot of money for a truck!"

Dan instantly agreed, "Yes, it is, and worth every penny of it, too. I barely made my margin on this one. And just for the record, it didn't put much of a dent in Mr. Ponyboy's cash reserves as far as I could see. I would judge he had two or three times that left in his bag."

Both men showed surprise at this, Thomas saying, several times, "Well, I'll just be damned..." he was about to say it a third time, when the look on his friend's face caused him to think better of it.

Charlie himself appeared a bit more worried now. "Harley didn't happen to say where he was headed when he left here, did he?"

Dan was adamant, "I mentioned to him that carrying around that much cash could be risky and asked him if he was headed home? He said, 'I need to have some cash. Not everyone's willing to take a check from an Indian... And no, I'm not going home. There's someone I've been meaning to look up for a while now. She's not from around here, so it's going to take some travel.' The man then transferred a duffle bag from his old truck to the new one and was out of here before I could wish him luck." Dan smiled at the two. "He's kind of a strange little guy, isn't he?"

Both Navajos nodded agreement.

~~~~~~

On their way back to Shiprock the pair was unusually quiet, Charlie being the first to bring up what was on both their minds. "Did you know anything about Harley winning any money?"

"No, but I did know he bought some tickets when he was up in Cortez last week. He told me he took a mule to the sale barn up there, and on his way back stopped in at the Ute Mountain Casino at Towaoc. That mule hadn't brought what he thought it was worth and he hoped to parlay the proceeds into something more in line with what he deserved."

"How did that work out for him?"

"He lost all but thirty-six dollars playing the slot machines and finally figured he might better invest what was left in lottery tickets." Thomas lowered an eyelid. "As you well know, Harley's no gambler. So, I guess I was pretty hard on him for wasting his last few dollars on such foolishness. That was the last time I saw him… And maybe why he didn't let me know when he won."

Thomas's story left Charlie in a quandary. "Hard to believe, isn't it? Harley Ponyboy is the last person on earth I would expect to fall into something like this. He's a hard luck guy if there's ever been one. Not that he doesn't deserve a break, of course." The Investigator smiled to himself and said, "When Arlene gets back from her vacation tomorrow, she'll be excited to hear about someone from out here on the Rez finally winning something." He looked over at Thomas and explained, "Down at the office we have a little pool that buys a few tickets every now and then. Arlene's in charge of it. She thinks it promotes team spirit and feels it somehow contributes to office morale."

"Have they ever won anything?"

"No."

Thomas nodded. "That's just what I told Harley...no one ever wins out here on the Rez... none that I've ever heard of, anyway."

"Well, you may have heard of one now."

"Yes, and I doubt he'll ever let me live it down, either. I wouldn't blame him if he never spoke to me again."

"You know Harley's not like that. I wouldn't worry about it. Why, I expect he'll have plenty to say to you the next time you meet." Both men grinned at this.

As they crossed the La Plata bridge, Thomas pulled his hat lower to shade a setting sun, then squirmed further down into his seat as he turned to the window. Watching the country slip by in a fading montage of gold melding to crimson, he turned back to frown at the Investigator. "You know who he's gone looking for, don't you?" It wasn't really a question.

"Eileen May."

"Sure, as Hell... He's had that woman on his brain since she first blew into town two years ago and tried to sell him that Bible."

"Well, Harley's a grown man," Charlie sighed, "I know he doesn't act like it sometimes, but he is," then sighed yet again. "I'd hoped we'd heard the last of Eileen. I'm afraid you're right though, much as I hate to think it." He silently worried this around for another minute or two. "When I get home, I'll call Fred Smith and see if he's had an update on Eileen's whereabouts. He mentioned a while back he still keeps track of her. Agent Smith never wanted to let that investigation go back then. He just couldn't put it all together at the time—not anything strong enough to suit the Federal Prosecutor anyway." Privately, Charlie thought the FBI man had always been convinced the woman was a cold-blooded killer.

"You never told me that..." Thomas stared off into the distance before saying, "Must have been more of your *privileged information,* huh?" He and Charlie had a thing about privileged information. He didn't believe in it, and Charlie did.

"I doubt you'd be able to convince Harley she's no good. He was pretty much gone on her from the first time they met. He's hardheaded as a billy goat once he gets something in his mind." Thomas had known the man a long time and was well aware of his foibles.

"Well, he's obviously got it in his head now to find her. I don't know how the man figures... Eileen was just using him all along and everyone knew it, too, except for Harley, of course." Charlie frowned, seemingly more thoughtful as he went on, saying, "He's never had much luck with women, has he?" He continued without waiting for an answer. "Starting with his ex-wife, Anita, a hardcase if there ever was one. He never really had a chance to experience any other women before that, none that he's mentioned to me."

"That's a fact. Anita, was his first and only real encounter with a woman... Until Eileen May came along and bedazzled him. That's when things went from bad to worse in my opinion."

Charlie wondered for a moment at Thomas's use of the word *bedazzled,* not something he would have ordinarily expected him to say. He credited the man's involvement in Lucy Tallwoman's recent political campaign for this and smiled.

Thomas, turning again to the Investigator sounded deadly serious, "Well, I guess we better find him, before he tracks her down and gets himself robbed…or worse. One thing for sure, there's no one else gives a damn, except me and you."

Concentrating on the road, Charlie slowly exhaled and then sucked in a deep breath, he knew where this talk was headed and turned briefly to gaze out the side window at the San Juan river, swirling with red mud from some errant up-country rain. *This is going to wind up being a real bitch* is what he was thinking.

Thomas, perceiving some reluctance in his friend's silence, was quick to forge ahead. "If you can't get off work, I'll go by myself…Harley doesn't stand a chance in Hell with that woman."

After a while, Charlie nodded. "I know… I'll get off, one way or the other."

2

The Windfall

Harley Ponyboy had seldom experienced any good fortune to speak of. Growing up in the *Tsé Bii' Ndzisgaii,* his early years were filled with isolation and hard work. Monument Valley was a tough place to make a living, especially herding sheep, which by their very nature are prone to misfortune. Little feed and scarce water can make for long days and lonely nights for a young boy charged with such responsibility.

His old aunt cared for Harley as best she was able but had known nothing but hard times herself leaving very little to help him with. These sheep, along with the woman's weaving of their wool, represented the only form of income left to the family. Harley's uncle, by marriage, was considerably older than his aunt, who was no longer young herself, not by any stretch of the imagination. Being his mother's only sister, however, she was duty-bound to take him in. To the Navajo way of thinking she was as much Harley's mother as was her dead sister. The old uncle, on the other hand, felt no such obligation and made that plain from the start. Harley saw the old man as unapproachable, unwilling to give him a chance from the very beginning. Try as he might, he was never able to make any headway with his uncle, who by now was caught up in his own mortality and considered him little more than an added burden.

Harley's greatest worry, however, was not his Uncle, but rather the mythological trickster Coyote, who seemed always to be nipping at his heels, biding his time, waiting to practice his devious magic. Coyote often came to him in dreams…in itself, a bad omen. Both cunning and nefarious, Coyote takes a relentless toll on those he sets his sights on; especially with those more superstitious outliers of the *Diné Bikeyahh.*

Despite all these things the boy, being of a naturally optimistic nature, eventually arrived at the conclusion that somewhere, there had to be a better world waiting. By the time he was of an age to be on his own he was determined to find that better place and to forever shed this lonely and desperately barren life. Over time Harley devised a plan by which he would head south to the town of Shiprock, thinking he might find a more reasonable way of making a living there.

"There is more of a future ta be had in town," he said. "Maybe down there I can do better than just herding sheep."

His uncle, now realizing how useful the boy had become and that the herding would now fall to his aging wife, seemed suddenly against the boy's leaving, declaring himself too old to be left with such work.

Harley's Aunt was well aware her husband's main concern was that she wouldn't have time for her weaving upon which their meager income depended.

For the sake of her dead sister, however, the woman encouraged her nephew to follow his heart, saying she would help him the best she could despite what her husband thought. She reminded the old man that this was her *Hogan*...and her sheep...and that this was the way it was going to be.

The young man hitchhiked away from the only home he'd known carrying his few possessions rolled in a heavy wool blanket, a last present from his aunt's own loom. Sleeping out under a culvert at the edge of Shiprock and eating only what little food she'd been able to send with him Harley kept the old woman in his prayers and swore he would never forget her. He did, eventually, find a job digging ditches for a construction company, work that suited him and paid a living wage. And in only a short time the boy had settled into a new and more gratifying life.

Naïve though he might be, Harley's honest and outgoing nature quickly made him new friends, and for the first time in his life he found himself socializing with people his own age. He then was convinced the worst might well be behind him, and that Coyote and his evil designs had been left in the red dust of Monument Valley.

In due course it was only natural the boy should fall under the spell of a local girl...from a good family and suitable clan, and he dauntlessly pursued the young woman to the limit of his meager resources. All this, despite hearing she was already promised to another person, an older man, and a Singer some said—more likely a witch, others thought—but an obviously dangerous man no matter who one believed.

Despite this older man's continuing threats, Harley, not one to be easily intimidated, finally convinced the girl they should marry, and in the face of everything remained strong in his resolve to make a go of it.

Then there came the curse by the former suitor, known now as the 'Witch of Ganando'. He vowed Anita would never give Harley a child and should *any* pregnant woman even his path, that person, innocent though she might be, would lose *her* child as well.

Anita, never a cheerful girl to begin with, grew even more petulant and complaining. Nothing her young husband did or said seemed to please her.

Harley knew her family had never considered the marriage a suitable match and had much preferred she marry the older, more successful suitor—still the good people allowed him to move in with them, as was the custom in those times. The young man consoled himself that he would now, at least, no longer be alone in his misery. But after enduring their daughter's whining and complaining for several weeks, the couple offered the pair an old and isolated trailer house many miles from their own place.

It was only a year or so later Harley met up with Thomas Begay and still being somewhat naïve, fell under the man's influence, joining him in his disreputable ways. It allowed an intermittent escape from Anita and some small excitement in an otherwise dull existence. There was nothing for it then…the die was cast, and he and Thomas became the scourge of the off-reservation bars and bootlegger hideaways. Fighting their way out of many a close scrape together, the pair formed a brotherly bond and came to rely on one another as such. As it turned out, when the situation called for it, Harley was a fierce and determined fighter and would generally give a good account of himself despite his size. Many a larger man sidestepped Harley Ponyboy knowing full well there is little glory in besting a smaller person. Should the larger man somehow lose, his reputation would surely suffer. This common barroom belief might allow some small but foolish person the courage to seek out bigger men for these very reasons. Many came to regret such a decision...but not always. As some ancient once said, "Often it is courage that wins the victory...and not the sword."

The two like-minded *Diné* spent more than a little time in jails around the country. From Gallup north to Cortez, and Ignacio west to Tuba City, the pair wandered the Four Corners like misguided knights of old. Professor Custer would later liken them to Cervantes's Don Quixote and sidekick Sancho Panza. The two Navajo were not alone in this skewed quest for enlightenment—the life was not uncommon on the reservation at the time, still isn't, should one know the sort.

After a while Anita tired of Harley's drinking, and became even more tired of putting up with Thomas Begay. More and more she was convinced it wasn't so much the witch's curse that was causing their troubles, but rather Thomas himself who was responsible. Even

23

after the man quit drinking, she had no use for him and thought him a bad influence on her husband.

Anita had, in fact, so soured on her life with Harley that she finally left him once and for all. It came about so abruptly and with such finality that it sent the little man into a downward spiral, driving him ever deeper into the bottle.

Thomas Begay, now miraculously the sober one, remarked, "If it weren't for bad luck, Harley, you'd scarcely have any luck at all." He meant this in the kindest way possible but Harley, having already heard it from others, allowed himself to be so strongly influenced that it eventually became a self-fulfilling prophecy. Through it all, the reclaimed Thomas Begay, possibly driven by guilt, stood resolutely in support of his friend. With the combined help of Charlie Yazzie and the redoubtable George Armstrong Custer, himself a famous drinker, finally convinced the young man to come under the wing of a local AA chapter. That organization came to the battle well tutored, and despite many a stumble along the way eventually sobered Harley up, leaving him with only the occasional fall from grace to account for.

Through all this adversity, the little man's traditionally rooted *hozoji* remained strong and his trust in the Holy Ones unshakable. Even Thomas Begay, traditionally minded though he was, found the man's faith remarkable.

Harley Ponyboy, in the nether regions of his mind had long suspected that should he only manage to hang on, he might eventually catch a break. When deliverance finally came, however, it had been so long a time in coming that he couldn't help feeling some distrust in his good fortune.

Perhaps the Holy Ones are, at last, taking some notice he concluded, thinking he had certainly prayed enough and might reasonably expect something in return.

This was not the first time Harley had occasion to think his luck had changed, only to see those hopes crumble. There had been another woman, after Anita, and she, too, had in the beginning brought hope of better days. Eileen May, despite having left almost as quickly as she had come, won such a place in his heart that she lingered there yet…sometimes causing him to do foolish things.

Smart, and oh so worldly Eileen had, even in her short time there, taken him apart and put him back together a significantly different person. The memory of her so pervasive he'd been unable to put her out of his mind. He constantly found himself wondering what she was doing… if she was still selling Bibles for a living? And, if she was, to what pass that might have brought her?

Perhaps, he reasoned, *this recent great gift from the Holy Ones was meant to be my key to the future…a future that might include Eileen.* Many was the dream he had of the woman and flashbacks of their short time together came to dominate his waking hours allowing him to think of little else.

~~~~~

Harley pushed back his breakfast plate—unable to shake the premonition that no one on the reservation should learn of his good luck, at least until he was certain it was not just a little joke of the Holy Ones...or... more likely, some trickery of Old Man Coyote.

As his food went unnoticed, Harley glanced again at the scrap of paper and with a cautious forefinger drew it closer. The wrinkles and creases did seem more pronounced. *What if the thing comes apart or becomes unreadable?* he wondered. *What then?* He suspected this could happen if he didn't quit handling it. Though the numbers were burned into his memory he still could not resist the recurring urge to verify and then re-verify the figures.

In Harley's mind there were still any number of things that could go wrong, and he wrestled with these possibilities as his ham and eggs went stone cold in a shimmer of grease. His forehead, now beaded in sweat, sent a trickle to form a drop at the end of his nose and he brushed this away with the back of a hand as he forced himself to look away from the ticket.

Work had been scarce. The last food in the house was that on the plate in front of him and this thought alone brought a pang of anxiety. Putting down his fork he peered through a dust-streaked window, his gaze settling on the old truck outside. He wasn't even sure it had enough gas to make it into town. A mind-numbing state of inertia had fallen over him, sapping his ability to think, or even function. Fear was what it was. Harley

Ponyboy was immobilized with self-doubt, frightened he might ultimately make a bad decision—perhaps the most important decision of his life. He'd heard of lives ruined by bad financial decisions and the thought brought him to the heart-pounding realization that he might not be up to the task. Truth be told, he was probably more worried of being made a fool, than anything else.

If only Eileen was here. But she wasn't, and due to his limited resources, he'd about given up hope of ever finding her. He had no idea where she might be. It had been several years since she climbed on the Greyhound headed for Salt Lake. Though she'd promised to write he'd not heard a single word. Oh, he'd tried reaching her at the address scribbled out in their final minutes together. She'd be at her Aunt Mary's place she promised.

When, finally, Harley screwed up the courage to write he'd received the letter back only to find it had been forwarded to yet a different small town, but even then, was stamped: "Not at this address." Not knowing what else to do, he was forced to leave it at that. His friends Charlie Yazzie and Thomas Begay and yes, even their wives, made it clear they thought this was for the best. All secretly agreed there was something very wrong about the woman and none ever found anything good to say about her.

Now on the verge of a great new opportunity, Harley remained determined no one should know this ticket could be a winner, not even his best friend Thomas, who had so belittled his chances when told he'd bought in. Thomas had come right out and declared, "It's crazy for a person to gamble their last few dollars with so little chance of winning," thus placing the whole business under a shadow of doubt. "Why, I've heard it's more likely a person would be struck by lightning!" And went on with this line of reasoning for some time—in the end so discouraging his friend that Harley became engulfed in uncertainty and came to regret squandering his money on something "so foolish" as Thomas Begay had proclaimed.

Even so, after a great deal of soul searching, Harley decided what it came down to was this: Someone was going to win... Where else can a person buy hope for a dollar?

3

Redemption

The new Chevy truck was so far beyond anything Harley Ponyboy had ever imagined he had a hard time believing it was really his. To his mind nothing even came close to owning a new truck and a red one at that. The intoxicating aroma of the luxurious interior alone was enough to give him a sense of confidence he'd never experienced. He had at last done something right. This was the epitome of success to his innocent way of thinking. He could, at last, show Thomas Begay what a little faith could do for a person.

He glanced at the bank bag beside him, secure in the knowledge there was yet more where that came from. The bank manager felt the prudent thing was to leave a portion of the winnings in a savings account right there in his bank. It was not as much as Harley had first envisioned. For one thing, the prize had split several ways, and for another, he had opted for the cash payout…that seemed best for someone leading the chancy sort of life encountered on the reservation. But even this wasn't the end of it; the lottery office insisted on deducting the considerable state and federal taxes right up front. It was the law, they said, but was something else Harley hadn't figured on. The amount left over *was*, nonetheless, more than he'd ever dreamed of having, and he gave fervent thanks to the Holy Ones each morning thereafter.

He was determined not to let greed get the best of him; that was not the *Diné* way of thinking. Pursuing more money or possessions than a person had need of might cause him to forsake the Beauty Way—followed by the inevitable loss of *Hozo*, which was just the beginning of that slippery slope. He'd seen it in others and was determined it wouldn't happen to him.

When he finally reached the little town in southern Utah he stopped to gas up and buy the chicken-salad sandwich he spotted in the cold case. Never having had such a sandwich before, he felt this might be an opportune time to see how he liked it. Upon paying, he asked the woman behind the counter where he might find the address on the bedraggled letter he handed over. She took the envelope, studied it through thick spectacles, and then shaking her head made that little clucking noise that might be taken for pity. "It looks from this letter's 'returns' you're having a little trouble finding this person. I know most people around here but not any Eileen May. This last address, down here at the bottom, isn't so far away though…" and she went on to explain in minute detail how to get there.

Harley sat outside the store in his truck, eating the chicken sandwich, which he found interesting, and going over the store woman's directions in his mind. This was becoming a lot more complicated than he had bargained for, but that only made him the more determined to see it through to some sort of conclusion, no matter how disappointing that might prove to be.

He found the neighborhood and drove to the rundown cinder-block house…indistinguishable from the gaggle of others with bare yards and peeling paint. He double checked the faded number on the door frame, parked and stood for a moment outside his truck to survey the neighborhood which quickly reminded him to lock the truck's doors. His moneybag, now wrapped in an old jacket, was stuffed under the back seat. He remembered Eileen talking about her Aunt Mary and became a little easier in his mind as he recalled the woman was a full-blood Navajo herself.

There were two older cars in the drive, one under a sagging carport with the hood up—engine parts carelessly strewn about the yard. The other a sun-faded silver Pontiac, looked even older but from what he could see, was the more likely of the two to be an actual driver.

A dog chained at the other side of the yard came from his makeshift shelter; it was a big dog, rangy and with a good dollop of pit bull somewhere down the line. The canine stretched and slowly turned its head from side to side, like a prize fighter loosening up…getting ready. Harley waited for it to come to the end of its tether—making sure there would be room to get by without being bitten. He had been around dogs like this most of his life and knew intuitively this one would do the exact opposite of what a person thought it would do. The two contemplated one another for nearly a minute, equally wary, each on his guard. A tentative wave of the dog's tail gave no indication of what was really on its mind. It was a dog that knew what worked and what didn't. The surly looking creature crouched slightly, barked just once, then launched itself the full length of the chain. Harley had it figured about right and stood his ground as the dog came up short with a frustrated growl—he had come close, and he knew it. The two stood staring at one another, close-up this time, each mentally calculating the odds of another try.

The front door creaked open and an older woman, obviously Indian, and most likely Navajo, stood just inside the screen-door watching. Harley thought he could see a faint resemblance to Eileen but knew this might be only wishful thinking. The woman called to the dog to stand down, which it seemed reluctant to do. Again, she shouted, and this time the big dog hung its head this time and gave way.

"He didn't get you, did he?" The woman spoke with a discernable Navajo accent, "I had to put a knot in that chain so he couldn't reach the mailman…I maybe should a made it a little shorter…" She threw a glance of approval the dog's way. "A person has to have a bad dog, living around here." She looked Harley up and down for a moment before turning her attention to his truck. This immediately seemed to lend the man much needed credibility and she motioned him on up to the porch so they could speak face to face.

He smiled inwardly as he glanced back at the Chevy and then moved up to the screen door.

Mary opened the screen slightly and peered out around him. "That's a nice truck you got there. Looks brand new to me."

Harley shifted a bit so she might better admire the vehicle. "Naa," he replied carelessly as though long accustomed to driving new trucks, "I've had it awhile." He held out the envelope with the address on it. "I'm Harley Ponyboy from down ta' Shiprock. I'm looking for Eileen May. I used ta know her down there on the reservation, but I sorta lost track of her over the last couple of years. She wouldn't happen ta be around, would she?"

Mary opened the screen wider and studied the envelope a moment before looking him up and down. "Ponyboy, huh?" From the corner of an eye she looked again at the Chevy, as though something wasn't adding up. "I've heard that name before. Eileen's going to be sorry she missed you, Mr. Ponyboy. My niece spoke of you now and then." The woman offered no impression of how favorable that talk might have been.

"So, she's not here now, then?" Harley wilted visibly, disappointed despite hearing Eileen had at least made mention of him. "I'd hoped she might be living with you. The last time I talked to her she said she was going to be with her Aunt Mary." He shrugged… "That was a while back, though..."

"Well, I'm her Aunt Mary, all right, Mary Chano, but Eileen didn't come to my place to stay when she left down there in New Mexico. She said she would, but she only stopped to see me for a few days and then went on to Seattle. She was up there a couple of years I guess."

Smiling, she admitted, "I've moved a few times myself since then." She waved a hand toward the horizon. "That girl likes to move around…changes her mind a lot…never stays long in one place. Maybe her father had some Gypsy blood in him. He was a handsome devil, plenty of charm too." She grinned, and Harley saw she was missing a lower tooth. "Not that the Navajo don't get around, these days. Still plenty of nomad blood in us too, I suppose." Pausing as though wondering what else she might say and not away too much about her niece. Finally, she shook her head and came right out with it. "She come through here a while back; said she was heading to Arizona—she had someone with her though, so she didn't stay long."

"She's not married, is she?"

"Eileen? God no, I'd feel better if she was…what with her running around the country and all. If she was married, she might settle down a little." She shook her head again and grimaced. "But she did have a man with her. He told me they were going down to the North Rim, you know, the Grand Canyon…said he'd heard there were a few end-of-season jobs opening up down there—college kids going back to school and all. 'They're always looking for maintenance people down there,' he said, and thought maybe Eileen could get on in the gift shop." Here, she lowered an eyelid and nodded in such a way Harley felt a shiver. "But you know, there was something odd about that man—like he was hollow inside, that's what my grandfather used to say about people like that—like they had no soul, he'd say."

Harley nodded at this, trying not to show his disappointment about Eileen being with a man. "I see…well, I hope things work out for her down there."

"My niece, you know, she's good with people, always puts on a good face; she'd probably do well at that sort of job down there in the Canyon…that is, if she was at herself. I was always surprised how young she looked each time she come through—no matter how long she was gone she would always look the same as before." Mary stopped for a moment, shook her head with a sad smile, saying, "But not this time. She looked bad this time. Not like her old self at all. It was like the life had gone out of her." Mary shrugged herself out of this with a shiver and couldn't help reminiscing back to better times, asking, "Did she ever tell you what her Indian name was?"

"Well, I asked her that one time and she just said it didn't matter anymore. She didn't like to talk about it, from what I could see. She did tell me, one day when she was in a good mood, 'Antelope Girl'…she said, 'that was my name when I was little,' but she said no one had called her that for a long time now."

This brought a smile to Mary's face. "I remember when we called her that. My father gave her that name, when she was still only a baby, barely walking and only a few months before he died, too. But, you know, that hasn't been her Navajo name for a long time now."

"So, what is her name now…her Indian name I mean."

The woman put her tongue in the space where the tooth had been, as though that might keep her from saying it. "No one outside the family should ever know that name now." Then seeing Harley's face fall, she took a deep breath and told him anyway.

"It is Falling Girl" she said, "That's how she's called among our family clans now." She waited for Harley to ask why.

But he didn't ask. He didn't want to know.

"You wouldn't happen to have a phone number or address for her, would you, Mary?"

"No, Harley Ponyboy, she never leaves me anything like that—says it's for my own good—whatever that means. She did mention once that she always lists me as her next of kin on her job papers and such. I guess that means I'm the one they'll notify when something finally happens to her."

"I see..." Harley felt a chill that made him suddenly uncomfortable and decided it was time to go. "Well, nice meeting you anyway, Mary. I'm glad we had this little talk. Your niece always spoke highly of you. I'll let you know where she is, if I find her." He turned to leave—checking first to make certain Mary Chano's dog was still where it was supposed to be.

Mary opened the screen and came part-way out. "Why don't you come on in for a minute, Harley, I got a pot of coffee on...you look like you could use some. You look wore out."

Harley mulled this over. It was a long way to the North Rim and with night coming on he would likely need some coffee before it was over. "Yes, I guess coffee sounds good...I could use some coffee, thank you."

At the table Harley couldn't help noticing how neat and orderly everything was despite the poor outward appearance of the house. He was thinking, *Aunt Mary may have had a man here sometime…maybe still does. Someone fixed this place up for her.* He could see no sign of it, if there *was* a man. A man generally leaves a mark of some sort and Harley was good at picking up on such things. "Have you been a long time off the reservation, Mary?"

The woman turned from the stove, smiling. "Why? Are you wondering if I still speak a little Navajo?"

"Eileen said you taught her some when you lived with her mom."

"I tried to, but her father didn't like it. He made me stop. He wasn't much of a father…or anything else, from what I ever saw. A few years ago, he killed a man in a barroom fight, and they put him in prison for doing it. From what I hear he'll be there for the rest of his life. As for your question, I've been off the reservation since I was a teenager—after boarding school, you know—we all had to do that didn't we? My father used to say 'Don't worry! You'll never forget how to speak your native tongue,' but they soon showed us different at boarding school. I've forgotten a lot… I can still get by, but it doesn't come as easy as it once did. I find myself searching for just the right word now. Hell, I even think in *Billigaana* these days." She forced a smile. "I never figured that would happen." She brought the coffee and then speaking in Navajo, looked Harley in the eye. "I remember Eileen saying you were raised traditional yourself."

"That's about right, I came up the old way I guess." Harley admitted this in old Navajo, mostly just to see how she would answer.

Mary took a sip of her coffee and smiled across at him, "It's been a while since I heard someone speak Navajo that way, it reminds me of my grandfather to hear you talk like that."

Harley chuckled, "I get that a lot, even on the reservation."

Mary's tone changed and became almost winsomely provocative, "Why is it you want to find Eileen, Harley? What do you think might come from that?"

Harley answered in English hoping to make himself clear to the woman. "I don't know, Mary, I guess I hadn't really thought about 'why' that much. She's just been on my mind lately…wondering what she's up to and all. I just wanted to talk to her. I'm in a place where I could make that happen now, so I just decided to have a go at it." He looked down at his hands and flexed his fingers. "I don't really expect all that much ta come of it, I guess."

Mary switched back to English, herself, "Well, Harley, you seem like a reasonable man to me…and an honest one, too. Eileen said you were, and now that I've met you, I can see she was probably right." She fidgeted with her coffee a moment more. "There's a few things you might better know about Eileen before you go running off down to Arizona after her." Her voice was not unkind when she said this, but there was enough steel in it to fix his attention.

He held up a hand and was quick to say, "I'm not really 'running after her,' Mary, I'd just like to see her again, that's all. Things are different with me now. I'm not like I used to be when she knew me back in New Mexico."

The woman saw she might have embarrassed the man without intending to and changed her tone. "The thing is, Harley, Eileen has been on her own since she was a kid and has had a tough go of it. She don't trust people the way you and I might...I doubt she ever will. She don't form strong attachments for people the way most do. That's the only way I know how to put it."

"I understand, Mary, I been on my own most of my life, too. I had it pretty rough myself. But that don't make someone a terrible person." Harley looked around the room as though trying to fix on something, then lowering his voice he went on with it, admitting, "I used to be bad to drink and get in fights when I was young, but I'm past that now." He smiled. "What do you know, huh? People can change after all, I guess. Me and Eileen just seemed ta hit it off down there for a while. And at the time, I didn't even have enough money ta buy groceries. I knew she was on the run...hiding out from some guy she used to go with." He paused and looked away, "Oh, I know she just needed a safe place to rest up and get things together again. But you know, I always thought there was more than that between us. She knew how ta make a person feel good about himself. Maybe it was all in my mind...you know what I'm saying? But I really think there was something there."

Eileen's aunt looked down at her hands and when she looked back, she had teared up. "You don't really know Eileen, Harley. She just seems to attract the wrong sort of people...always has." She smiled and quickly added, "Present company excepted, of course." Mary reached over and touched his hand, searching his face while running her tongue across her upper lip, giving the impression she knew something he didn't, something she was hiding. "I guess you could say Eileen finds it exciting to run with dangerous people. Her own mother told her it would get her killed some day. Those two never got along and didn't see or talk to each other for several years. Before Alma died, she told me she gave up on Eileen a long time ago." Here she stopped and lowered her voice, as she leaned into the conversation. "I guess I'm about the only one who's ever really cared for that girl—but that's our people's way, isn't it? It's always a sister that takes on the burden when the mother can't...or won't. My grandmother used to say, 'All are sisters in the clan, and all must be mothers to one another's children.' Eileen comes and goes, never stays long...then it's off to the next adventure. I'll always be here for her, she knows that. She knows she still has a mother here. I been the one looking out for her since she was sixteen. But, you know, when I think back on it now, I can't see where I've ever done her any real good."

Mary sat back in her chair with a nearly imperceptible nod of her head. "I see now that you care for her, too. Maybe you'll have better luck...but, Harley, this much I do know...in the end, it won't make a damn bit of difference. Eileen is what she is, and no human I know will ever change her."

It took Harley a moment to get past this. "Well… Mary, I just need to see where we stand, Eileen and me, satisfy myself that I tried this one last time…no matter how it ends up. When she and I met that first time, down there on the reservation, I didn't have anything much to offer except an old trailer-house parked out in the dirt, and a long way from town. It's a wonder how she even made her way out there. That was all I had back then. I never expected Eileen to stick around for that, and I didn't blame her when she didn't. It's different with me now, though. I've come up in the world some. She needs to know that at least. I would like to help her if I can."

"Well, Harley, I will say just this last thing, and then I won't say no more about it. When Eileen first came back from New Mexico, she told me her friend, I think his name was…Claude…from the Bible Outreach Center down there in Phoenix. He was thought to have killed an old man from Teec Nos Pos, waylaid him for his money, Eileen said, and told me Claude died getting away from the law. But she knew something about the killing of that old man that no one else did—she told me that herself. I get bone-cold chills when I remember the look on her face as she talked about it. I didn't ask her no more about it…I couldn't stand to hear any more. Whatever it was that happened down there. I wish she'd never mentioned anything about it. I wake up sometimes at night and can hear her talking about it. It makes my skin crawl to be honest about it."

Harley stared at the woman, his face not betraying the thoughts rushing through his mind. The two sat silent for a bit, him not knowing what to say, and Mary Chano all talked out.

He drank the rest of his coffee, declining a second cup, saying it was getting late and he had to get on the road. He rose and moved toward the door feeling suddenly sick to his stomach.

"Harley…

He turned to see a worried look…

"Yes, ma'am…?"

She took a deep breath, bit her upper lip a little, and then let the air out leaving only a sad little smile. "Oh, nothing, I guess…" She pointed a finger at the door. "You watch that dog on your way out, now, he'll try to fool you if he can."

"I'll keep an eye on him, Mary."

"Well then… You take care of yourself, Mr. Ponyboy. Be careful down there in Arizona. There are bad people everywhere these days, and if any are down there, Eileen will likely be right in the middle of them."

Nodding a goodbye, Harley touched the brim of his hat to the woman, his mind still awash with unanswered questions. But now, at the back edge of all this, there ran a trickle of icy fear. *What if Mary Chano is right and I have been wrong all this time?*

~~~~~~

Eileen's aunt watched as her visitor opened the door to his truck and saw him feel around under the back seat before climbing behind the wheel. He sat there a moment, staring down the road toward the highway, looking even smaller perched up there in the big truck. She hoped he had a gun under that seat; he might well need one should he find Eileen. That Robert Rafferty she was with was a hard man. She had warned Harley as best she could—but she knew now he was going down there, no matter what. He would be on his own down on the North Rim.

There was another thing she might have told him…almost did tell him, in fact, but caught herself just in time. It wasn't her place to tell the man something like this. It wasn't something that would kill him, after all…not right away it wouldn't.

4

Reunion

Harley Ponyboy, drowsy now, was finding it hard to stay awake at the wheel. These new Chevy trucks, even at speed and over poor reservation roads, were so quiet and luxurious he wondered how anyone could stay awake driving at night. He'd finally cranked up the radio and turned it to the Indian station. KTNN—Voice of the Navajo Nation. The DJ was playing chants with plenty of drums and sometimes a flute or two. Mesmerizing. The weatherman broke in with storm warnings for the Kaibab.

A wind was already kicking up, dead out of the North, too. Whistling its way down Bryce Canyon looking to take a little rip through the Kaibab Indian Reservation—catch those Piutes unaware.

Harley was looking at the little tourist note on his service station map. Barely two hundred square miles total, The Kaibab was one of the smallest Indian reservations in the southwest. Only about a hundred and ninety-eight people lived there, it said, less than one person for each square mile. *Them Piutes better watch out tonight.* Harley smiled into the darkness. *I hope that's enough Indians ta keep that little patch from blowing away.*

By the time he reached Glendale, Utah he figured the wind to be gusting over sixty miles an hour and promising to do better before morning. When the skiffs of windblown sand and dust sifted across the road, he thought he could feel the Chevy's lift in the turns *If it gets any worse, I'll have to stop and pitch some dirt in the back.* Then remembered he didn't have a shovel. *Big rocks would work but that will beat the hell out of the bed.* He wouldn't have thought anything of this with his old truck, but with this new Chevy he was unwilling to go that far, just yet.

Concentrating on the white line was hypnotizing, twice he caught himself dozing off despite the wind. He switched the radio to KOMA "The Mighty Koma in Oklahoma" 50,000 watts of radiated power. When atmospheric conditions were right it could be heard all across the western United States. Livewire-Radio… He ran the volume up till the truck fairly vibrated with the voice of Charlie Tuna and the latest Top Forty rock and roll… No one did it better.

Harley had never been so far off the *Dinétah* and was now reduced to a dependence on the service station map he'd picked up earlier. The chicken salad sandwich was all he'd had to eat this day and it was wearing thin. Still he refused to stop for food, thinking eating might make it even harder to stay awake. The wind buffeting the big red Chevy was the only thing keeping him on his toes. At the Mount Carmel Junction, the blowing dirt grew so thick it caused him to miss his turn and he was half-way to Hurricane before he realized what happened. He could see now how the town got its name.

He backtracked to pick up 67, south of Kanab at Fredonia, on the Arizona line. That's when it really started blowing. It was past midnight, and the lack of sleep was affecting his judgment. Twice he thought he saw a wolf-like apparition float across the road…just there, beyond the lights…ghostly, dreamlike and of course, impossible.

There hadn't been a wolf in this part of the country for nearly a hundred years. When he was a boy, the old men talked of desert lobos occasionally working their way up out of Chihuahua and Sonora state. But the stockmen on both sides of the border took a heavy toll and only a few reached this far north even back then. More likely it was just another trick of Old Man Coyote who could make himself appear as most anything should it suit his purpose.

Approaching the Kaibab National Forest, the wind blew harder yet but with less dust as the altitude increased. Harley figured he might be only an hour or so from the North Rim but thought it best he should arrive after daylight when the Park businesses would begin opening.

When he saw the Forest Service sign for the Jacob Lake Campground, he thought he should stop and get some sleep. He wanted to be fresh, *not worn out by the storm when I get there.* He pulled into the entrance not knowing what to expect, but after reading the posted notice decided ten dollars was too much for a couple hours sleep. The facility was primitive, even as campgrounds go in that country; he had no need of a fire pit or picnic table. And it was not that he couldn't afford to stay in a campground now, but he remembered passing a Forest Service maintenance track only minutes earlier. His lifetime of frugality won out. What Harley told himself, was: *This way will give me a little more privacy...and then, too, it's free.* Harley was having a hard time adjusting to his new affluence and its seemingly unlimited choices.

Stretching out on the front seat he dozed fitfully through the final hours of darkness awaking stiff and cold just at dawn There was a doe and her fawn standing not far in front of the truck. The wind had died almost completely away. The two muleys had probably stayed hunkered down during the storm and now wanted their breakfast. Deer don't like wind. It makes them nervous when they can't hear danger approaching...that's why they have those big *mule* ears...they lose that obvious advantage in the wind.

The doe walked off as he opened the door and her fawn followed, only to stop and stand thirty or forty feet off, nose lifted to his scent, trying to see what he was up to. Harley watched them for a long moment before turning into the trees to relieve himself behind an old-growth ponderosa. He returned to the truck twisting and stretching to loosen up. The doe and fawn were still there, unafraid. They had grown accustomed to people around the Forest Service facilities and found them interesting.

Back in the cab Harley squinted at the bank bag and thought, *This might be a good time to do something with this money; it seems silly to have all my eggs in one basket.* Harley had never owned a chicken and couldn't remember seeing a basket of eggs. The thought had just popped into his head, probably from the banker as he explained why Harley should leave some of his winnings right there in his bank.

Smiling now he took five hundred dollars from the bag and carefully divided it between his wallet and two front pockets. Where money was involved, even Harley knew to be cautious among strangers; a caution he had come by the hard way and thus had never forgotten. *It's the hard lessons you don't forget* he thought to himself as he found the screwdriver he wanted lurking under the seat.

Loosening the kick panel on the passenger side of the cab, he stuffed the cash bag well up inside then made sure the carpet was tucked neatly back into place at the bottom. He reached behind the front seat and pulled out his small duffle, rummaged around for his second-hand revolver, the Colt he'd picked up at a pawnshop on his way out of Farmington. A Detective Model .38 Special…on a larger frame than the stainless S & W Charlie Yazzie carried…on the rare occasion the man remembered to carry a sidearm at all.

Harley had never owned a handgun himself yet felt an added measure of confidence just having this one handy and despite the hope he would never have to use it. Nonetheless, he put it in the glove box thinking he should keep it where he could get at it…the same place Charlie Yazzie kept his when he traveled.

He hadn't forgotten Mary Chano's final warning about her niece keeping chancy company. Maybe that was true and maybe it wasn't. He'd know soon enough, one way or the other.

The little lake that gave the area its name was nowhere in sight. Being the end of the season, Harley reasoned the lake might have dried up, or maybe it just couldn't be seen from here. The small store across from the campground would surely be open by this time. He could use a coffee and perhaps something to snack on, but only until he found himself a proper breakfast.

On the road, and caught up in his thoughts of Eileen May, the scent of pine and cool mountain air lifted his spirits, causing him to murmur a few words of thanks to the Holy Ones. Pointing the Chevy down 67 he reveled in the response of the big V-8. Harley turned it loose, anxious now for the North Rim and some word of Eileen.

As it turned out, he had timed things about right and drove into the parking area just as people began straggling in toward the lodge. It was mid-week and well into the off season. He was surprised to see so many tourists already trailing in—people from all over the world by the looks of them. The big tour buses were already lined up in front of the main lodge and disgorging their cargo. Harley's hat and boots drew admiring glances from a small group of Japanese tourists, several of whom smiled behind a hand in passing. Harley touched the brim of his hat and nodded in return. As a twitter ran through them, several gave a slight bow. Harley, not to be outdone, acknowledged this with a nod that was almost a bow and smiled back at them again.

Inside the gift shop there were already a few people browsing and he stood back a little to see if he could spot Eileen. She was nowhere to be seen as far as he could tell, but there was a cashier busy at a register toward the back and he headed that way.

Edging his way through the display counters and knots of gawking looky-loos he waited for a lull in traffic then put on his best face and took off his hat to approach the register. The haughty attendant, tastefully attired and with every hair in place, took a sip of coffee from a hidden cup. She didn't appear to be in a happy mood, not surly or rude, but rather just disconnected as she surveyed the steadily growing crowd of tourists. Seeing, Harley approach she forced a smile and setting the cup back in place, daintily patted her mouth with a tissue. There was a name tag on her blouse declaring her Manager. He could see no other name on the tag leaving him with the impression the place might be subject to a high turnover.

"Can I help you?" She was clearly expecting the usual question concerning the restrooms...or where there might be a drinking fountain.

Harley bellied up to the counter and smiled affably. "I was wondering if you might have an Eileen May working here?"

The woman frowned, looking sharply around the room before answering. Then apparently satisfied no one was listening she gazed down her nose at Harley with a tight-lipped smile. "And who might be inquiring...?"

"Ah...well, I'm Harley Ponyboy from Shiprock, New Mexico. Eileen's aunt Mary told me she might be working here now."

The woman, taken slightly aback at this, recovered herself and with a quick intake of breath, said thoughtfully, "No, I'm sorry, Eileen doesn't work here anymore...she did for a while, but apparently didn't find the work to her liking. She's been gone well over a month now, almost two months, actually."

Harley looked down at the counter with a defeated nod of his head. "You wouldn't happen to know where she was headed, would you?"

The woman hesitated, as though weighing the query against her first impression of the man, but after a moments reflection relented; he appeared harmless enough, and she was inclined to take pity on him. "I'm afraid I don't know where you might find her now. She just up and quit one day; left without giving any reason or notice of any kind." The woman was obviously still angry over this breach of protocol and didn't bother hiding it. Eileen May had caused her a good bit of extra work, running off the way she did, and she was not the sort of woman to forget it...it was a thankless job to start with. Looking the sad-faced little man up and down, she lowered her voice, "I don't know if it's true or not, but I've heard there was something about an altercation Eileen was involved in, at an employees' get-together at a local campground. There was said to be some drinking, I guess." She let the elegant fingers of one hand flutter to her mouth, saying conspiratorially, "Who knows what actually happened, but that was the gist of the story that was going around."

Harley thanked the woman and had already turned and walked some distance away when she spoke softly from behind.

"I'm just sorry for the baby, that's all…"

He stopped mid-stride and turned to look back, but she was already talking with a customer who was grinning over a plaster wall plaque—a local artist's depiction of the iconic tourist attraction, no doubt.

THE GRAND CANYON OF THE COLORADO
One Helluva Hole!

A fresh busload of tourists were pushing their way into line and the cashier obviously now had her hands full. Harley didn't bother going back…he doubted he'd heard her right…that couldn't be what she said.

Outside the building a blinding sun was just up above the far rim caused Harley to blink a time or two as he meandered, downhearted, through yet another gaggle of tourists lining up to hear a Park Ranger speak on the geology of this world-renowned wonder. A young man sporting horn rimmed glasses and carrying a notebook, pulled a pen from the plastic pocket-protector on his flowered shirt and began scribbling down the speaker's name for future reference. Turning to his less than excited female companion he exclaimed, "This is just going to be great! Don't you think, Doris?"

The woman gave a weak nod and looked away with a puckered brow. One might have guessed they were at the end of their honeymoon...forever.

Approaching the parking area Harley did a double take at the sight of Thomas Begay sitting nonchalantly on the tailgate of the red Chevy patiently thumbing through a park brochure. He didn't bother to look up even knowing he'd been spotted. Harley wasn't surprised the man didn't acknowledge him. He could see now that any sort of reconciliation would be on his own head alone and wondered why it always happened this way. He went to stand directly in front of him.

"What took you so long?" Harley asked point-blank.

Thomas, not looking up from the brochure or offering the slightest sign he'd heard, turned another page before replying, "Charlie didn't wake me up to drive when he said he would...that's exactly why we're late. Don't let him tell you any different either."

Harley shook his head. "So, Charlie came, too?"

"Yeah, he said he wouldn't miss it for the world."

Harley almost smiled at this but didn't, knowing it would compromise his position.

"Where is the 'Investigator'?"

"He's in there, same place you were...I figured he'd be out by now, he must have run into some good investigating somewhere." He looked up finally, "Did you find her?"

"Who?"

Thomas just smiled.

Harley hefted himself up on the tailgate and wondered idly if the previous owner might have installed a lift kit on this truck. The tailgate seemed a good bit higher than he was used to. Thomas Begay's feet were barely touching the ground.

"Did you see the Grand Canyon yet?"

"Naa, we were waiting on you…I was hoping we'd get a chance to throw you over the edge."

Harley nodded. "I wish you boys would throw me over. I doubt I'd have the nerve to jump on my own…not sober anyway… I've thought about it some, though."

Thomas grinned finally. "Well, little man. we'll see what we can do about that when Charlie gets back." and then punched him on the arm, but easier than he usually did. The tall Navajo stood and stretched his neck to see past the tourists queuing up.

"Here comes Charlie now." He shaded an eye with one hand. "He looks tired, don't he, Harley? I told him I should be doing more of the driving last night…it's my goddamned truck. We'd damn sure got here sooner if he'd let me take the wheel. I swear, he drives like an old lady."

Harley watched the Investigator come down the steps. He looked more than just tired, to him. The man looked pissed. "So, he didn't drive his company truck?" Harley always called his official vehicle the "company" truck, knowing it got on his nerves. Charlie would say, "How many times do I have to tell you, Harley, it's not a company. It's Legal Services…Tribal Government, for Christ's sake."

Thomas laughed. "No, Charlie still claims he can't take an official Tribal vehicle out of state. He did once if you'll remember, then got in trouble for it." Thomas snorted, "And he's the head of Legal Services now, too… The man should be able to take that truck any damn where he pleases…I know I would." He looked directly at Harley for the first time. "But, that's Charlie for you, isn't it? A stickler for the rule book if ever there was one." He took a deep breath, thinking suddenly how good it smelled up here at eight thousand feet, *ponderosa pine is mostly what it smells like.* "So, anyhow, I had to borrow Lucy's truck. I think I got an injector going out on mine. It'll be ok for her to drive back and forth to town. I just didn't want it to quit us half-way to Hell and gone."

"Where're you parked, Thomas?"

"Farther than I wanted to walk to see a big hole." he replied grumpily, "Have you seen those plaster casts they have for sale in the gift shop... They must be selling like hotcakes. I've seen two or three come by here already."

Harley nodded he'd seen them and asked again, "So, where'd you park?"

"It's about a mile up the road, I guess." Thomas glanced over at the line of tourists. "I can't imagine this many people coming all the way out here in the middle of nowhere to see something like this."

Harley studied the crowd a moment before offering an opinion, "I would imagine these people are from pretty far off and don't get to see a really big canyon every day, like we do."

As they talked, Charlie Yazzie was working his way through the crowd and was now within hailing distance. He didn't appear particularly excited by anything he had learned—if he'd learned anything at all. The Investigator raised a hand as he caught Thomas's eye.

Thomas folded his brochure and slipped it into his back pocket thinking Lucy Tallwoman might like to look it over when he got home. He hoped she wouldn't want to come take a look at this thing for herself though. He couldn't imagine why anyone would.

Like his friends, Thomas wore boots and a Stetson hat, but with his hair in a traditional bun at the nape of his neck, and a turquoise-set Concho belt wrapped around his middle. It would be hard to mistake him for anything other than an Indian, and most likely a Navajo.

"*Yaa'eh t'eeh,*" he called to Charlie—mostly just for the benefit of another small group of Japanese tourists who were watching politely from a short distance away. Thomas had heard these people found Indians interesting. He figured they might like to hear some Indian talk...and they did.

Charlie rolled his eyes at the pair and saw Harley raise a middle finger to him in greeting. *It's a wonder one of them hadn't held up a hand and just shouted, "How!" for the benefit of the tourists.* He'd bet it crossed Thomas's mind; that's just the way the man thought.

He smiled across at the pair as an uncontrollable urge came over him—raising his right hand, palm out, he *said* it for them. "How!" he declared in a sonorous tone, and loud enough for the excited little group of foreigners to hear. A ripple of chatter ran through them along with a delicate clapping from a few of the ladies. Some of the older children touched a hand to their mouths in embarrassment. The Japanese, young and old, have long been fascinated by the American West, many being quite knowledgeable when it came to the various tribes and the places they once roamed. This was not the same group Harley had encountered a while earlier, but they, too, recognized Indians when they saw them and were delighted at the slightest interaction.

Not one of the three *Diné* cracked a smile. Glancing a last time at the Japanese, Thomas saw a few of the older ones bow and watched as Harley returned the gesture with a slight inclination of his head. Everyone smiled this time.

"Let's get out of here," Thomas grinned, "Before I decide to scalp someone; that should really make 'em set up and take notice."

The three loaded up in Harley's red Chevy for the congested ride to the other parking lot and Lucy Tallwoman's Ford pickup. Harley searched Charlie's face for some clue as to what he might have learned at the lodge but was too busy dodging tourists to pursue it.

Charlie had just opened his mouth to speak, when Harley decided he couldn't wait any longer and spoke first.

"I'm guessing you boys already talked to Eileen's Aunt Mary, huh? That's how you knew where to find me, huh? What I can't figure out is how you found where she lived up there in Utah. I never told anyone about her." He pinched back a frown as he glanced over at the two.

Charlie grimaced at the steadily increasing herd of people heading their way; most likely from the outlying rental cabins. "Yes… Agent Smith put us onto Mary Chano; she was his last known contact for Eileen." Charlie thought it best he didn't mention that Fred expected to be informed of Eileen's whereabouts should they run across her.

Even so, a look of mild alarm crossed Harley's face. He spat out an explicative to show what he thought of Fred's investigation. "He's never going to give up trying to tie her to that old man's murder, is he?"

"Fred's just keeping track, Harley, that's what the FBI does. 'Keeping track' is part of their job." Charlie thought a moment longer before deciding exactly how much more he should say, "We talked to Mary, all right, and the funny thing is, she had apparently spoken to her niece only hours before we got there."

Harley slapped the steering wheel whispering between clinched teeth, "I had a feeling that woman might hear from Eileen a little more often than she let on."

The Investigator held up a finger which he wagged back and forth and said, "You know, Harley, it could have just been a coincidence that Eileen happened to call when she did." Then seeing the look on Harley's face was forced to admit, "On the other hand you could be right, too." Charlie was here to help the man, not to antagonize him.

"Well, I already talked ta that lady in the gift shop; she wasn't much help...just told how Eileen had some trouble up at a campground the night before they left."

Thomas couldn't stand it any longer and nudged the Investigator with an elbow. "So, did you learn anything at the lodge, or not?" He elbowed his friend. "Harley here didn't seem to find much out."

Charlie smiled and shook his head. "Harley didn't talk to the right people. And he doesn't have a badge on his belt, that always seems to help."

Thomas shook his head as he grinned at the Investigator. "Once you're off the reservation that badge isn't worth the tin it's printed on, Big Boy, and you know it."

Harley was waiting to get a word in. "I'm telling you two I talked to the very woman Eileen worked for..."

"Well, who you should have talked to, Harley, was the outfit's bookkeeper. Eileen had a partial payroll check coming and at some point, would have to send them a forwarding mailing address if she wanted her money. The bookkeeper told me she'd tried every way in the world to have him pay her what she had coming the morning she left. The man finally convinced her it didn't work that way. Her check would have to come from the main office and there wasn't any way around it. Eileen left in a huff but then only a couple of days later sent them an address—she needed the money apparently." This said, Charlie still didn't sound overly optimistic, "There's no guarantee she's still at the address she gave them."

Harley was adamant. "I'll be needing to know where that is. I'm going after her no matter what, and I don't care how long it takes neither."

Thomas grinned. "You're not exactly batting a thousand here, *Hastiin*. Maybe Charlie and I better tag along, for moral support, if nothing else. It looks to me like you could *use* a good investigator on your side."

Charlie jumped in, "Just for a couple of days, Harley, maybe not even that. It's really not that far from here...where she's at I mean...and if she hasn't already moved on." The Investigator brightened considerably when he noted, "It's almost on our way home anyway, Harley."

"Where is it?" Harley was immediately suspicious. He knew the two were trying to put him off Eileen's trail, and he wasn't having any of that.

"Just south of Page—back on the reservation, near Kaibito. She must know someone there that she can stay with. I do recall Mary Chano mentioning she has cousins down that way. Charlie, more thoughtful now, added, "She may have figured there would be repercussions from that little set-to up at the campground. The bookkeeper knew all about that apparently. He mentioned it right off and said it wasn't her boyfriends's first brush with Park Security either. I'm guessing that thing up at the campground isn't their only problem. I can't see any other reason for her to leave like she did—Kaibito isn't much of a place from what I remember...unless you're on the run."

Thomas feigned surprise. "Hey, Kaibito's not far from Navajo Mountain, maybe we could run by my

Uncle John Nez's place...we haven't seen him in a while." His brow furrowed into a frown. "Last I heard, he and Marissa weren't getting along so well. I hope that's worked itself out by now. I liked Marissa, for a white woman, she's a good person."

Harley nodded. "I wondered how long that would last—her being an anthropologist and all; they're pretty nosey, you know, that's what the doc says. And we all know John Nez is a private sort of person when it comes to some things." Harley, too, liked Marissa, but always doubted she could stick it out in so isolated a place as Navajo Mountain. Even *Diné* women often didn't take to that lifestyle...unless they were raised there...and didn't know any better.

Thomas had to agree, "Uncle Johnny isn't the easiest person to get along with either; he's been a little edgy this last year or so. I think being on the Tribal Council and all that responsibility might be too much pressure." He looked off into the distance and said thoughtfully, "It's kind of nice though, having two family members on the council now, it might give a person a little lee-way, if you know what I mean?" The thought caused him to smile. "But getting back to Uncle John... The last time Lucy talked to him at a Council meeting, she thought he seemed a little distant. She says he's well respected by Council members, and way popular in his own district, too. Of course, she's always stood up for Uncle John. And there's no doubt we owe him. He nearly raised me, and we've stayed pretty close over the years." John Nez was a good man to have on your side. Everyone knew that.

Charlie thought for a moment and then added, "Your uncle might know this cousin of Eileen's. I'd judge he knows just about everyone in that part of the country."

Harley thought all this talk about John Nez might make for an easy out. *I don't need these two tagging along and messing things up.* Raising a finger to the pair, he asked, "How about this? How about I go talk to Eileen, and you two can drive on up there and see John Nez? I'll bet he'd appreciate that. If I can't connect with Eileen, then I'll take a run on up there, myself, and you can help me figure things out from there. Why wouldn't that work?"

Charlie turned to look at Thomas, who was already looking his way and smiling. "I suppose we could do that, Harley. There's a phone at the Chapter House at Kaibito. If things don't pan out, you could use it to leave a message at the Chapter House at Navajo Mountain. It's near John's place and there's always someone wanting to curry favor with John Nez. They'd get word to us I'm sure."

Thomas saw the Investigator was just messing with Harley—playing good cop, bad cop. He guessed *he* was supposed to be the 'bad' cop and jumped right in, taking up where Charlie left off.

"But, here's the thing, Harley, Uncle Johnny might well know those people down there at Kaibito, and maybe have some idea of what we're getting into. You know, before you go jumping in over your head like you usually do. We all owe John a visit, anyhow. He's always been there for us when we needed him. It won't take more than a few hours to get up there and find out what he knows…could save us all a lot of trouble down the road."

"Thomas is right! And if Marissa's gone, John Nez could maybe use a little cheering up anyway." Charlie knew the man was a pretty tough old bird and seriously doubted he would have any need of cheering up; but he also knew how easy it was to play on Harley's sympathetic nature.

Both men were fully aware Harley would rather not have them hanging around in the event he found Eileen May. They could understand this but were not going to let him get in over his head on this one. Not with Eileen May. They intended to keep an eye on him whatever it took…and regardless of whether he liked it or not.

Harley shrugged this off, "I don't want to miss her again. As far as we know, she might be getting ready to leave right now."

Thomas pretended he didn't think so, saying, "She's running out of people who will take her in, Harley. She'll likely be at her cousins for a while yet. Her paycheck might not have even reached her this soon, reservation mail being what it is. And then there's that yahoo she's hooked up with. He sounds like someone who could turn out to be a real wild card."

Harley brushed this last aside but had to admit he wasn't yet sure what he would even say to the woman when he did find her. But whatever that turned out to be, he wanted to say it in private. He might need a little time to figure all this out, he couldn't deny that. He'd at least like to have it all straight in his mind this time around.

This could be his last chance to reconnect with Eileen. Despite what his friends thought, he didn't want to spend the rest of his life wondering what...*might have been.*

"What about it, Harley? Let's run up there and see Uncle John?"

Harley stared right through the pair. "You two must think you're talking ta some kind of idiot. I've got the damn roadmap right there in the glove box—we would have to go right past Kaibito to even get to Navajo Mountain."

Charlie had only been to Navajo Mountain once himself and even then, it was by another route. He didn't have a clue...

Thomas, though, knew very well they would have to go by Kaibito. Still the last time he'd passed through, there wasn't even a sign or a post to put one on.

The pair exchanged glances as they came up on Thomas's truck, and Charlie finally realized Harley knew what he was talking about.

In the face of this, Thomas finally caved. "Okay Harley, you have it your way. We'll stop off in Kaibito and find out where the Hell the woman is, and if we locate her, me and Charlie will just stay in the truck while you talk to her."

They pulled even with the truck, and the three got out then stood around while Harley checked his oil.

Charlie, giving a silent nod, nudged Thomas toward his borrowed pickup, calling after him, "Since you don't want me driving, I guess I'll have to ride along with Harley. We wouldn't want him getting any ideas about running off without us, would we?" He grinned as Thomas opened his door and added. "He might just outrun that Ford, should he happen to make a break for it."

Thomas smirked, "Maybe he'll let you drive partway, Big Boy, if he does, I'll catch up to you pretty damn quick."

Harley shook his head, laughing now, and motioned Charlie to get in. *If these two think they can screw up this thing between me and Eileen...they got another think coming.*

Thomas mounted up and gunned the Ford's engine a couple of times to let them know he was ready. He had set this truck up himself, it was fast, and it was full of gas, he seriously doubted Harley's red Chevy could outrun it for any distance.

5

Foiled Again

With Charlie Yazzie calling the shots from the roadmap and Harley Ponyboy driving the lead vehicle, the three Navajo worked their way back up Highway 67 then across Alt 89, to circle up and around the wildly beautiful Marble Canyon on the Colorado, then crossed the famous 'Navajo Bridge' where they rejoined State Highway 89 for the twenty-three mile run north to Page, and back onto the Navajo Reservation. Depending on how far out Eileen's cousins lived from Kaibito it would probably be coming on evening before they got there. They had stopped in the bustling little town of Page to fuel up and grab something to eat. By that time, Charlie had spent a good deal of time checking out Harley's 'unit' as he now referred to the Chevy. Something he'd no doubt picked up from Dapper Dan's sales lingo. Charlie agreed these new models were much improved over his two-year-old Tribal issue. It had taken him years to work his way up the ladder at Legal Services and become next in line for a decent truck. And while his truck was slightly used when he got it, he had, up until now, been happy with it.

Harley patted the dash and gave him the side-eyes. "So, how do you like her, Charlie, not bad, huh?" And then, almost to himself, "Now that I have the money, I'm going to take care of this baby, I'm going to check the oil every chance I get— no more missed oil changes like before, neither. Dapper Dan himself told me, 'Harley,' he says, 'This unit could last you ten or fifteen years if you keep up with the maintenance.' I'll bet old Dan's right, too. My old truck hardly ever got serviced…and look how long it lasted. This truck could easy make it longer than that." Harley stopped to catch his breath but was then right back into it. "Of course, Thomas already told me that old truck was on its last legs and that him working on it now and then was the only thing that kept it going." He paused to catch his breath but not for long.

"That's why I traded it off…Dan knew it wasn't worth much and I don't blame him." He patted the dash again, "This is one of the best Chevrolet trucks Dan Murphy ever got in…told me so himself. Belonged to a little old man right there in town. The old fellow hardly ever drove it, according ta Dan. He died though, and his daughter traded down to a used Cadillac convertible. I can't imagine anyone wanting a 'soft-top' in this country, can you? The sun's bound to eat it up in a hurry, and the wind would beat a person to death with the top down; not to mention, any rain that got in could put an end to your electrical accessories. Dan said he'd seen it plenty of times." Harley was running on…hoping to stave off any further conversation about him and Eileen. He had his mind made up on that subject and didn't intend to discuss it any further, not even with Charlie Yazzie, who was well educated and pretty much gave advice for a living.

The Investigator nodded amiably enough and tried not to smile. It wasn't hard to figure out what Harley was doing, and he knew in the end it wouldn't work. Charlie considered himself a trained interrogator and knew a lot of tricks to get people talking. It shouldn't take long for Harley to turn loose the things he and Thomas really wanted to know.

When he finally did run out of words Charlie was ready for him. "Harley, Thomas is afraid you might be a little ticked off at him for saying you couldn't win that lotto like you did. But you know he was just trying to look out for you, don't you? He didn't mean any harm by it."

Harley couldn't hide a look of satisfaction at how that had turned out. "Well, I guess he knows better now, don't he?"

"Yes, he does. I expect he might even apologize at some point. In fact, he came right out and told me he was going to. He doesn't apologize very often, Harley...not to anyone...but that's just Thomas." Charlie got a faraway look in his eye. "I thought he was going to apologize to my new receptionist the other morning, but he didn't, just the opposite in fact. No Sir! For *anyone* to get an apology out of Thomas Begay is a rare thing, that's just so you'll know, and not be disappointed if he doesn't."

Harley frowned as he murmured, "Don't you worry; I won't hold on ta my breath waiting for that ta happen."

Charlie gazed out the window at a distant cloud shrouded mesa, gouged by dark canyons on their own run through time, leaving behind only whispers of those things no human remembered or could ever understand. There was a note of sadness in his voice when he finally turned back to the driver. "That's good, Harley. I wouldn't hold my breath either, knowing Thomas like we do... He's not an easy man to figure out."

Harley smiled to himself, *these two are going to find out I'm not that easy to figure out either.*

Dark anvil headed clouds were boiling up to the north, beyond the far edge of the mesa. Thunder Birds, big and bold waiting only for the wind to set them sailing south to deliver their heavy cargo. In this country, no one place could count on rain even when it looked inevitable. The geography alone made that impossible. Much of it would depend on where these black-bottom thunder-bumpers came undone, and that, no man could foretell.

The radio mentioned a chance of heavy showers toward evening for this area, but Harley doubted they would be a problem where they were going. The forecast did, however, distract him long enough that his mind finally broke free of those torturous memories of Eileen. Where would he finally draw the line when it came to this woman? Had he only imagined they'd shared any sort of real connection? He didn't want to wind up looking foolish, especially in her eyes. That would be worse than simple rejection.

From the corner of an eye Charlie watched as his friend grappled with these thoughts and couldn't help feeling a twinge of conscience. He and Thomas should, at least, have talked with him about Eileen...even knowing it wouldn't do any good.

Harley seemed to be deep in some internal conversation with himself but didn't appear anywhere near a resolution. Not one he could live with anyhow.

Stretching and yawning as though waking from a short nap, Charlie turned, lifted an eyebrow at his friend, and asked pointblank, "Harley... Do you want to talk about it?"

Harley kept his eyes on the road refusing to answer.

"Well, how about I drive for a while, then?" He glanced in the rearview mirror to make sure Thomas was keeping up and he was.

Harley flexed his fingers, one hand at a time, and then regripped the wheel. "No... I'm good for now, we only got about another hour before Kaibito." He said this with a finality he thought would squelch any further talk aimed in his direction. But there was that thing gnawing at him, and this was probably as good a time as any to bring it up. "I'm wondering why Mary Chano was willing to talk with you and Thomas about Eileen? She could see by your badge you were some kind of law."

Charlie thought about this for a moment before easing into it. "I got the impression she was worried about what might happen down here if you did find Eileen."

Harley thought back to his conversation with the woman and saw it was so. "That did seem to bother her some when we talked. She seemed like a nice enough lady, I guess."

"She probably hadn't talked to her niece at that point, but after Eileen called her, Mary was left with the feeling she was being mistreated by that man she was traveling with...Robert Rafferty...was it? She mentioned Eileen had bruises she didn't want to talk about and seemed afraid of Rafferty. By the time they left Mary knew the man was in some serious sort of trouble. That's why they didn't stay any longer than they did. ...they're probably still on the run right now. Maybe because of that trouble up at the campground, but more likely, something a lot more serious than that."

"How did you know about the campground thing? The lady at the gift shop told me, but I never said anything to Thomas or anyone else about it."

"The bookkeeper told me...it's the sort of thing that makes the rounds pretty quick in a small community like that. It may have been more serious than you thought. It seems this Bob Rafferty as he calls himself, pulled a knife and cut someone."

Harley frowned and nodded. "That would explain them heading for Kaibito, wouldn't it?"

"Maybe."

"What else did Mary Chano say?"

Charlie hesitated, looking out the window again and wishing there was some better way to put it. "She thought you might find more trouble down there than you could handle. She said she wouldn't have told you where to find Eileen, if she'd known then just how bad a person her Niece was hooked up with."

Harley's jaw tightened as he shook his head in denial. "Well, we don't know any of that for a fact. It don't make no difference anyway. I came to see Eileen and I intend ta see her—and that's all there is to it."

Charlie saw it was futile, trying to talk the man out it; they had come too far. Harley had declared himself now and he wasn't a man to back down, once he set his mind to a thing. Talking wouldn't stop him, yet no matter how it played out, Charlie was glad he and Thomas decided to come along. Harley's good nature to the contrary, Charlie had seen him *lose* it a time or two. He doubted even Thomas could prove a mollifying influence should things hit the fan at this stage of the game.

It was midafternoon and only a few miles from Kaibito when they saw the old woman standing alongside the road with her thumb out and even at this distance, looking worn out. There was a shopping bag at her feet, and she was shading her eyes with one hand as Harley pulled to a dusty stop beside her. Charlie Yazzie understood, even in this day and age, no one should leave a person just standing alongside the road in such country. She was on Charlie's side and he rolled down the window smiling.

The woman waited there a moment studying the truck. She didn't know anyone with a new truck like this but when she saw the cardboard dealer-plate, figured someone might have got lucky. When Thomas pulled up behind them, she looked back through the dust and saw he had San Juan County plates. *These people aren't from around here*, she thought, and squinted an eye at the man rolling down the window.

"Yaá et t'eeh," Charlie called and then, in his best Navajo, asked if she needed a ride into Kaibito.

She returned the greeting, and then answered in a loud voice, "Yes...that is where I am heading all right. I have had to walk twice already today, and it was a long time between rides. I am starting to get a little tired..."

Charlie nodded, "The back door is unlocked...hop in." and then added, "you can put your bag back there, too." He had seen her eyeing the pickup bed.

Harley looked over at him and whispered, "She was thinking she would have to ride back there behind the cab, that's how it's usually done out here when someone offers you a ride. She thought that might be what we expected."

The old woman dusted off her long skirts and gave the shopping bag a good shake as well. Carefully arranging her things on the back seat, she got in and shut the door, saying, "I don't want to get this new truck dirty. I've collected a lot of road dust today." She was chuckling to herself as she said this, and then seeing Harley looking at her in the rear-view reassured him, "I got most of it off though. I took a wash over there at that stock tank."

When the woman had settled herself in the seat she reached in her bag for a small sack of hard candies and held it out to the two in the front. Harley peered into the bag and plucked out a red one with hardly any dust at all. He popped it into his mouth as he drove. Charlie held up a hand and declined, "Bad tooth, none for me thanks."

Harley looked surprised. "I didn't know you had a bad tooth, Charlie."

The Investigator, looking straight ahead, rolled his eyes but said nothing.

The old woman extracted a candy for herself, rubbed it clean on her sleeve and carefully put the sack back in her shopping bag before asking, "You boys aren't lost out here, are you?"

"No...not yet. Harley, here, is just looking for a person he knows. She's supposed to be visiting down this way." Charlie pulled a small piece of paper from his shirt pocket and read off the name of Eileen's cousin the bookkeeper had given him the day before. "Her cousins are supposed to live right around here somewhere." He squinted at the paper. "You wouldn't happen to know a Dwight Redhorse, would you?"

The old woman didn't even have to think about it.

"I know everyone out here—most of them since they were born," she laughed, "I know Dwight and his wife Lilly, all right. They live a good bit farther north of town. They don't come down here much...sort of stay off to themselves. They are the kind who think they can live like people used to live fifty years ago and from what I hear, they don't seem to need much to do it." She smiled at the thought. "I heard they had someone staying with them, but no one seems to know who they are. I never have seen any sign of them down here." She moved closer to the window and tilted her head to glance skyward. "The weatherman says we might have some storms blow through here later—that could bring rain. But when it comes to the weather in *this* part of the country, those radio guys don't know any more than you or me. If it does rain, though, you might have a little trouble getting in and out of Dwight's place. Kaibito Creek can get up pretty damn quick if it rains up-country. There's a sand wash or two that sometimes floods should things hit just right, too. That would be something you should watch out for." She looked back at Thomas's Ford and nodded, "You might want to take both of these trucks in case one of you has to pull the other one out." She snickered again. "But if you don't think that'll happen, you can leave this pretty red truck in my yard till you get back. Both our trucks are broke-down at the moment. I'm sure my boys would like to have this new Chevy sitting in the front yard to attract the girls." She slapped her knee and laughed.

Harley looked at her in the mirror. "Why didn't your boys thumb a ride into town for you? Are they too young to go by themselves, Grandmother?"

"Oh, no, they are plenty old enough. They offered to go for me, but then I would have to give them the money." She looked down at her shoes and chuckled softly to herself before answering, "They might have come back drunk, or not come back at all for a long time. Then we still wouldn't have the things we need, and no money left to get them with either. They are pretty good boys, you know, but they can be bad to drink when they get their hands on some money."

Harley nodded back at her, knowing full well what she was talking about. He glanced her way again and changed the subject "I don't think we'll get much rain down this way, Grandmother, but you could be right about farther north. That's good advice about taking two trucks, it's always good to have someone around to pull you out, or whatever."

Charlie saw right away that Harley meant to forestall any notion of him leaving his truck with anyone, and secretly wondered to himself, *Harley might have some of his money hidden away right here in this truck.* Earlier, when being shown the Chevy, he hadn't noticed anything but an old blue duffle, lying open on the backseat and with only a few articles of clothing in it...and a small bag of snacks on the floor behind the driver's seat. It didn't look like there was any kind of money bag in either one. Dapper Dan had mentioned Harley leaving with a considerable amount of cash in a bank bag. He shook his head, thinking, *I'll bet he's hidden it right here in this truck.*

The Investigator sighed and thought to himself, *there was a time when you could leave a vehicle anywhere in the back country, even alongside the road, and not have to worry about anyone messing with it— but not anymore, like the song says, the times they are a changing.*

The old woman pointed up the road to the turnoff and with Thomas close behind, directed them to pull off in front of a compound made up of several older trailers and a double-wide. A goat-proof fence surrounded the property and from out of nowhere several large dogs came loping up, barking nonstop right up to the gate. When they recognized the old lady, they immediately shut up and stood with their tails between their legs, watching as she unloaded. When finally they saw she had nothing for them, they retreated to the double-wide where they whined from under the porch and cast hidden glances at the old woman.

Those dogs made Harley think of Mary Chano's dog back in Utah...people always had a dog in this country...likely from the very beginning when the first people came here, they had dogs. He was one of the few he knew without a dog. He only had mules and they are animals who don't as a rule like dogs. It takes a long while for a mule to get used to a new dog without trying to stomp on it. He only had the one mule left now and it was especially unreliable in this regard. A city dog wouldn't have a chance with it. Harley thought he might just shop around for a better natured mule now that he had the wherewithal. He wouldn't mind having an animal he didn't have to re-break each spring. Yes, he thought, *I might well have to get a dog, now that there is a reason for a little added security around the place... now that I can afford to feed one.* All this money was nice to have, but he could see it came with its own cost in trouble and added responsibility. Things he'd never had to deal with before and, going forward, he wasn't sure how he was going to get through that part of it.

The old woman gathered her things, and looking back, gave a wave to Thomas Begay who returned it with a grin. She turned back to Charlie's open window and offered a hand to shake, which he did.

"I sure do thank you boys for that ride. I was about all wore out. There was a time when that little old bit of walking wouldn't have bothered me none…just getting old I guess." Then lowering her head so she could see in the window she looked across the cab at Harley, and again thanked him for stopping then pointed a finger up the road and past her house, saying. "Just you stay on this road till you see a two-track that turns off to the left and crosses the creek. Follow that road up the canyon there and Dwight's place will be on the left side. They are the only people up that way now…you can't miss them." She stood by the gate until they started down the road…still waving goodbye.

6

Disappointment

Kaibito Creek wasn't any problem when they crossed it. But several miles on there was yet another wash, this time coming in from a more westerly direction, and running a good bit more water. Even Thomas thought it prudent to get out and survey the situation before attempting any sort of crossing. He'd been fooled a few times in places just like these. Going to the edge he studied the rushing water for several minutes. It would be up to him and Harley to make the decision; it was their trucks that might be risking a swim.

Charlie stood back and let the two talk it over. Gazing across the wash at what lay ahead: overgrazed greasewood flats for the most part—but then lifting to barren ridges cut by deep arroyos. Farther north lay considerably rougher terrain soaring to the horizon. Fortunately, the trucks were both four-wheel drive and Thomas's at least, was well supplied with chains, tow ropes, and a Hi-Lift jack mounted behind the spare wheel. He had made sure of all these things before leaving home. Two spare gas cans were snugged to the bed's side rails—he'd checked them when they stopped for fuel in Page. It would take more than this sand wash to stop them.

Harley watched as Thomas threw a small stick in the current, gauged the speed and then went back for a shovel to probe the bottom—mainly gravel he announced, "She's solid enough to cross as long as we don't slow down too much at the start." He examined the bank across from them and judged the swift moving water to be already receding from its highwater mark.

"We're good!" he decided, slapping Harley on the back as he went past. "I'll go first. I wouldn't want to see that pretty red truck go slipping off downstream...with you two in it."

Harley grinned. "Right!" and then called back to him, "You're not just afraid you'll need me to push that Ford on across, are you?"

The closer they came to finding Eileen the higher Harley's spirits rose. Both friends hoped he wasn't setting himself up for a fall.

Both trucks crossed without incident, though Harley's Chevy did slip a little sideways about midway through. *Too light in the rear-end* he figured, and once again made a mental note to add some weight when he got back. He'd never really had the money to fix a truck up the way he'd wanted...but he did now, and this would be one of the first things on his list. On the other hand, he might not have to drive these reservation roads much longer. He was giving some thought to moving into town or maybe just a little way out, like Charlie. Maybe a few acres with a little irrigation. He could see a whole new life in the offing—depending on how things played out with Eileen.

The second wash they came to was even easier. The sky to the north was clearing, and the water here had already gone down, leaving only a few inches of sandy mud. They didn't even stop to reconnoiter this time. Hitting it hard they splashed across in grand style. Both trucks now covered with mud and the new Chevy lost its shine as they worked their way toward the Redhorse camp.

Harley was growing more nervous the closer they got. "Charlie, take a look in that glovebox and hand me my shooter."

"Your what…?"

"You know, my gun, I'm thinking I'd best be ready should we run into any trouble. There's no telling who or what we'll find up there. People living this far out aren't used ta strangers dropping in on them—that Rafferty fellow could have them stirred up, too."

"I didn't know you owned a gun. Harley?"

"I didn't, but I do now. I picked it up at a pawnshop as I was leaving town, a .38 like yours except it's a Colt."

Charlie pursed his lips and stared at the little man. "Harley, do you really think you are going to need a gun up there—you've got me and Thomas for backup?"

"Did you bring your gun?"

"No, I didn't think we'd need one."

"And Thomas don't have one, neither, does he?"

"Not that he's told me about."

"Then hand me the damn Colt, Charlie." He turned to look him in the eye. "Things are different for me now. I'm beginning to see how foolish I've been all these years."

"How so, Harley? Are you feeling a little insecure about your money already?"

Harley's eyes went instantly to the side panel next to Charlie's feet then returned to the road with a nervous jerk when he saw his friend had guessed his hiding place. "Well, when a man finally has a little something, he has to be a bit more on his guard, not everyone you run into these days is going to be what they seem."

Charlie smiled to himself. *This, is why Harley Ponyboy can't play a winning hand of poker, or even tell a lie...especially when the chips are down.*

"How much cash have you got with you, Harley?"

Harley replied instantly and without thinking. "Thirty-five maybe thirty-eight thousand depending how much is left...I've had some expenses... Oh, and a few hundred walking-around money here in my pocket."

"Do you think it's a good idea to be running around the country with all your money right here with you?"

Harley lifted his eyebrows in surprise. "This isn't all my money, Charley... I've got a bank account now, and one of those safety deposit things with money in it too."

"So, how much was your share of that winning ticket, Harley...all told I mean?" Charlie didn't mind asking, just as Harley wouldn't have hesitated to ask him.

With a beatific smile Harley admitted, "I'm not really sure at this point, Charlie, there's still some tax things to figure out and a bond I had ta put up for insurance; you know my driving wasn't too good for a while there. The accountant the bank steered me to has been helping me with the details. He says he'll know for certain in a just a few days…then I can start looking at some investments…according to him, the worst thing I can do is leave it lying around thinking the interest will make a difference." He pointed a finger, "Do you have any idea what interest rate the banks are handing out these days? A man could go broke waiting on that to add up."

"So. You have no idea how much you'll wind up with?"

"Not as yet, I don't. Right now, my guy's guess is— and he seems pretty sure about it—is that the net will be in the neighborhood of five-hundred and fifty thousand… maybe a little more. To be honest he kinda lost me at ten grand, that's what I needed for the truck."

Charlie grew quiet, astounded at so much financial acumen, and terminology, from a man previously unsure where his next meal was coming from. The Investigator raised his head and sniffed a time a or two. "I wish Thomas was here so he could hear this for himself. I would love to watch him turn purple."

"I know, I can't wait ta tell him myself."

They were both still thinking of Thomas and smiling when they were reminded by the beep of a horn that the man was right behind them. Harley looked in his side mirror and saw their friend vigorously pointing off to the left. So engrossed in Harley's good fortune had they become, they had nearly missed the turn to the Redhorse's camp.

Thomas, with his head out the window, backed up a little, and then scowling at the two, pointed his chin at the little cluster of earthen colored dwellings, almost invisible backed against the distant canyon wall.

Harley reversed the truck and pulled up beside him. Charlie rolled down his window.

Thomas was still frowning and clearly in a state.

"Were you two taking a nap? I've been trying to get your attention without honking—I been flashing my lights for nearly a mile! You were about to run clear past the place. So much for just dropping in on these people unannounced."

Charlie couldn't help grinning over at him. "Remind me to tell you how much money Harley has whenever we get a minute."

Thomas spun the truck in reverse raising a small tornado of dust for them to back through as they made the turn.

Laughing and rolling up his window Charlie looked over to see Harley laughing along with him. This was almost like old times and he was suddenly glad he'd decided to come along. The three of them were due a road trip together.

Thomas hung back a little as Harley went on ahead, easing his way up into the camp's yard before honking his horn. There were two old style *hogans* of slanted cedar posts plastered with mud, and close by, a shabby prefab dwelling showing its age. The weathered siding on the prefab blended remarkably well with the two *Hogans*. The usual collection of derelict vehicles were scattered about in the way children might abandon toys that no longer work. None appeared to have gone anywhere recently.

In a patch of weeds beyond the far *hogan*, a milk goat was staked out on a long chain. She looked up at the sound of the horn and stared with jewel-like yellow eyes; visitors were rare, and her curiosity instantly became aroused. She offered a tentative bleat toward the newcomers and then stood stamping her feet as they came closer.

A man working a small field had stopped to watch as well. He leaned on his hoe and studied the two trucks now sitting in the yard and almost to the door of the nearest *hogan*. As Harley, and then Thomas, shut off their engines, the man clad in ragged coveralls still had not made a move toward the house, nor did he wave or call a greeting.

Harley stepped down from the mud-splattered Chevrolet only to reach back inside to honk the horn a second time, making sure the man had seen him and hurry himself along.

He stretched and swung his arms to loosen up; he wasn't used to driving for so long a time and was feeling it now in his shoulders. As he looked around, he thought it odd there was no dog.

Watching the man come up from the field…nearly hidden now in the tall weeds…he saw him hesitate and study his visitors from the shorter distance. Harley waved and smiled to further encourage the man who, seeing there was no way around it, reluctantly knocked the mud off his heavy grubbing hoe. Bringing the hoe along with him he turned to the house with a tired shake of his head. He wore a sweat-stained hat of no discernable style and limped a little as he stepped through a broken-down fence, eyes darting this way and that as though keeping his options open. A raft of grey clouds scuttered across the sky to hide the sun and adding to the austere and impoverished air of the place.

Harley again raised a hand to wave. Before the man could respond, however, the door opened with a raspy screech, but loud enough to signal Harley of this closer option.

The man in the field saw the door open, as well, and for a moment seemed to consider returning to his work...but then continued grimly on toward the house. The woman standing in the door was neither young nor old, with that early patina of age acquired through untold hours spent outdoors and far removed from the niceties of town.

Though seeing the man in the field was already headed their way she nonetheless motioned vigorously for him to hurry himself along.

Harley turned now to the woman thinking she must be Lilly Redhorse and called a pleasant greeting in old Navajo, which he was certain she would understand.

It was a moment longer before the woman answered, glancing again at her man doggedly trudging up the path. She obviously thought it best to wait for him. Her English was not so good, should something go awry she might require some help figuring things out.

She returned Harley's greeting but with a measure of caution and then again, motioned for the man to hurry.

Harley took the initiative, "I'm Harley Ponyboy, come ta see Eileen May, if she's here."

The woman's voice cracked as she replied in a reedy voice, "I thought that might be who you are… Eileen talked to her Aunt Mary yesterday and Mary said she thought you would probably be along sooner or later." Like most older Navajo, the woman took her time and thought things through as much as possible before committing herself. She'd come to understand her words were sometimes subject to misinterpretation and might be hard to call back.

The man with the hoe had, by this time, come up beside his wife, and scratching his jaw in thought, looked Harley over with a polite curiosity. "I heard you say you are Harley Ponyboy. I'm Dwight Redhorse. We been expecting you."

Harley wasn't quite sure what was going on and was somewhat surprised these people knew he was coming. He glanced back toward the trucks at his friend's faces peering from half-open windows and obviously trying to hear what was being said. Harley turned from the woman to stare at the man, who seemed now to be taking the lead.

"What I was asking…is if Eileen May is anywhere about. I would like to speak with her if she is."

The older man took a moment before answering, though he had rehearsed his words on the way up from the field. "Eileen is my cousin.' He said quietly, "She and her friend left early this morning…gone to find work, they said. My son drove them to the Chapter house to pick up a check she was expecting, and then figured to take the two of them on to Tuba City to catch the bus." He turned slightly and pointed. "That's their car over there in the weeds—as you can see, it doesn't have any license plates—my son thinks it might be stolen. The old thing barely made it here at all, and now goddamn it, refuses to start." This about exhausted everything he knew pertaining to Eileen's whereabouts and reason for leaving. Straightening his shoulders slightly he turned back to the woman hoping she would jump in and take it from there. When she didn't, he forged ahead on his own. "My cousin Eileen left something here for you, Mr. Ponyboy."

Harley had almost never been called *Mr.* before, yet he had now been addressed in this manner twice in two days. What was so different about him now? Was the smell of money so strong on him, or was it the new truck that demanded this token of respect?

About this time two shabbily dressed little girls appeared at the open door, one only slightly larger than the other. Then, peeking around the side of the smaller girl, an even smaller boy, a toddler still unsteady on his bare feet. His hair stuck straight up in the air and his nose was running. He wore only a T-shirt and shorts tied with a string at the waist.

Catching sight of the children, the man pointed a finger at the older girl. "Here now, you girls, get little Harley back inside. You know he's not supposed to be out in this cool air. He's already sick and here he don't even have a coat on."

For a moment Harley Ponyboy wasn't sure who the man was referring to and then looked again at the children. Harley wasn't a common name—he'd seldom heard it on the reservation. "Harley?" He said, surprised, and loud enough everyone could hear.

The woman shooshed the three youngsters back inside, but he still could see them, their heads, one above the other like stairsteps peeking out along the edge of the open door. He watched transfixed, as the tiny boy pulled loose from the younger girl and scurried back out. Despite his size the child was surprisingly fast and managed to elude the older girl who, now with one hand over her mouth, was making a grab for the little deserter. She missed the boy, then giving up she dragged her smaller sister further inside, knowing they would surely be held responsible. Skirting the woman as well, the little boy toddled directly toward Harley Ponyboy, bare feet slapping the mud like a duck. Then clutching on to Harley's pantleg he looked up, curious to see who this stranger might be. Harley smiled down at him—it might have been the smile that caught the boy's attention—or maybe hearing him say his name had attracted the child.

Harley reached down and touched the little hand, now firmly attached to his pantleg. The child sniffed his runny nose and looked up with a little smile of his own, a smile remarkably like that of the man he was holding on to.

Dwight Redhorse let the hoe drop from his hand and covering his mouth as he whispered to his wife, "I never saw him do anything like that before. He usually don't take to strangers." Dwight was unaware small children are often drawn to people who smile, and many times are prone to respond in a like manner.

The man in the coveralls nudged the woman and whispered something else. She stepped back and went into the house, where they could hear her raise her voice at the two girls. Returning in only a moment or two with a sealed envelope, she thrust it into Harley's hand along with a plastic bag of disposable diapers.

"Eileen wanted you to have your boy now, she said, she can't take care of him no more." She threw a sideways glance at her husband before going on, not quite sure how she should put it. "Eileen…she's going through some 'health' problems right now…she's just not up to tending to him." Lilly Redhorse stopped talking then, as though she might have already said too much, or maybe not explained things as well as she might have.

Her husband was quick to add what he thought might help. "Eileen's Aunt Mary sent us a message down to the Chapter house saying you were a good person and should be the one to have him. Mary knew that baby wasn't being taken proper care of. She said she offered to take him herself when Eileen was up there at her place. But Eileen told her no, he belongs with his father. 'Maybe the two of them can make something of each other,' is what she told her."

Harley stood dumbstruck, staring from one to the other of the ragged couple, and then finally down to the baby clinging to his leg. The little fellow was wobbly but holding on with a firm grip, the other fist in his mouth, he didn't waver as he looked up at the man.

Harley was sure there was some part of this he hadn't fully understood…that he'd somehow missed the most important part…something so vitally important that if known, would instantly make everything clear. He looked down at the envelope and studied his name written in Eileen's own hand. It was the closest he'd come to her in a long time and he ran a finger over his name several times. Shaking his head, he folded the envelope in half before putting it in his pocket. He somehow couldn't bring himself to read it right there in front of everyone, afraid he might not be able to keep his emotions in check, and that seemed important right now.

The husband had a softer look in his eye when he said, "I'm guessing you didn't know about this boy? Mary Chano is my clan cousin, she said she didn't think you knew about this boy. Eileen probably thought you wouldn't want to see him…or her again. I guess that's what she was thinking. She's not herself right now. I doubt she can take care of a baby the way she is." He looked down at the ground. "She wants you to have him now."

The woman moved closer to her husband. "We might have kept him if no one came. My husband is related to Eileen by *blood* and clan." She said this last in a reproachful way and stared the man down, ashamed he wouldn't own up to being blood kin. "There isn't anyone else that can take this boy. It would fall to us to care for him if you hadn't come along. We really can't afford another child and might someday have to turn him over to Child Services…much as we'd hate to do that you understand." She was clearly embarrassed to admit these things but thought it something that needed saying regardless how it might reflect on them personally.

Thomas and Charlie, watching intently from open truck windows were still unable to understand what was going on. The two of them watched befuddled as Harley reached down and took the boy up into his arms. Looking into the baby's unwashed little face for the first time, he whispered in his ear, "Hi Harley..." Smoothing the baby's tangled hair, he confided, "I guess it's just you and me now." He glanced at Lilly Redhorse and then asked, more curtly than he meant to, "Where is the boy's clothes?"

"You are looking at them. I burned all they brought with him...they wouldn't have done you any good...wouldn't even made good rags," she said, looking self-conscious and a bit humiliated. "What he's got on there are hand-me-downs from my girls."

Harley nodded then, embarrassed for the woman and not knowing for sure what to say. Reaching in his pocket for his money he peeled off two, one-hundred-dollar bills.

"I appreciate you folks holding onto this boy for me," he said, handing her the money.

The woman at first made as though she might refuse the bills, but when Harley raised a hand to block that notion, she nodded and tucking the money in her skirt, then abruptly turned back to the house without saying another word. Her husband, feeling ashamed himself now, stood only a moment longer, staring first at the boy and then at Harley, but finally he, too, turned and went into the house, pausing only to wave a weak goodbye over his shoulder and closing the door firmly behind him.

Harley turned toward his friends and breaking into a lopsided grin, hefted the child up for them to see, and then laughed at their expressions. At the Chevy he went to the passenger side and said simply, "Scooch over Charlie, you'll have to drive while I hold onto my son."

Charlie slid over so flabbergasted he was unable to say a word.

Thomas Begay got out of his Ford and came up to their window grinning. "From what I could see, it looked like you just bought yourself a kid, Harley?"

Harley still in a state of wonder, smiled back at him. "I guess, in a way, I did…" He straightened up with a chuckle, saying, "Now you'll have two of us to deal with."

Charlie, who up until now hadn't uttered a word, finally found his voice long enough to say, "Boys, if we're going to get back across that wash while there's still some daylight, we'd better get going. It can't be more than a couple hours on to John Nez's place. I expect he can put us up for the night, at least." Then handing the new father a paper napkin left over from lunch he twitched his nose a couple of times, as he pointed at the baby.

Harley wiped the boy's nose and gave him a hug.

Charlie grinned finally. "Well, at least you didn't have to shoot anybody to get him." Then he sniffed delicately and declared, "That baby needs a fresh diaper."

Still smiling, Harley wiped the baby's nose again and reached in the back for his wool-lined jacket, which he draped around the boy as they pulled out of the yard.

"That's not all he needs, Charlie, but I'll see that he gets it...and more. Maybe I can make up for some of what he's been through." He didn't know much about babies but figured he had plenty of time to learn.

Harley understood now what the Holy One's reason had been, making him wait and have all his luck at one time like this.

The Holy Ones had known what was coming all along.

7

The Quandary

There were dollops of suds splashed everywhere and Harley Ponyboy was nearly as wet as his son who was wind-milling water and squalling at the top of his lungs. The washtub on the kitchen table was erupting in spumes of soapy water, causing the onlookers to move their chairs back. Halfway through the spectacle, John Nez suddenly threw up his hands and slipped out the door. When they heard his truck start up and drive off. All three men exchanged glances. Thomas Begay figured his uncle could no longer stand the commotion and just up and left.

Charlie who felt himself well tutored in the ways of parenting, sat thinking how glad he was that he no longer had this sort of thing to look forward to each night; his two children, Joseph Wiley and Sasha, took their own baths now...and even Sasha, went to the bathroom by herself.

Looking harried, yet happy, Harley turned his head to Thomas—hovering there in the background with a towel over his arm. "I hope we didn't run your Uncle off with all this racket. But I doubt anyone would want to be around this boy much longer the way he was."

Thomas laughed. "I wouldn't worry about it. It'll give Uncle Johnny a chance to see what he's been missing all these years."

Harley, with a final check of the boy's ears, stood his son up and poured a pitcher of warm water over his head, then pulled the surprised boy from the tub to fold him in the towel Thomas held out.

Charlie Yazzie thinking it high time he took a part in all this, stepped up now to throw the baby's clothes, such as they were, right in the bath water where he started scrubbing them with a bar of soap.

Thomas rigged up a line across the kitchen and after a quick rinse, the clothes were wrung out and hung to dry over the woodstove. "There, now, these duds will have a nice cedar smell to them," he announced.

The sound of John Nez's truck pulling back up in the yard alerted them to his return. Not more than thirty minutes had passed since Thomas's uncle had left and already, he was back, and with a paper bag filled with clean clothes for the now smiling and cooing Harley Jr.

John held up the bag. "My neighbors that help with the cows when I'm gone have all kinds of kids—but none as small as your little guy anymore. His wife said some of these should fit him, though. She had been meaning to take them to the community 'Free Box' but hadn't got around to it yet."

John Nez had never had children of his own, but *had* helped raise his brother's only boy, Thomas Begay, whom he was pretty certain, had been more trouble than any two or three regular children. He still had a feel for what a child needed, and in this case knew where to get it.

By the time they had the baby wrestled into an oversized girl's nightgown and Harley had figured out how to fit one of the new-fangled disposable diapers, the baby was worn out and falling asleep sitting up, a tiny smile on his round little face.

Thomas eyed the baby with satisfaction and noted, "It's a good thing we got some food in him first, or I'm pretty sure we'd be doing that bath all over again after he ate." He grinned, "He's a stubborn little varmint when he gets riled up, ain't he?"

Charlie smiled over at the boy and murmured. "I wonder who he gets that from?"

Harley beamed at this. "He's a chip off the old block, all right, that's for sure?"

John Nez sat silently watching, hoping this last statement proved to be right. Harley Ponyboy was a good man, and despite past failings, John thought this situation boded well for both these two Ponyboys and thought, *Harley might become an even better man for the sake of this boy.*

He only wished it had come a little sooner for both of them.

~~~~~~~

Charlie woke to the sound of a calf bawling and for a moment couldn't figure out where he was to hear such a racket. His first thought being it was the baby squalling somewhere. He rolled over and looked out the little cedar framed window. It was the sound of John Nez's laughter filtering in that put the morning into perspective. He had to smile as he recalled Harley giving his son a bath in a wash tub. Fully awake now, he looked across the *hogan* John kept ready for visitors. A few rag-tag relatives had on occasion, wanted to move in and live right beside John Nez, thinking he was rich now that he was on the Council. John told them no, saying he had to have that place available for those who came to talk about council business and air their grievances. Not many bothered to come so far to see John these days and Charlie was glad they had taken advantage of the opportunity to connect with him again and see how he was doing.

There had been no sign of Marissa...nor had anyone mentioned her the entire time they'd been there. Charlie figured John Nez would say something when he was ready...or not. The couple had been married for a while now and had lived together for even longer. While the relationship was reported to have its ups and downs, it always seemed to Charlie Yazzie that it was working well enough, all things considered.

From the very beginning, Marissa was only there off and on, either traveling the reservation collecting information for her latest paper or giving talks about the Navajo to various academic groups interested in the culture. While no longer teaching, she was still highly sought after for speaking engagements across the country. As anthropologists go, she was considered quite a reliable authority. Some had initially rumored it around that this was what brought her to take up with John Nez in the first place and surmised the woman would most likely leave when she had all the information she needed. But those who knew them best saw there was more to it than that. There was a bond there, they said, despite no one being able to figure out what that might be.

John Nez was often gone on council business himself and for days at a time, too. He was sometimes required to meet with Congressional committees in Washington and on several occasions had been gone more than a week. It wasn't your average marriage…but then it never could be. While mixed marriages had become more common on the reservation and now more accepted, these two were still considered an odd couple by any standard—often drawing questioning stares from the more traditional denizens of their district. The small-town Whites at the edge of the reservation were even less tolerant.

Only those people who left the reservation to live in distant places escaped the kind of scrutiny experienced right there in their home country.

Charlie roused Thomas and they made ready for breakfast, whatever that might prove to be. Harley Ponyboy felt it poor manners to impose on a person's hospitality too long. And especially not this far from a source of provisions which had to be stockpiled and sometimes rationed should supplies run low. Harley had bought several bags of groceries in Page when they took on fuel and now hoped this would be enough to make up for what they'd used. John Nez waved away any thought of payment, saying he was well supplied, and they should feel free to stay as long as they liked. Hospitality runs deep in the traditions of the Navajo people.

Charlie and Thomas came out into a sunrise so clear and cool they immediately felt invigorated and started for the big *hogan* at a brisk pace. Thomas was first to catch sight of John Nez carrying the baby in his arms, apparently headed to the corrals to show him the new calves.

The Councilman called to them, saying, "Harley is making breakfast—you should go on up there and eat." I'll be along directly," he said, as he perched the little boy on the top rail of the corral for a better view. The child had not seen calves before. He was clapping his pudgy little hands together and laughing, urging them to come closer.

Thomas held up a hand and stopped to watch. "That boy's a dead ringer for Harley—don't you think?" He said this as though he was afraid there might be some doubt.

From the very start Charlie had considered the baby's lineage a near certainty and affirmed this now when he noted. "I don't know how he could be any more like him. I know it's hard to tell at this age but there's a definite and strong resemblance there. No one can deny that." He, too, was watching the boy now and nodding affirmation of his own words. "I thought about it on the drive up here last night." He stopped to consider an added inducement. "Not to mention the boy's age, and the timing seems to fit, too."

"Right. That crossed my mind as well. I figured up the time she'd been gone and how old little Harley is now…it all adds up." Saying this, Thomas turned again toward the big *hogan*. "Harley didn't happen to say anything about the letter Eileen left for him, did he? It would be interesting to hear what the woman had to say. The more I think about it though, there still seems to be something not quite right about this whole deal. Everything just seems to fall into place so easily…almost too easily if you get what I'm trying to say."

They were almost to the door—Charlie halted a moment before going in and put a hand to the back of his neck, rubbing that place that tightened when some intuition cautioned him; he was missing something. About to open the door he stopped dead in his tracks and abruptly declared, "I think I'm going to fire Ben Benally's daughter when we get back."

Thomas didn't know what this had to do with what they'd been talking about but was, nonetheless, quick to agree it was a good idea. Secretly, he couldn't help wondering what "Big Ben" would have to say about it. It was almost certain someone would wind up paying a price, and he hoped it wouldn't be him.

Harley turned from the stove as the pair entered the fragrant *hogan*; the satisfying smell of bacon frying and coffee perking filled the air and drew them to the table.

"You boys kinda slept in late this morning, didn't you?"

There was no denying this and not caring to dignify the jab with an answer, the two sat themselves down in silence. There was a pot of coffee on the table and places set with cups at the ready. Only after they'd poured their coffee and fixed it with canned milk and sugar did they feel up to taking the conversation a step further.

Charlie was smiling as he asked, "How was that boy of yours this morning? There for a while, last night, I thought you might drown him. I'll bet that was his first bath in a wash tub."

"It looked to me like it might have been his first bath of any kind." Thomas was also smiling when he said this, but when Harley turned from the stove, it was plain the comment saddened him…still, Thomas made no effort to apologize.

With a lopsided grin, Harley let it pass and admitted, "He hasn't had the best of care for sure, but like I said last night, I intend to make that up to him." He then returned to his cooking, talking over his shoulder as he worked, "But you know, Eileen hasn't been feeling well of late. Her cousin Lilly told me that herself. I'm afraid Eileen might be worse off than they think…letting this baby go like this."

Thomas glanced at Charlie and shook his head behind his friend's back. "Did Dwight or his wife say what they thought was wrong with her?"

"No, they didn't. To tell the truth, I don't think they knew." Harley was fishing out the bacon and piling it on a paper sack to drain. He then dumped a mound of sliced potatoes and onions into the hot fat before putting a lid on the skillet. There was a platter of scrambled eggs keeping warm on the back of the stove, and he eyed a small pot of oatmeal on the back burner before turning it off. Oatmeal was something he thought his son might be able to handle this morning. In his opinion, Harley Junior hadn't been ill at all, just poorly tended to. Being taken over by all these strangers hadn't seemed to faze the boy one bit, which made Harley suspect he'd grown used to being passed along. He half-turned to the table while keeping one eye on the stove. "I opened that envelope Eileen left for me as soon as I got up this morning." He said this matter-of-factly and with little expression or rancor of any kind. He lifted the lid on the skillet and checked the potatoes, flipping the steaming mound just once to let the other side brown. Harley was a middling cook but could produce a good meal when he set his mind to it.

After a moment or two of silence, his friends decided he didn't intend to say any more about it. Then Charlie noticed a tear slip down the man's cheek and decided he was experiencing some tug of emotion. He and Thomas remained looking down at their cups waiting for him to gather himself.

When, finally, the man went on, an aura of melancholy had taken hold, causing him to pick his words more carefully—even the tone of his voice belied the Harley they knew.

"There was a couple of things in that envelope... One of them being a signed paper saying Eileen *relinquished* all custody of one Harley Ponyboy, Jr. (age thirteen months) to his natural father, Harley Ponyboy, Sr. an enrolled member of the Navajo Nation." At this point he paused to brush away the hint of another tear, but his voice grew stronger as he went on. "It wasn't all that official looking to me, but at least it's something, I guess."

Charlie said, "I'll have a look later, Harley, and see what can be done with it—it's probably binding enough for the present, should no one contest it."

Harley drew himself up. "I can't think of anyone that would question it. No one seems to want this little guy anyway. As far as I can see, none of Eileen's people have any way of taking care of him."

"I don't think that's going to be an issue. I doubt there's anyone who would go up against the kind of legal front you can afford now." This was the lawyer coming out in Charlie and both men knew he could be counted on to see Harley's claim defended, should it ever come to that.

Thomas Begay was quick to speak up then, anxious to get on with it so they could move along to breakfast. "You better turn those potatoes again, Harley... What else was in the envelope?"

Harley reached in his shirt pocket and pulled out a photograph which he tossed over to the table before returning to the food.

Thomas picked it up and studied the signed photo for a moment and then without comment, passed it to Charlie.

Charlie noted it was dated not long after Eileen left the reservation more than two years previously. Turning the photo over he saw it had been taken by a professional studio in Washington state, and was just signed, "Love ya!" and below that in a flowing hand:

"Eileen."

She looked good in the picture, yet Charlie doubted she would look like that now, two years of hard living and a baby could make a big difference in a person on the fast track. There was no actual dedication on the photo and Charlie guessed few would believe she'd meant the sentiment for Harley specifically. He glanced up from the photo to see Thomas's face turn grim as he scrutinized their friend. Thomas Begay was having bad thoughts about Eileen May, and this wasn't the first time, either. He had not trusted the woman from the beginning and had never made a secret of it, even to Harley Ponyboy.

~~~~~~~

Later that morning on the way back down from Navajo Mountain and their visit with John Nez, Charlie along with Harley and the baby riding shotgun, were once again running out ahead of Thomas Begay's Ford. They decided on Route 16 south through Navajo National Monument, continuing south on 98 past the Shonto turnoff, then hit 160 before angling northeast to Kayenta. A straight shot to Teec Nos Pos would then leave them only a two-hour run back to Shiprock and home. There are few direct routes to *anywhere* on the reservation and going 'roundabout' is a way of life for those traveling the outer reaches.

Just before Shonto, Charlie who preferred to drive rather than hold little Harley who was feeling his oats, so to speak, spied a pickup stopped alongside the road with its hood up. Harley Ponyboy saw it at the same time and nodded to Charlie, inclining his head to indicate they should pull over and see what the matter might be. Helping a traveler in distress is a long-honored tradition in the culture of the *Diné,* and one that is seldom ignored even today.

A long-haired boy, looking to be in his early twenties, was leaning into the engine compartment of an old pickup truck that had clearly seen better days. The boy turned their way with a discouraged frown. He had obviously exhausted his mechanical knowhow and now seemed glad to hear help approaching. Charlie pulled up alongside and with his window down, asked if the young man needed help.

"I was on my way home…" the boy waved an arm toward Kaibito, "and the damn thing just quit on me. It had run fine all the way to Tuba City and back…it has plenty of gas and oil in it…I don't know what the Hell it can be!"

Charlie, having been in this position himself a few times, nodded sympathetically. Thomas Begay had pulled over behind them and was out of his truck and already close enough to hear what the boy said. He was the mechanic of the bunch and was already mentally ticking off the most common problems and a short list of possible cures—he'd seen a lot of sick vehicles in his day and his diagnostic ability in these cases was well known among his friends and neighbors.

Harley Ponyboy, still holding the baby, got out and came around to join the group, peering under the hood and clucking to himself which was about all the help he could offer.

The young man looked at the baby and without thinking said, "Hi, Harley," and gave the child a little wave. Then it hit him, and his look of surprise turned to concern. "Uh...what are you guys doing with little Harley there? That's my cousin Eileen's boy?"

Big Harley tightened his grip on the tyke and with a smile explained, "This is my son. I've come for him. I'm Harley Ponyboy...Senior, " he added with a grin.

The Boy stood scratching his head, silently staring from the man to the toddler, suspicion fading somewhat as he studied the resemblance between the two. The baby smiled back at him and jabbered something in an unknown tongue.

As the light bulb went off in Harley's head he squinted at the young man. "You are Dwight Redhorse's son, aren't you?"

Thomas nudged Charlie Yazzie and whispered. "What are the odds? Right?"

Charlie looked out across the desperately lonely country stretching to the horizon. "I'd say the odds are pretty damn good—we haven't passed another car in more than thirty minutes—there's just not that many people out here, Thomas." The Investigator then stepped up and pulling the badge from his belt, held it up for the young man to see, then identified himself, saying, "Harley here is who he says he is, and he has a letter from Eileen May relinquishing custody of little Harley. We were just up at your place yesterday and picked the boy up. Your parents will explain everything when you get home."

The badge worked its usual magic and the young man immediately seemed to relax, telling Charlie his name was indeed Jason Redhorse.

Thomas jostled his way in to study the engine, going over each suspect component with a practiced eye. Smiling, finally, he reached across to push the distributer wire further up into the coil. *Why someone would mount that coil upside down... Gravity alone would allow the lead to work itself out on these rough roads.* Motioning to the boy he called, "Get in and give it a try now, Jason."

The boy jumped to comply and the truck, which had no muffler, roared instantly to life which in turn startled the baby who clouded up with a frown and opened his mouth with a yell. Harley jiggled him up and down a time or two assuring him in a soft voice everything was all right—it worked, and in only a moment he was jabbering happily at the noisy truck.

Harley stepped up to the Redhorse boy's window and asked, "So, you took Eileen and her friend into Tuba City to catch the bus?"

The boy nodded. "Eileen had to cash her check first so she could fill up my tank. Her boyfriend, he didn't like that, said it shouldn't take more than a half-tank to get me home. Eileen jumped right down his throat, 'We're filling it up!' she told him." Jason looked Harley straight in the eye. "That guy's a jerk and I can tell you he didn't like little Harley much either—thought he was too much trouble, I guess. That may be the reason Eileen left the baby behind. It's a good thing you came for him—he'll make a fine little boy once he gets settled down in one spot for a while. Hell, he's already been more places than I have and I'm twenty years old."

Harley's mouth tightened as he struggled to control his voice. "Those two didn't happen to mention where they were headed, did they?"

"They were talking about Tucson, I guess the man had some relations there from what I could figure out. He called it his 'safe house' whatever that's supposed to mean."

Charlie, who was listening to all this, moved up beside Harley and put his hand on the windowsill. "Jason, what was that man's last name, do you recall?"

The boy pursed his lips. "Eileen mostly just called him Robert, but once, I heard her use his last name; Rafferty is what it sounded like. I wouldn't count on that being his *real* name though...he was a pretty shifty character from what I saw of him. And I would bet that car they came in wasn't his either." He chewed on his lower lip a few seconds and then said, "I hope Eileen dumps that guy once they get where they're going. I'm beginning to feel afraid for her."

Harley's face turned to stone as he patted the baby, who obligingly burped in his ear.

Thomas closed the truck's hood and stood to the side as he called to Jason Redhorse over the sound of the engine. "I'd put a dab of something on that coil wire to keep it from working out of there again." He said this knowing the boy probably wouldn't get around to it...not until it left him at the side of the road again, he wouldn't. It had dawned on him why the coil was upside down. They most likely cut off the frazzled end of the wire so many times they had to turn the coil upside down for the shorter lead to reach. Poor folks had poor ways, was his final judgement…and he could relate to that.

Charlie kept his hand on the sill as though holding the vehicle back a last moment while reaching in his shirt pocket for one of his cards.

"Jason, should Eileen get in touch with you folks I would appreciate it if you could give me a call at this number." Just leave a message if I'm not in. I'll get back to you; Harley would like to stay in contact with Eileen in case he has questions about the baby."

The boy scrutinized the card. "Legal Services, huh? Sure, I'll let you know if I hear anything, Mr. Yazzie. I'd like to keep up with how little Harley's getting along anyway."

Charlie then looked up and down the road both ways, tapped the sill a couple of times and motioned the boy onto the highway.

The young man gave Thomas a little salute as he passed and his grateful thank-you carried back to all of them.

Harley waved Jason goodbye while lifting the baby's arm up and down, causing *him* to wave as well.

Charlie turned to Thomas and with a quick 'thumbs up' indicated they were all set to go. The three men and a baby were soon back on the road and headed for home.

Earlier, before leaving John Nez's place, they had made a small bed in the back seat for little Harley but had so far been unable to keep him in it due to his constant efforts to explore and make his way back up front…that's where the people were. Now, however, it was clear the little fellow was winding down and on the verge of falling asleep. Harley was then able to take the wheel for a while, leaving Charlie to keep an eye on the boy as he slept in the back.

Soft music from a Utah station's easy-listening program filled the cab, and the two men, each with his own thoughts, traveled without speaking for a few miles. Harley set the cruise control on the long straight to Kayenta and was finally able to relax a little. Keeping his eyes straight ahead he chuckled deep in his throat. "If we didn't have little Harley back there, I'd show Thomas what this truck can do."

"Well, good that you are already thinking that way…about the baby, I mean." Charlie smiled. "Having a baby depending on you makes a person think about a lot of things they might not otherwise considered."

Harley hesitated a moment before saying, "I just wish I'd had a few minutes with Eileen…to let her know how things are now…what with the money and all. I think I might have changed her mind about a few things."

Charlie nodded reluctantly thinking to himself, that things had, so far, worked out better for his friend than he thought possible. Still, he was left with the impression Harley intended to find the woman despite all. That worried him. Had she known about Harley's recent windfall in advance, there might have been an entirely different outcome to the recovery of the child— and not one in Harley's best interest. Eileen May had now fallen even lower in his estimation. As far as he was concerned, she was in a downward spiral that held little promise of any sort of future with Harley and her son. As soon as they were back home, he intended to find out who this Robert Rafferty really was, and whatever else Agent Fred Smith could dig up on him.

"Harley, it seems to me Eileen can only complicate you and your son's life right now. She's obviously unable to help herself let alone helping with the boy in any reliable way. As I see it, you're pretty much the only person that baby has left; it will be up to you to put him first going forward."

Harley's hands tightened on the wheel and his voice became deadly serious. "I'll do whatever it takes…you can count on that. I don't want this little guy winding up like me when I was his age."

As sincere as Charlie knew his friend's intentions were, he still worried Harley might not be prepared to face the inevitable challenges that lie ahead.

8

The Adjustment

Robert J. Rafferty had a lot on his mind, but he was accustomed to that and good at prioritizing. He didn't find any of this daunting but admitted to the situation being more complex now. Eileen May had provided them both a new opportunity...and a serious liability along with it.

The two had met at a down-at-the-heels pub on Seattle's historic waterfront, both obviously Indian, and that alone proved an attraction. Each hoped the other might be of a local tribal affiliation, one that might provide a little cover. As it turned out, their ethnic ties lay more to the Southwest—Eileen with a Navajo mother, and Robert a mixture of several tribes in southern Arizona. Neither had been raised on a reservation and both shared an inclination for a more modern and freewheeling lifestyle. They lived by their wits and were first and foremost, opportunists. This latter affinity proved to be the cementing factor. When first they met, Eileen was working in a church funded nursing home and all things considered, seemed to be doing quite well. With her own apartment and a little money in the bank she was, to all appearances, a self-sufficient woman on her way up.

The chance meeting had been a stroke of luck in Robert's view and he quickly parlayed his shrewd grasp of the woman's less obvious vulnerabilities into an increasing dependence on his incisive emotional support. He was intelligent and clearly well educated, though at the time he had no visible means of support he talked a good story, saying he had several irons in the fire and expected good things from that.

Things went along smoothly enough for several months, but eventually Eileen was finally forced to admit two things to the man; first that she was embezzling at work to finance their escalating lifestyle, and secondly, that she was pregnant…and had been for some time…from before she left the reservation, in fact. She had been in denial long enough that when reality did finally set in, it was too late to remedy either situation.

Robert, not one to give up a good thing on a trifle, rationalized this chain of events by saying it shouldn't be all that long until Eileen was back at work—whatever that work might prove to be—and in the meantime he was willing to step-up as their sole provider. He found this an opportune time to mention that he, too, had certain legal problems, including outstanding warrants for his arrest. He then came to the rather tardy conclusion they might need to lie low for a while, but still didn't clarify what his undisclosed warrants involved.

To Eileen all indicators suggested Robert's problems were serious ones. Serious enough, it was decided, that the only fix was a quick departure for more distant, and hopefully, friendlier climes. Ultimately the couple was obliged to flee Seattle and as it turned out, only steps ahead of the law.

Robert had often promoted himself as a talented gambler—given a reasonable bankroll to start with, of course...and should the competition not be too stiff. Using what funds Eileen had squirreled away as a stake, they boarded a bus back to Salt Lake where Robert immediately ferreted out a few backroom poker games on the seamier side of town. It was a life Robert was familiar with and thanks to a few nefarious little side gigs and a run of pure luck with the cards, he was able to provide reasonably well for the two of them. That is, until the baby came when, of course, things became more complicated.

Eileen's recovery proceeded slowly and with the added drag of caring for an infant and all that entailed, things gradually went from bad to worse. Robert heard there was work further south...one possibility being on the North Rim of the Grand Canyon...seasonal to be sure and late in the season at that, but something, nonetheless. He felt they were again pushing their luck and a change was in order should they have any hope of staying ahead of the law. A two-day stop at Eileen's aunt's house had not been in Robert's plans but Eileen insisted, saying she might be able to hit Mary up for a small loan as she had from time to time in the past.

Though Robert had a few hidden resources Eileen knew nothing about, he would later come to look back on Mary Chano's later intervention in her niece's affairs as one of the major turning points in his life.

~~~~~~~~~

At their new jobs on the North Rim the couple settled into their quarters as comfortably as possible, being careful to maintain what they considered a low profile. Robert working as a groundskeeper and maintenance person and Eileen finding work in the gift shop, mainly stocking shelves and cleaning up. An elderly woman whose husband was in a park management position, offered to care for little Harley during the day…saying she missed her grandchildren. Their life had leveled out somewhat, leaving them both feeling a little more secure and in truth, verging on boredom—until that fateful night of the employees' "end of season get-together."

By this time both Robert and Eileen were itching for a little social interaction, something that didn't involve tourists Eileen insisted. Convincing themselves they were short timers, anyway, they felt they might as well indulge themselves a bit. Their next-door neighbor agreed to watch the baby for a few hours noting her husband was hosting an interaction group for the Park Service that night, and she'd be alone and unable to sleep in any case.

Eileen assured the woman they wouldn't be long, and the couple were then on their way for a relaxing night out. They weren't surprised to see some drinking going on despite alcohol being banned in the government campground. The party started off well enough and Robert was soon among coworkers from the maintenance department and well in his cups. When one of the older hands made a play for Eileen, Robert felt the irrational urge to defend her honor—his first instinct being to pull a knife on the surprised interloper. He then proceeded to inflict some minor damage before three of the man's friends were able to pull him off. The upshot was that the man, though not seriously injured, declared his intention to prefer charges the next morning.

Once again the pair, with little Harley in tow, hurriedly gathered their few possessions and headed for the only refuge Eileen could think of.

Her cousin's camp at Kaibito was isolated and the Redhorse family were simple people who wouldn't ask too many questions. After being there, a few days, however, and seeing how the people lived, Eileen shuddered when Robert said they might have to spend the coming winter with her relatives. Even if the Redhorse family were amenable, Eileen felt the prospect abhorrent. She was certain a winter with her clansmen would drive them both to the edge.

When Aunt Mary called the Chapter House and left a message for her niece to return her call, Eileen sensed a change of luck. She returned the call to learn of the much more affluent Harley Ponyboy's search for her. This changed everything. But it was Robert that most discerned the feeble ray of light in their heretofore interminable vortex of darkness.

Now, if what Eileen's Aunt Mary indicated in her phone call was true...and Robert had no reason to believe otherwise... this Harley Ponyboy might be just the break they needed. One that had all the earmarks of something that fit his skill set. Privately, he was afraid something better might be long in coming. The man had to suppress a smile when he thought of Eileen's infatuated bumpkin admirer from the reservation—the father of her illegitimate brat—and knew this might well prove their way out, or rather his way out. The possibilities threw a whole new light on their difficulties and for the first time in weeks Robert had high expectations for the future, and just in time too. He had almost decided Eileen was at the point of diminishing returns, or in words she would understand, "More trouble than she was worth."

Should the woman decide to play along with this new opportunity, however, he would have to rethink that...but only for the time being, of course.

9

The Dichotomy

Once Harley Ponyboy set his mind to a thing, he seldom wavered until satisfied he'd made his best effort. He began by outfitting himself and his son in the latest in western wear. Some of it a little over the top his friends opined, but well-deserved everyone agreed. Harley then made the rounds of everyone who had done him past favors making certain they were all well remembered. Feeling better in both body and spirit, he proceeded out to the Begay Camp to look in on Thomas's father-in-law, a Singer of some reputation despite his declining health. According to Lucy Tallwoman, her father had been doing a bit better of late and thought this partially due to his involvement in the new medical trial she'd fought tooth and nail to have him enrolled in.

Old Man Paul T'Sosi, as he had now come to be known even to his friends, had long served as Harley's mentor and spiritual advisor and Harley wanted to see what this old man thought of his son, even bless him if possible, and offer whatever guidance he thought might be useful. There was the matter of a Navajo name for the boy for one thing, that alone would take some guidance.

Probably some small ceremony would be the thing...attended only by their closest friends. These were heady days for Harley Ponyboy, and he was making the most of them.

Driving up to the Begay's new house, still only a few years old, he noticed the absence of vehicles and first surmised there might be no one home. Their two children would be in school, of course, but it would be unusual to find no one at all there.

Harley honked the horn before hefting his son from the now washed and sparkling Chevy truck, then made his way around to the kitchen door. If Paul was in the big house this time of morning, he would most likely be in the kitchen drinking coffee. Harley first knocked, then pounded on the door. He looked at his son and tightened his grip on the boy, "Stop squirming around, Harley, you're not getting down out here." He smiled into the frowning little face and declared, "I don't feel like chasing you around this morning."

A soft voice from the old *hogan* behind him inquired. "Are you talking to yourself now, Harley Ponyboy?" Paul couldn't see what Harley was holding in front of him, but there was nothing wrong with the old Singer's hearing.

Harley turned, grinning hugely as held out his son for the old man's inspection.

"I heard you'd found yourself a baby, Harley. Bring him in here so I can have a look at him."

In the dimly lit *hogan,* Harley stood the boy on a chair next to the table. Paul cocked his head and leaned closer, the better to see the boy. "There has been some talk that he might not be yours..." The old man was a plain talker and these days cared little for how it might be taken. "But now that I see him for myself...there's no doubt in my mind whose boy this is. I have seldom seen such a likeness at this young age. Does he talk?"

Harley reached out and gently poked the boy's shoulder. "Say something to Paul, Harley." The boy grimaced and cut loose with a squall that made the old man jump back.

"I guess that's going to be about it for now," Harley picked the boy back up. "He talks to *himself* every now and then, but no one has been able to figure out what he's saying."

The toddler quieted down and with a somber face watched the old man's every move, then finally losing interest, turned away to focus his attention on the *hogan* itself and the many interesting things hung about the walls, in the shelves and even pushed under the beds.

The old man smiled as he studied the boy. "Set the boy down Harley; the stove is cold and there's not much he can get into. Let him look around... He may never see another old place like this." Paul's daughter was constantly after him to move into the new house with the rest of the family. But he said, "No. Your mother and I lived here a long time. We raised you here, and I have good memories of those times when I'm in this place. No one ever died in this *hogan,*" he went on, "so there is no reason to give it up." He glanced around the room, seeing things only he could see. "These old time *hoogans,*" and here he used the old Navajo way of saying it, "are part of the earth, and holy to old people like me. I intend to die right here—then they can tear it down if they want."

Harley nodded his understanding; he'd heard it all before and knew the old man's family would play hell ever changing his mind.

The old Singer pulled at an ear to recall what they had been talking about. "I wouldn't worry about this little man not talking. He will eventually let you know what's on his mind…it's just a matter of time… I was a slow talker myself. And now just look at me!"

The two men then spent over an hour discussing how best to help this boy stay on the Beauty Path and keep his *hozo* right. This, Paul thought, was the only way he could understand who he was and allow him to connect with his people.

When Thomas finally came, he brought word that Charlie's wife, Sue, thought she had found just the right property for their newly affluent friend. Only a short distance from their own place, and considerably nicer, she'd said, with a twinge of envy. Thomas grinned, "It's the place the preacher owns…the one with the guinea hens." He smiled at this and said, "He told Sue those guineas go with the place, too."

Harley was excited about the news; not the guineas, particularly, but he remembered the place being a good one. Only weeks ago, the thought of him living there would never have entered his mind.

Upon hearing that Lucy Tallwoman was still stuck in town on Council business, Harley decided not to wait but rather to catch up with her and the children another time. Then they could take their time getting acquainted with his son. He talked on with Paul and Thomas for a few minutes, mostly for politeness sake, then excused himself, saying Little Harley was getting cranky and ready for his nap. *Charlie Yazzie should be getting off work soon* he thought. *We might be still be able to take a quick look at the Preacher's place this afternoon.*

Harley stopped in town to buy ice cream cones for the two of them, and saw the boy look surprised when he touched his tongue to the icy treat. He had obviously not had ice cream before, and Harley worried for a moment that he might still be too young for something like this. It was too late—the boy wouldn't give his up without a fight. Harley relented, justifying his decision, with the thought that Navajo children are often allowed their way...should it not be something that would kill them outright.

By the time the boy finished the cone he was a mess and looking drowsy; a trip to the restroom was required to put him back in order. The wash job woke the boy back up and the new sugar-high caused him to babble the rest of the way to the Yazzie place.

Charlie had just pulled into the drive when Harley fell in behind him. The Investigator was already out of his truck and standing patiently at the steps waiting for Harley to cajole the boy from the front seat. The baby, looking through the windshield, wasn't sure he wanted to leave the truck. He was tired of new places and the red Chevy was beginning to seem like home, it was dry and quiet...and smelled good, too.

Charlie eyed the two with a smile. They were dressed alike in stiff new Levi jeans, and pearl button shirts along with matching hats and boots to complete the picture. The son was a near replica of the father...except for the dried ice cream on his shirt.

The Yazzie children, Joseph Wiley and Sasha, came running from the house, laughing to see the tiny boy dressed in big people clothes. They immediately whisked him back inside to show their mother. Sue was at the stove, putting a pie in the oven, and had to sit down in a chair—she was laughing so hard at the sight of the baby dressed up in 'big people clothes'.

Outside, Charlie was still smiling when he said, "I guess you heard about Preacher's place being for sale. They're already moved out for the most part, just tying up some loose ends, and then they're off to some foreign missionary thing for a few years. They left a key with Sue if you want to see the place." He grinned, "She told them you might pay cash if you liked it well enough."

Harley nodded thoughtfully at this and then assumed a more serious air. "I would think they might consider knocking off a little for cash, wouldn't you guess?"

"That's a good thought, Harley, I was just thinking the same thing, myself." What Charlie had actually been thinking was *Its funny how quickly money can affect a person's outlook. Harley Ponyboy has come a long way in a very short time.*

The house turned out to be well beyond anyone's expectations, with fresh paint everywhere, shiny hardwood floors and custom-built bookshelves in the living room. Due to the Preacher's dutybound obligation to the unforeseen missionary call, the home was reluctantly being offered nicely furnished …virtually turn-key. The surrounding acreage, too, was well kept, including any number of mature fruit trees and even an older barn in good repair. The attached set of corrals, everyone agreed, were a huge plus. The only drawback anyone could point to, being the obnoxious flock of guinea hens, no one had been able catch. The birds were obviously determined to stay on, welcome or not.

That night at dinner all anyone could talk about was the new place their friend might be buying. Sue Yazzie was almost as excited as Harley. "Wow, ten acres, with eight in good pasture. You'll have room for some mules now, Harley."

"Yes, I will, and I've already got my eye on a couple of good ones. I'll have to get me a horse trailer first though, everyone needs a good horse trailer to haul stuff around in anyway. I've borrowed Doc's a few times but have always wanted one of my own." Harley fairly beamed at the thought of all these things now within his grasp. "If this deal goes through that place will suit me and little Harley to a T. Why, I might even get him a few sheep and a couple of goats to herd around. He needs to know where he came from." He looked over at his son in Sasha's old highchair—the boy now fast asleep, his head lying on the edge of his plate—worn out by the two older children who even now were pointing and smiling at the little fellow.

Sasha piped up, "He'll have to have a puppy, too, Uncle Harley, you know, for herding those sheep." Everyone chuckled at this and allowed as how she might be right.

Charlie listened to the chatter and smiled to himself, *How typically Navajo all this talk is, hardly a word about the house itself, which was far better than his own; it was mainly just about the land and the livestock it might support. That was the Diné way of thinking.*

"Harley, tomorrow morning I can call those people up and put in an offer if you like. They don't have it listed yet and should be happy to make a deal before they leave and not have to work long-distance with everything from a foreign country." He scratched his head. "I know a realtor who can draw up a contract for a reasonable fee. I'll look it over for you, of course, but I trust this guy. Sue and I bought our house through him."

~~~~~~~

The following morning Harley showed up at Charlie's office as agreed and went over an offer Charlie felt equitable for both parties. After giving it a lot of thought Harley decided he didn't want to low-ball the people, for fear of losing out on what everyone agreed was a great opportunity. He had left the baby off with Sue, who was more than willing to take care of him for the morning.

As the two men sat talking back and forth, Charlie's intercom flashed an incoming call on his private number. The voice on the line was Agent Fred Smith at the FBI office in Farmington. Charlie listened for a moment and thought he might better continue the call later in private. "Ah...yes, I'll have to get back to you on that Fred. I have someone here in the office at the moment." Putting down the receiver he turned back to Harley Ponyboy, who was visibly pleased the Investigator thought this deal important enough to take precedence over a call from Fred Smith, and not a casual one from what he saw in Charlie's expression.

Turning back to the business at hand the Investigator tried not to sound hurried when he said, "Harley, I'll make sure this offer gets to the seller this morning and hopefully we'll hear something back by this evening."

Harley smiled and nodded, saying, "Well then I guess I better be getting back to pick up little Harley; he can be a hand-full, you know."

Charlie laughed. "I expect Sue can handle him all right." He rose from his chair and passed Harley a copy of the proposed contract, then mentioned, "Sue and I are looking forward to having you for a neighbor, Harley. We both hope this house deal works out for you and the boy."

"Things are moving pretty fast, huh?"

Charlie could hear the excitement in his friend's voice, but thought he caught a hint of uncertainty, too.

"You're doing fine, Harley. I think you're handling everything as well as you possibly could. You're going to be all right with this…just take care of your son and don't let the rest worry you too much. It's all going to work out." Charlie followed him out to the front office where he watched through the window as Harley stopped at his truck, looking up at the sky as though he might be saying a little prayer…or offering thanks…or maybe just checking the weather.

Leaving the office Harley paused beside his truck, drew in a great draught of the chill morning air, and finally looked off past the smokestacks on the San Juan. Only a faint trail of steam rose from the generating plant and the turquoise sky shone clear and clean, a sure indicator of the coming winter. *I hope Charlie's right about all this. I hope I don't wake up to find this is all just a dream.*

Arlene motioned her boss over to the reception desk, her face radiant. "Mister Yazzie, is it true Harley Ponyboy won the Lottery drawing…you know that's the rumor going around, don't you?"

The Investigator nodded his head. *It sure doesn't take long for news of something like this to get around out here.* "Well, Arlene," he paused to think how best to confirm the rumor without making too much of it. "I guess he did win something all right. Though I have to tell you, it wasn't as much as some people think." This was a poor effort at subterfuge. He knew it, and so did Arlene.

"But isn't this something! Harley Ponyboy is a rich man now." An almost spiritual aura crossed Arlene's face as she considered the possibilities. "I guess we'd better get to filling out our tickets here at the office."

"Arlene, you do know about 'lightning not striking in the same place twice', don't you?"

"Yes, I do, but we're not talking about lightning here, Mr. Yazzie. We're talking about someone like Harley Ponyboy up and winning the Lottery." She placed a finger alongside her cheek making her words seem more confidential. "And if it can happen to Harley…it can happen to anyone…it's a big reservation."

Charlie sighed and walked away shaking his head, but halfway back to his office he stopped and then retraced his steps. Then with a solemn wink, laid a dollar down on Arlene's desk. "Put me down for one of those tickets, Arlene." *What the Hell, she could be right.*

Back in his office, he took time to realign his thoughts with the earlier call from Agent Fred Smith, the one interrupted by Harley Ponyboy's real estate offer. He hoped Fred wouldn't be put out over that. It meant a lot to Harley. Picking up the phone he dialed up the FBI man, Fred had sounded upbeat when he called, maybe he, too, would have good news this morning.

Still eyeing his phone as he worked, Fred Smith knew exactly who was calling. "Charlie? Sounds like you had a busy weekend." The FBI Agent couldn't keep the smile out of his voice. "That Grand Canyon's something, isn't it?"

"I suppose it is, Fred, I really didn't get to see much of it." He was grinning himself now. "I'm guessing you got my message about Robert Rafferty and Eileen May?"

"I did, and it didn't take long to come up with something once we had the name. Rafferty's an alias, but one he's used before, so we at least had something to go on. His real name is Robert J. Maldone, better known as R.J. in the little town outside Albuquerque where he was raised. He has relatives on the White Mountain reservation in Arizona, too."

Charlie hardly had time to say, "Hmmm…" before the agent went on, the excitement in his voice almost palpable.

"This guy doesn't land anywhere for very long. So, I'm guessing those two may not be in Arizona much longer either." There was the sound of papers being shuffled. "Here's the troubling part, Charlie, while the man has several outstanding warrants against him—at least one of those for felony assault with intent—there's also a two-year old arrest and hold warrant as a suspect in the disappearance of several women. All in either Arizona or New Mexico. All Native American—no remains ever found, so the investigation appears to have stalled and probably for that very reason: no Corpus…so no Delicti."

Charlie rolled the familiar term around in his head *no corpse, no crime*. Eileen and her new boyfriend might prove more dangerous than he had first thought. "What's your next move, Fred?"

"I'm waiting for that determination from our Phoenix office. Once they have a little more information, they'll decide how to handle it. The local Sheriff's office in Albuquerque had a rap sheet on Maldone, along with a list of relatives he has contacted in the past. We're looking into those people on the White Mountain reservation, as we speak. He's been known to hole up down there before." The Agent paused. "It appears Eileen May could be a little out of her element this time…and probably doesn't even realize it. I talked to the Federal Prosecutor in Albuquerque this morning. He said despite what Maldone may think—they haven't forgotten him—in fact, they've recently come up with what they think are viable grounds for a violation of the Mann Act, and if nothing else, feel they can get a fresh warrant for that alone. It would at least put him back under the gun." He raised his voice slightly for emphasis, "Maldone is moving to the top of the Bureau's list, Charlie. He may be as vicious a killer as we've seen in some time." It was clear the Senior Agent was looking forward to taking this man down and fully realized this might be his last chance.

Later that afternoon, recalling the conversation, the Legal Services Investigator thought, *Assuming Fred's long-held suspicions are true, Eileen May might be the sort of person that could take this Maldone guy on...and survive.* Charlie himself was firm in the belief there was more to the woman than anyone knew. The other thing that occurred to him was *Eileen might try to contact Harley. Especially if she knew he had enough money now to make him worth the trouble.* The bottom line, unfortunately, was that this mean even more troubles in store for his friend Harley Ponyboy, and possibly not far down the road, either.

10

The Plot

Eileen May was sick…sick unto death…was the overly dramatic term that crossed her mind. Still reeling from the effect of her last dose of *medication,* she badly needed help and only Robert Maldone was capable of that. His reservation relatives, while not happy with the prospect of taking them in, had nonetheless, stepped up, not fully knowing the liability they were letting themselves in for. They were, however beginning to suspect their clansman's troubles might be more serious than previously thought. The brother-in-law was soon hinting that it was time they moved on, even offering a little monetary incentive in that direction.

Eileen now convinced that for her there were only three possible options left to consider…each one heartbreaking in its own way. The first would be easy enough and the most pleasant should she be able to convince Robert to turn loose of her medication—but it would be, oh so temporary, and leave her to face the same evil dilemma again and again.

The second solution, going cold turkey, would be more difficult, maybe even impossible at this point, and even then, might not result in a lasting solution.

The third possibility was the most frightening, it would be quick...and guaranteed permanent...yet require an inner fortitude she was not sure she could muster in her current state. She just wasn't sure she was ready for that yet.

It was only human nature that Eileen should choose the easiest and more pleasant of the three—and that, of course, is what she did.

~~~~~~~

Robert smiled as he put the needle away; in only a few minutes Eileen could be helped into the car and barely even know what was happening. When she woke in the morning, she would be far away, and with not the slightest idea how she got there. They'd been with his in-laws for days now and while it had given him time to perfect a plan, it was time they moved on and put that plan into practice. As evening fell and with his brother-in-law and family gone grocery shopping, the time was at last right to make his move. The wife's car had been left in the shed beside their miserable little house. He needed that car. It didn't bother Robert that he would be crossing the last relative off his list of safe havens. If this latest plan worked, he wouldn't have to worry about that for some time.

~~~~~~~

Dawn found the fugitive couple already north of I-40. Staying to the backroads, Robert had pulled into several isolated campgrounds intent on lifting a fresh set of plates. It had occurred him they would be better off ditching the telltale Arizona tags and go with out-of-state plates for this latest acquisition. But that shouldn't take long—not for him it wouldn't.

This little detail had taken more time than he'd allowed, putting him somewhat behind schedule. It couldn't be helped, however, there would already be a report out on the Arizona plates. The man eventually spotted what he was looking for in the outskirts of a small town only a few miles from the New Mexico border. Just the thing he'd had in mind. Where they were headed, New Mexico tags would fit right in…and so would they. He hurried to make the switch. More cautious in the coming dawn, he was thinking, *It will be daylight soon and from here on in we'll have to take extra care to avoid the slightest attention from the law.*

Staying to the backroads and within the speed limit he had taken the time to pay strict attention to every niggling little traffic sign, and while necessary in his opinion, it was beginning to wear on his nerves. When Robert was nervous it was in his nature to turn mean, and there was nothing to be done for that. He gave the sleeping Eileen a grim smile as he thought of the messy business ahead.

Northbound at the eastern edge of Arizona he at last eased into the little town of Window Rock, Capital of the Navajo Nation. He drove to the back lot of a likely looking motel and parked between two eighteen wheelers, drivers yet asleep in their cabs.

Leaving Eileen sleeping in the backseat of the car, he grabbed what little luggage they had and took it through the back entrance to check in.

Leaving their bags in the room he returned to the vehicle only to find Eileen, now awake and steadying herself at the back edge of the car…throwing up in the oil-soaked dirt of the parking lot. Not a pretty sight nor was it an unusual one for this area, people returning from the nearby bars of Gallup made it a common enough occurrence. The big truck next to them fired up with a roar; the driver, staring down from his seat, shook his head and with a disgusted sneer on his face pulled out for his day's run. Robert watched to see if anyone else had taken notice and seeing no sign of this, he took her by the arm, guiding her through the back entrance of the motel. Inside their rear facing room he dragged her to the window looking out on the back lot and again studied the parking area. He double locked the door before pushing her toward the bathroom.

"Clean yourself up, Eileen, and put on a fresh shirt…you smell."

The woman, bleary eyed and unsteady on her feet, grimaced, as she kicked off her shoes, and then stumbled toward the lavatory with a flip of her hair, still mumbling incoherent threats. She shut the door behind her, and he heard the lock click, then the sound of water running.

Sitting himself on the edge of the bed, Robert turned on the television in time to catch the local newscast, watching to make sure he wasn't part of it. Eventually satisfied they hadn't made the area news, he waited through the commercials, certain now the missing car, or campground theft hadn't been newsworthy. And even then, he felt uncomfortable here on the *Dinétah*—vulnerable, might be the better word. Eileen wasn't aware of it, but he had a history here and knew there might yet be warrants out in nearby Gallup.

It was several years since he'd left his good job there, along with the opportunity to pursue his other proclivities here on the reservation. Then only to flee north to Seattle and a new beginning. He had promised himself he would stop, that it wouldn't happen again, but it did, even in the Northwest. Still not much had come of it. He was becoming very good at what he did. Even so, this sort of thing had been so much easier here on the reservation. Easier than anywhere else. Reservation Law Enforcement had been thinly stretched from its inception and even now it was not a serious deterrent, should one know his business. With this upcoming Tribal Fair, the local police would be even less effective. It would be a week of general confusion, chaos even should things get out of hand, which they might, depending on how much booze got smuggled into town.

Should the two keep to the low profile he envisioned they should be nearly invisible for the next few days.

He'd been lucky to find a room so easily—in less than two days the Navajo Nation's Fall Fair would be kicking into high gear and people would be pouring into town. These rooms, commonly booked from the year before, would again be filled. Fortunately, he'd been able to negotiate a small financial arrangement with the desk clerk and now, thanks to the money his brother-in-law had given them, *they* had one of those coveted rooms. He eyed the phone beside the bed, then shook his head at the thought, *That could be dangerous—convenient though it might be—it was too early to be taking so foolish a risk. There would be time enough tomorrow to find a pay phone.*

Eileen had called her Aunt Mary from his brother-in-law's place as soon as they'd arrived in Arizona—to see if Harley Ponyboy had found her cousin's camp, and if he had taken his son away with him as they'd hoped. From what he could hear of the conversation her aunt did most of the talking, Eileen making only the occasional little exclamation of satisfaction. When she hung up, she was smiling.

Later when Robert questioned her, he found the news encouraging but lacking in detail.

Mary Chano told Eileen that two men had come to her place looking for Harley Ponyboy and had questioned her as to the whereabouts of her niece, apparently already knowing that's where their friend would be heading. One of those men, Mary said, was full of questions, yet careful what he said in return. The other, a tall taciturn Navajo, kept his thoughts to himself, saying very little the entire time. He did, however, in a lax moment, let slip that their friend was not a poor man and hinted of a recent windfall. That's why they were trying to find him, he said, before he came to some harm because of the money—making Mary think it must be a considerable amount.

It was plain that Mary felt some sympathy for Harley, but at the same time thought he might be the one to help Eileen with the child. To Mary Chano, the man seemed the type who might take on some responsibility in that regard. Still, her major concern remained focused on her niece and Eileen and her continuing welfare down the road. With her recent phone call, she suspected her niece was in desperate need of help.

Robert had immediately guessed Eileen was not being totally forthcoming about the talk, and that there might be information she was keeping to herself. Further questioning, however, failed to reveal anything along those lines. The woman seemed determined not to give anything else away.

I may have to hold back her 'medication' he thought, *but one way or another, I'll find out what's really going on. When she's in a better frame of mind, we'll have a good talk.* He would reason with her, of course, make it clear how this plan of his could mean an entirely new future for them both…yes, he would say, "for them both." But if it came down to it, and she left him no choice, he would get rough, and this time he wouldn't be easy with her like before.

~~~~~~~

Eileen, came from the shower wrapped in a towel and finding him gone, thought Robert probably had gone for food, neither of them had eaten since the day before and even in her current state she thought a little something might do her good. Robert had mentioned several times that the two of them shouldn't be seen in public together if it could be avoided. No, she was certain he had gone looking for breakfast.

It was cool in the room and she rifled among their open bags before throwing on one of Robert's clean flannel shirts and then dug out a fresh pair of her jeans. She was aware Robert had a pistol, taken from his brother-in-law's house on a whim, but it was no longer in his bag and she thought she knew why. It was lucky for him he had taken it with him. Though her mind had cleared somewhat, a nervous edge was beginning to build. She really hadn't been thinking clearly for days now, making memories of the past, all the more painful.

She knew Robert had a small supply of product laid back—it was his fallback, he told her—and while he had remained generous with her for the time being, that could change, should things not go his way. For the present, however, she was afforded this small window of cogent thought…before her skin began to crawl, the whisperings began, and darkness enveloped her once more. Then there would be no getting away from Robert, not without outside help there wouldn't.

~~~~~~~

Robert Maldone sat in the small cafe drinking his coffee and nervously awaiting his 'to go' order. He tried to keep his thoughts away from the thirtyish something waitress wiping down the nearly deserted counter.

When she thought he wasn't watching she would occasionally look his way with a half-smile.

Robert Maldone missed this game and couldn't help smiling at this little subterfuge. Not that any good could come of it, interesting though the possibilities might be. Too much depended on things going smoothly over the next few days. He was in dangerous territory, and while the chances of anyone recognizing him were slight, the thought still brought a quickening of breath and glimmer of perspiration across his upper lip. He didn't have time for this, too much depended on keeping a clear and uncluttered mind. Still, each time he looked up she seemed to be glancing his way again, longer each time; then would quickly turn back to her work, knowing now he was watching. *Yes,* He thought, *there was definitely something there, no doubt about it now, she knows I have my eye on her.*

When she brought his coffee, Robert was quick to notice the white circle on her ring finger and couldn't help wondering what story might go with that. *Ah, so many opportunities and so little time.*

Finally, the woman took the bag from the order window and carried it to the cash register where he saw her make a note on the check. Looking over at him she motioned that his order was ready and then smiled expectantly as he came up front. She slipped the check inside the bag without a word. Making change, she handed that over, then purposely not looking back, turned and made her way to the kitchen.

Outside, Robert stopped on the corner to retrieve the note which he read with the hint of a smile, then wadded it up and dropped it in the gutter. That would have been all he needed—for Eileen to find this when she was most vulnerable.

He thought of the other woman who had thrown away perfectly good lives on no more than this? The phone number had its own little niche in his mind and would now be impossible to forget.

~~~~~~~~

Eileen propped herself up on the bed and glancing at the television, watched a commercial for the up-coming Navajo Nation Fair. Window Rock's major attraction of the season would commence in the next few days. This caught her attention, and as she watched scenes from the previous year's celebration with its throngs of people, it occurred to her this might be why Robert picked this particular time and place for their staging area. There could be an opportunity here somewhere, even for her. If only she could keep her head straight long enough to take advantage of it. But then, taking advantage was what she had always done best.

When Robert returned with breakfast the conversation began pleasantly enough. He asked how she was feeling and nodded sympathetically when she replied, "A little headache is all."

In the beginning Robert had assured her a bit of 'medication' would help ease her anxiety at leaving Little Harley behind. They would be traveling fast from now on, he'd cautioned, and it might be in the boy's best interest to remain there with her cousins and in a more stable environment, *deplorable though the conditions might be.* Muddled as her thinking was at the time Eileen agreed, and had left the child with hardly a goodbye and little sign of emotion.

Now, Robert continued to smile encouragement as he began explaining his latest plan, one he assured her could set them up for a long while to come. "We'll have to cut back on your 'medication' I'm afraid. I think you can manage without it…you haven't been on it so long that you can't wean yourself off…with a little help, of course. Oh, it might be a bit rough for a day or so, but in the end, you'll find you no longer need it." He paused to gauge the expression on her face and could see she was not convinced. "The plan I have in mind is going to take both of us working together," he warned, "and we'll both have to be on our game to pull it off." He waited for a response, and when none came, his face grew tight with displeasure and a frown signaled possible consequences.

Eileen took her time now, knowing her choice of words would be crucial. "I'll give it a try…I guess we'll just have to see how it goes."

"It can only 'go' one way, Eileen, what little product I have left will have to go toward funding us now." He paused for emphasis. "Until we can see a little daylight here, this is how it will have to be." A grim smile pulled at his lower lip as he assured her, "It won't be long, I promise." And then before she had time to think, he changed the subject.

"How about, in the morning, the two of us take a little day trip out to that trailer house you said Harley lived in? The fresh air and change of scenery will do you good. Maybe we can catch him home and have a little face to face chat to get the ball rolling."

Eileen wasn't convinced this was a good idea and pretended she wasn't sure she remembered the way out there. Robert's rough reply and threatening attitude soon convinced her otherwise. As it turned out she was able to find the place with no problem.

Pulling up in front of the old trailer a sudden wave of nostalgia colored the woman's thoughts, not so much for her time with Harley Ponyboy, but rather for the refuge the place had afforded in that uncertain and dangerous time. She'd whiled away the hours concentrating mainly on herself, recouping physically, and mentally planning the next phase of her life, a plan that was later working quite well... until she ran into Robert Maldone.

"It doesn't appear your boyfriend's at home?" Maldone touched the tip of his tongue to his upper teeth, disappointed, and at odds with what his next move should be.

"No, it doesn't," She said, hoping her satisfaction at this turn of events was not too apparent.

"There's a note on the door. I'll just jump out and see what it has to say." He took the keys with him and she watched as he peered through the trailer's window for a few moments. Robert came back smiling at the note in his hand. "What a dump... I can't imagine anyone actually living out here."

"I've lived in worse..."

"I'm sure you have," he offered without the slightest rancor, and continued to smile as he read the notice a second time, committing it to memory.

"What's it say?" She hadn't thought Harley's place all that bad at the time. Not that she had been there very long, but still...

"It's a mail forwarding notice. How considerate of the poor bastard. This is going to save us some time. I hope he wasn't silly enough to spend *all* his cash on a new house. We might just have to take that, too."

Eileen could see a whole new facet being added to Robert's plan. And it was ugly. Maybe too ugly even for her. She had almost lost herself in this new twist, when she realized the man was speaking again—quietly now, making himself sound even more sinister, and this caused her to turn to him with a start.

"Do you think this is a good idea? It's going to make things all that more complicated, I would think. You know, it would seem to me..."

Robert held up a finger and shook his head—he didn't want to hear it.

"What say we take a run by this new place of Mr. Ponyboy's and have a little look-see. Get the lay of the land, so to speak, maybe get some idea of what the man's really worth. That could come in handy, wouldn't you agree?" Robert couldn't quit smiling as he went on, "I'll call the County Assessor's office in the morning and find out a little more about this new place of his." The man sounded almost euphoric. "This could turn into a gold mine, properly handled."

Eileen felt unaccountably queasy at this, the thought of taking *everything* from Harley had never entered her mind. Yet, now, in the cold hard light of reason, she had to admit it would be silly not to, should the opportunity present itself. She was no longer thinking in the interest of Robert Maldone, or even as a joint concern…but now, strictly in her own regard. She was becoming more convinced than ever that she could pull this operation off by herself. And if not by herself, she knew who she could count on to help. It would be tricky, not to mention the considerable risk. There was suddenly no doubt in her mind, that it was not only doable, but had probably become necessary. She couldn't help feeling she was at a crossroads, and that this was her make or break moment.

On their way back into town Robert watched for some sign of rebellion but saw nothing of the sort. In fact, it seemed there had been some sort of acquiescence on her part that might assure a better relationship going forward. Not that he would countenance anything less, of course, but still this apparent acceptance boded well for the endeavor and at a critical time, too. Things were looking up, in his view.

They found the address with little difficulty and drove by and then stopped for moment to take a quick look. They drove on up the highway to a turn around and then back. The second time Robert pulled over for a longer look at the place. There seemed to be several cars parked around and some activity, a party underway maybe, or perhaps a family gathering of some sort he conjectured out loud.

"He doesn't have much family and only a few friends as far as I know." Eileen, too, studied the place a moment and then seeing someone looking their way, ducked down low in the seat indicating they should go. "We should leave," she said. "I don't want to be recognized. There could be several up there who might know me."

11

Coyote Lurks

It was the women who insisted there be a housewarming for Harley Ponyboy's new home...and then planned it to suit themselves. Just close friends and family they insisted, knowing full well the man's friends were his only family. Lucy Tallwoman took charge and along with her best friend Sue Yazzie, took the bulk of the preparations in stride. Everyone would bring a dish, that was customary, and it was made plain there were to be no gifts. That early decree was modified somewhat when Old Man Paul T'Sosi reminded Lucy that Harley's son was due a naming ceremony and that this would be as good a time as any. The women quickly agreed and then included the ceremony for Little Harley as well. This set off an additional flurry of preparations. The men had little say in any of this and went along with everything as planned.

Charlie's Aunt Annie Eagletree insisted she would again fresh killed beef from her own herd, and the Begay children were quick to pony up a spring lamb. Caleb said he and his sister agreed it was important they contribute from their growing flock. They were old enough now to assume that traditional responsibility and both Lucy and Thomas were proud to see them step up. This was how respectable people brought their children along, knowing everyone should share according to their ability. It was only common sense to reinforce one's *hozo* in such a way. There would be too much food, of course, but it was anticipated that leftovers would be divided among everyone there.

Professor George Armstrong Custer made it known he would pick up all the drinks and ice after leaving his office in Farmington. He was as happy as anyone for Harley, though sad he might be losing a valuable employee. From what he'd heard, Harley would probably not have need of a job anytime in the foreseeable future.

While Paul T'Sosi agreed to oversee the barbeque, he declined Harley's suggestion he throw a couple of guinea hens on the grill. "I don't know anything about those loud-talking birds, Harley, nor do I want to know anything about them."

Harley had previously mentioned to Thomas that the guinea flock, inherited from the previous owner, had grown out of control; he declared something needed to be done. The birds ran loose on the property and roosted at the top of several tall cottonwood trees. They had proven to be constantly on the alert and impossible to catch. Harley admitted they were great watchdogs but noted the paint on his new truck was beginning to suffer. Both the Yazzie and Begay children had tried and failed to corral the birds. Baby Harley found the chase hilarious and couldn't stop laughing, and this, of course, made everyone else laugh, too.

When the designated Saturday morning arrived, the women showed up early, knowing full well Harley would need all the help he could get—putting the house in order and prepping his son for the small ceremony in his honor. Through all of this the boy seemed sociable enough but hadn't been exposed to so many people bent on making friends with him. It wasn't that he was shy but that he was sometimes unpredictable. On one occasion he had reached out and grabbed a store clerk's long hair and wouldn't let go. That was embarrassing. Harley was constantly wondering what else he might have up his sleeve. Even with the older children keeping an eye on him, the child remained somewhat of a wildcard. Harley likened the boy to a mule—there were people he liked and people he didn't—and with that same streak of stubbornness in him, too.

As the cooking got underway the men, as usual, gathered around the grill and talked quietly among themselves while the women busied themselves bringing out food and setting up the serving table. Thomas's daughter Ida Marie Begay, being the oldest of the children, was given grownup duties. She, in turn, kept the two bigger boys running back and forth to the house for those always forgotten yet essential items no one seems to remember until the last minute.

Thomas Begay had twice turned to look down the drive, appearing more concerned each time; finally nudging Charlie, he whispered "That green car was parked at the end of the drive earlier—then left for a while...now it's back. I wouldn't have noticed if it hadn't been for those guinea hens raising hell down there in the pasture."

Charlie glanced that way. "Probably someone looking for an address or maybe they heard a house was for sale up this way."

"Could be... There was a man and a woman in the car first time they showed up, now I can see only a man. I guess it could be some of those religious people that go around talking to everyone in the neighborhood. They like to split up to cover more ground, I guess... It could be some of them folks."

Charlie turned and had taken only a few steps in that direction when the car started up and backed up onto the highway, pausing there only a moment before tearing off in the direction of Shiprock.

Thomas Begay watched it go rubbing the back of his neck, and then asked, "Did you see that? Now, there are two people again. That woman must have been staying out of sight or something. That's a little odd, don't you think?"

"Well, maybe she just didn't feel well and that's why they stopped...and now, she's better."

"Maybe..." Thomas wasn't convinced. "What do you hear from those FBI boys lately, anything new on Eileen and her boyfriend?"

"Only that the agents sent to Robert's relatives down in Arizona apparently missed them. Evidently, the two took off in one of their own family's cars when they left, too."

"Those two are really something... Did Fred say what kind of car they made off with?"

"Well it wasn't the one we just saw, if that's what you're getting at. His brother-in-law's car was a white SUV with Arizona plates."

"I doubt that means much with those two. It sounds like they change cars on a regular basis." Thomas turned back to the party with a half-smile. "I guess those guinea hens, kind of come in handy now and then, huh?"

"They're hard to get past, I'll grant you that, but I expect Harley would be better off getting himself a dog...a big one."

Thomas grew serious. "I wouldn't mention anything to him about this just yet, Charlie. He's still a little nervous about this whole thing what with the baby and new house and all."

"I won't say anything, no need to get him stirred up. But I will let Fred know we might have some lurkers up here." Charlie had taken special note of his friend's tone of voice. Thomas had a sixth sense about these things and over the years Charlie had learned to pay attention.

The Investigator's thoughts were abruptly diverted by Paul T'Sosi beating on a pan to call everyone to eat. The old Singer took a few moments to say a blessing, one Charlie guessed was from his time working for the Episcopal Missionaries. He had been with them a long time and some of it had obviously rubbed off.

The old man also offered a Navajo blessing for Harley's new house and then chanted his own rendition of a *Blessing Way* prayer in old Navajo—even those who didn't understand all the words felt the power in it.

When Paul sat down, people were ready to eat, grabbed plates and gave themselves over to the food.

Looking around the familiar faces, wreathed as they were in smiles and fragrant wisps of cedar smoke, Charlie couldn't deny some vague feeling of loss for those ancient Tribal traditions he'd left behind. He didn't regret the time he'd been away at school or his more modern outlook on life, but still he was happy to be back among his people and more aligned with the Beauty Path.

When everyone finished eating, Paul stood once more to announce it was time to have the naming ceremony for Harley Ponyboy's infant son. He went to Harley and reached out for the boy, who hesitated only a moment before going to the old *Singer*. Smiling, Paul held the little fellow up for everyone to see as he intoned the blessing. At the end, stroked the boy's hair with an eagle plume and announced his new Navajo name.

"His father wants him to be known as *Jadi Ashkii* which in English means Antelope Boy. It is a good name and will be easier for him to pronounce than some. It's not to be spoken lightly or where strangers might hear it to some evil purpose. When he is older, he may earn a different name, but for now we in his inner circle of life will know him as *Jadi Ashkii*."

Harley had never mentioned to anyone that the boy's mother's Navajo name was Antelope Girl. Still he wanted his son to carry this small part of her with him while he was young. He would be sure the boy never learned his mother was now called Falling Girl by her people—sometimes referred to as a *Yóó'a'hááskahh*, which means one who is lost.

Paul handed little Harley back to his father, who was now busy accepting the many small gifts offered to commemorate the day. Paul T'Sosi's contribution was a small beaded medicine bag the boy might someday wear around his neck—just like the one the old man had given Joseph Wiley on his naming day, also the same was a small bird point tucked inside, but this one was of black obsidian and not chert. One thing Little Harley's medicine bag would never have was a desiccated bit of his umbilical cord. Only his mother knew where that might be; if she had ever known at all.

Professor Custer presented the boy with a little handmade silver ring, set with a Morenci turquoise stone showing tiny gold threads running through it.

And Lucy Tallwoman gave a light shoulder blanket, so beautifully woven the crowd went silent at the sight of it.

There were other gifts, too, and Harley put them all in a bag for later. He would, in time, explain to the child who had given each one and the meaning or purpose of each. Harley's heart was full as he watched the sparks fly to the stars and he sent with them his most fervent wish for his son—a life walked in beauty and the gift of *Hozo* to make him one with his people.

~~~~~~

The next morning as Charlie drove in to work, his thoughts turned to the events of the previous evening and this time he was having second thoughts regarding the strangers at the end of Harley's drive. Like Thomas, the Investigator was becoming more convinced now that they were not yet rid of Eileen May. Her Aunt Mary would almost certainly have made mention of Harley's recent change in circumstances. And he suspected now that might well be what brought about Eileen's change in thinking toward her son...and maybe even for Harley Ponyboy, as well.

Although he felt Harley was, at least for the time being, on firm enough legal ground with the informal custody release, he was just as sure it could still be challenged by the right lawyer. What Charlie couldn't get out of his head was the growing premonition that Robert Maldone might push Eileen into some scheme to extort money from Harley. Even more troubling was Agent Smith's assessment of Robert's possible ties to the disappearance of various women over the years. This could well mean Eileen herself was in imminent danger.

All in all, it was beginning to look like life was about to become much more complicated for anyone connected to little Harley, Jr.

The Investigator was barely ten minutes late, but Arlene was already waiting with a message she said came in at the stroke of eight. She handed it to him saying, "Sounds like the FBI has something for you this morning." She raised her eyebrows. "Agent Smith said it was urgent you call as soon as you came in."

Charlie took the message and walked back to his office, thinking *Here we go*...

"Fred...? Charlie here, what's up?"

"Charlie, we've had a new development in the Robert Maldone case. As I mentioned previously, our people in Albuquerque have been going over old case files they believe Maldone might be implicated in. Their report out this morning makes it clear he could have been involved in as many as five, and possibly seven disappearances going back over six years. For three of those years he was working construction in Gallup and putting himself out there as a member of the Navajo tribe. At least three of the missing women were from the surrounding area, all on the Navajo Reservation."

"Fred, is there still no word of any sort of remains, or at least some forensic evidence that points to there even being remains?"

A heavy sigh preceded the FBI man's reply. "No, nothing yet. The Bureau's had leads, even recently, but nothing seems to pan out. They have, however, been encouraged enough to expand the investigation based on a possible new witness. Two additional agents have been assigned to the case, one a forensic expert fresh out of Quantico and the other some hotshot from the Denver office. Apparently, there's been a recent outcry from various Tribal media sources regarding missing women and the ongoing abuse happening on every reservation. It's hard to say how effective all this might be, but it could cause enough concern to get things rolling."

"New witness? What's the story on that, Fred?"

There was a slight hesitation. "The Albuquerque office isn't releasing any information on that yet, Charlie, still waiting for verification, but I'm hoping to hear more in a few days. One of the new agents is working on that. It could be nothing, of course, only time will tell. I'll keep you in the loop."

Charlie smiled, thinking to himself *Fred knows more than he's saying but may be bound by a privileged information mandate.* Charlie was fairly certain of it now. It would come out eventually, assuming the witness proved credible.

Just as Charlie hung up the phone and fell back into his usual morning routine, Arlene rapped at the window.

He motioned her in wondering *What now...*

"Come on in, Arlene." She was tall for a Navajo, almost as tall as Thomas.

"Sorry, Chief, I know you're busy, but Harley and Thomas are out front, and they have Little Harley with 'em, too... Isn't he a cutie?" The woman twisted her mouth in a cautious smile. "I offered to watch him up at the front desk, but Harley insisted you'd want to see him in the outfit he'd just bought." She raised an eyebrow. "They're dressed in matching father and son get-ups. Definitely cute."

Charlie pursed his lips to avoid smiling. "Just be sure you mention how loaded down I am this morning, Arlene, and that they might want to make it quick."

"Will do. Chief."

"Oh, and Arlene... don't call me Chief... I had enough of that at the university."

"Gotcha, Boss, I was watching that 'Cuckoo's Nest' movie last night on TV... I guess I wasn't thinking." The woman backed out with a little bow and headed for the front desk giggling to herself.

Charlie had the feeling he was verging on another wasted morning. He looked up at the clock. *It's too early for lunch at the Diné Bikeyah; not that it would matter to these two.*

The trio came in with Thomas in the lead. He seemed a little embarrassed as he cast an eye back at the Harleys. Both again in matching new outfits. Black hats this time, with flashy new red scarves around their necks. Big Harley was beaming, but Little Harley, hat scrunched down around his ears, had a set to his jaw and didn't appear all that happy.

"Come in... Come in and have a chair boys." Charlie put on his best face. "So, what brings you people into town this morning? Clothes shopping, I'm guessing."

Harley was, unashamedly, carrying a diaper bag over one shoulder and Little Harley in the other arm. He sat the bag beside his chair without the slightest show of embarrassment. Reaching down, he gave the bag a quick pat. "I'm trying to be careful with this, there's some bottles of milk in there I'm hoping to keep cool." A shade of doubt crossed his face as he said, "The lady at Health Services says I should be weaning him off the bottle, but me and him has already had a couple of pretty good fights about it. I don't think he's ready to give those bottles up yet. That woman did give me some vitamin samples though. She said they'd keep him perked up."

It was all Charlie could do not to laugh.

Thomas had a tight little grimace at the corners of his mouth and stayed looking straight ahead. He was remembering all the barroom fights he and Harley had been in over the years and now couldn't suppress the vision of them walking into a bar—Harley, with a diaper bag on his shoulder.

Harley put his son on the floor and proudly guided him toward the Investigator's desk. The boy had become much quicker on his feet, and definitely spryer than when Charlie first saw him over in the Kaibito. He looked healthy now and with a glint of mischief in his eye that hadn't been there before.

Charlie held out a hand to the baby who warily drew back and said in a loud voice, "No!"

"I see he's learned how to talk some." Charlie was still smiling at the child as he continued to hold out his hand.

Harley shrugged, "Uh... well that's mostly all he says for now, but he can say Da-da, too, when he wants something bad enough. He'll be talking in no time according to the Health Services Lady." He tried not to sound prideful when he added, "She said he's as fine and healthy a baby as she's ever seen and that he looks just like me, too." Then with a wry smile, "It's that Deer Clan woman, Darlene, that used ta like me a coupla' years back."

"What, she doesn't like you anymore?" Charlie pretended surprise.

"No, Darlene does still like me, but she already has three kids of her own." Harley thought this explained the situation as well as could be expected.

Thomas spoke up, "Of course... She doesn't know Harley's rich...yet," he chuckled and then said, "Lucy told him not to tell anyone that he was well off until he was pretty sure they liked him for himself, and not just the money." Thomas reached out with the toe of his boot, nudging little Harley closer to the Investigator. The toddler scowled back at him, but when he spotted the shiny badge clipped to Charlie's belt everything seemed to change. And the Investigator was quickly able to make a new friend. Smiling now, the baby willingly let himself be taken up on Charlie's lap where he was told what a good boy he was. Charlie allowed him to pull the brightly polished badge off his belt. The boy examined it minutely before putting it in his mouth, obviously thinking anything this pretty must also taste good.

"I hope he don't chew all the chrome off that thing," Thomas was only half-smiling when he said this and further noted, "What we really dropped by for, was to invite you to lunch at the *Diné Bikeyah*. We're going to go look at some saddles this morning, but we'll be back about eleven. You know how we like to beat the lunch crowd. Harley says it's all on him and that you can have anything you want, too. You wouldn't want to pass that up, Charlie. You could have one of those big T-bone steaks they have over there." He said, by way of an added inducement.

Harley was grinning and nodding his head, as he gathered up his son and then slinging the diaper bag back over his shoulder prompted, "We'll see you there... right?"

Knowing this was his friend's way of repaying past favors, the Investigator saw no gracious way to refuse.

He glanced up at the clock—and with a sigh of resignation finally agreed, "Eleven it is, then. I'll meet you boys over there." And then looking down at his lap, Charlie frowned and said, "Harley, I think that boy needs a dry diaper."

Charlie watched them stop at the desk so Arlene could chuck the baby under the chin a final time and assure his father how lucky he was. Several others in the office stepped up to say hello and congratulate Harley on his recent Lotto win and pat Little Harley on the head for luck. Then the two men and the boy trooped out the door—the child, now deciding he liked being the center of attention, had to be dragged along by the hand while voicing his displeasure in no uncertain terms. Outside, the little group paused. The men were surprised at how quickly the temperature had fallen. A chill in the air, along with a low bank of clouds drifting in from the northwest promised the possibility of rain. All indicators were now for an early fall.

12

Hard Sell

Robert Maldone knew it wouldn't be easy talking Eileen into his carefully planned, albeit risky, scheme. For one thing, the danger to her son would have to be downplayed. And for another, when the chips were down, he couldn't be sure the woman wouldn't put her own best interest above that of the common good. There was only one way that could end. He had hoped, in Eileen, that he'd found the perfect partner, tough, smart, and initially seeming quite loyal. But that was in the beginning, before her deceptive nature revealed itself. When the baby came along, he was finally forced to see things in a different light.

Dragging a child around with them didn't fit Robert's plans at all. He and Eileen both had good reason to stay on the move and this meant keeping a low profile. The child could only complicate that. He would have to stay on Eileen's good side for the time being, but probably not all that long. Later she could be dealt with as the liability she had become. After all, he reasoned, it wouldn't be the first time he'd had to go to such lengths. There had been others who hadn't worked out...but they were gone now, and without a trace. Though he was declared a person of interest in several of those investigations...nothing had come of them, and to his way of thinking this meant the authorities still hadn't a shred of any credible evidence, nor did they know where he was. Traveling with a woman helped, of course, and yes, having a child along may have been a plus at times, but the trade-offs weren't worth the trouble. He had decided now that the sooner he made the most of this new opportunity and then divested himself of Eileen, the better off he would be.

~~~~~~

Eileen May was not nearly so foolish as to think herself safe with someone like Maldone. She'd known for some time what the man was capable of, yet remained convinced she was clever enough to avoid whatever it was he had planned for her. As for her son she had for the most part been able to put the child out of her mind entirely. Robert's *medications* had helped with that. Now she thought of the boy only in the vaguest terms, when she thought of him at all.

These things aside, she had to admit Robert's plan was a good one, well thought out, and not that hard to achieve for one of his skills. She had every confidence he could carry it off. Nonetheless, her mind continued exploring other options, weighing alternatives, one against the other. It was only after some serious soul searching that she was forced to admit the best course for now was to just play the thing out as he'd planned it. She had no illusions as to how much of the plunder would fall to her, almost certain it would either be very little…or none at all. And should that be the case, she would have to act fast.

There might be a way out of all this uncertainty, but her timing would have to be impeccable and when she did engage, it would have to be with the mental acuity and internal fortitude to carry through. There would be no turning back, nor second chance should this be the path she chose.

The idea she should meet with Harley and attempt to separate him from enough money to satisfy Robert Maldone, was at first unsettling, but the more she thought about it the more it appealed to her. This was something only she could do—who better to do it? If she could pull this off, it would put an end to all the uncertainty. They would walk away with a considerable amount of cash and without the sort of exposure they could ill afford. She had not intended to give up custody of Little Harley quite so easily. It had been Robert who thought it important she set the hook immediately, explaining it was not, after all, a legal document and could be recalled should she decide otherwise. Secretly, Robert knew that was not likely to happen.

He told her validating Harley's claim to his son would help create a bond which would assure he'd take the boy along with him and then be reluctant to give him up. Should Harley express no interest in the boy and walk away, there would be little point in carrying the thing any further.

As it turned out, Robert had been right about the custody release and its effect on Harley. Now they had a firm grip on the boy's father, and should Eileen be as persuasive as Robert thought she might be, the entire process should be a done deal. Should Eileen not be successful, however, then Plan B would become necessary. That would be a whole different jump-up.

Despite her apparent indifference, Eileen was, nonetheless, loath to see Little Harley put in harm's way.

When asked again about the child's safety, Robert replied, "Don't worry yourself, Eileen. Should it come down to it, every precaution will be taken to protect the boy. And need be, I will handle the entire transfer myself and insulate you from the process completely. Now how does that sound?"

This was the first she'd heard that he might handle the exchange himself; it wasn't part of the plan, and she didn't like it. The problem was she would then be left not knowing what was happening or to whom. Still, she said nothing, thinking it too early to make a fuss over something that might not even be necessary. In her own mind Eileen was confident she could convince Harley in some amicable way to go along with a monetary settlement in return for an unassailable claim to his son.

Late that afternoon, Robert left Eileen at the motel saying he had to scout for a different vehicle. What with the fair in full swing, he felt there were plenty of opportunities of that sort available and now was the time to avail themselves of a fresh ride—the town was full of them, he said.

Robert had always felt the secret to being a successful car thief depended on one of two things: having a solid buyer lined up in advance, preferably a professional chop-shop that would pay cash and could be relied on to quickly dispose of the vehicle in a secure and untraceable manner. Or, as in this case, a vehicle taken to facilitate just a certain operation. An older low-profile vehicle worked best to his way of thinking. Here again the key was to keep it only long enough to complete the job, then ideally, it would be torched. All of this required advance planning, along with an experienced and skilled hand, all of which Robert Maldone had in abundance.

It was late that night when Eileen, already asleep, heard Robert return. Barely awake and through half-closed eyes, she saw he was only lightly dressed, without the heavy coat he'd left wearing. He showered, changed clothes and left again, only to return within the hour when he came directly to bed and slept soundly through the night.

The next morning while Robert shaved. Eileen turned the television to the news and was immediately caught up in a story on one of the Gallup stations.

A woman had been found dead only hours before, apparently burned to death in a stolen car—just outside of Window Rock. Details were sketchy at this early hour, but the young news anchor promised updates as more information became available.

Robert came out, shaving cream still on half his face and listened as he watched the video clip of the still smoldering vehicle. "Well isn't that a shame." He shook his head in disbelief. "The car must have caught fire. What a terrible way to end one's life."

Eileen watched his face and despite the concern in his voice, saw not the slightest hint of emotion. When he returned to the bathroom to finish his shave, the woman was overcome by a shudder that left her trembling uncontrollably. She rose shaking, and so weak she had to fumble with the knob before clicking off the television. She then sat huddled on the edge of the bed, desperately trying to regain any measure of reasoning that might convince her it wasn't him. Logically, she had heard nothing to tie this woman's death to Robert Maldone. Yet some undeniable intuition convinced her it was probably so.

13

Investigation

FBI Agent Fred Smith's unrelenting dedication to the pursuit of cold cases had become legendary among coworkers at the Bureau. And Fred had taken a serious interest in both the Robert Maldone and Eileen May files. Official opinion was that neither case would have come to anything had it not been for the couple pairing up in Seattle. The two crossing paths was the catalyst which caused them to appear on the FBI's radar.

While the Albuquerque office had kept separate tabs on each of them over time, Agent Smith agreed Eileen's case probably would have stagnated had it not been for her association with Maldone. It was now Robert Maldone who held the Bureau's unflagging and more urgent interest.

The upturn in all forms of abuse and the disappearance of women on the reservation was growing, and at an unprecedented rate. Native American Rights groups had now taken up the banner of these women—increasing pressure not only on local Tribal agencies, but on Washington committees charged with looking into the reported atrocities. Legal Services Investigator Charlie Yazzie had long been on the frontline of local investigations into these cases and continued to work closely with other Tribal agencies and the FBI, to sort out the growing case load filtering through his own office. Tribal Police were most often the first to receive these reports, Officer Billy Red Clay being charged with passing this information on to Federal officials. Not many complainants from the reservation were comfortable going directly to the FBI. A long standing cultural disconnect kept trust in the Bureau from gaining momentum. Senior Agent Fred Smith was working to change all this but so far it had been slow going. Not that Tribal Police were thought reliable confidants by the bulk of the population, but at least they spoke their language—both figuratively and literally.

When Fred Smith dropped by Charlie's office late the next afternoon, the Investigator knew something out of the ordinary was afoot. Seated across the desk, the FBI man appeared to be putting his thoughts in order as he withdrew two folders from a briefcase and laid them out side by side on the desk before even broaching the reason for his visit.

Charlie pushed his own paperwork aside and waited...

"We've got somewhat of a situation here, Charlie." The Agent said this in the manner of a person unsure how he should begin. As he flipped open one of the files, he pulled out the top sheet but hesitated before passing it across the desk. "Here's the thing, my friend, the

Federal Prosecutor in Albuquerque has notified us to back off the Eileen May case for the time being—I'm talking about the murder of the old silversmith, Benny Klee, over two years ago, in which Eileen was not only not charged, but later exonerated completely. While this was due to several mitigating factors at the time—the bottom line was: there wasn't enough hard evidence to prosecute the woman." It was obvious the Senior Agent found this original determination distasteful even now. "That was the prosecuting attorney's decision at the time, Charlie, and we had to accept it. Their office either couldn't, or wouldn't, put a case together back then, which in turn led to the courts eventually finding another party guilty. And, since that person was already deceased due to an automobile accident, there was little pressure to appeal the ruling." Fred stopped for a moment to catch his breath and let Charlie ponder where this talk was headed. He retrieved a file photo from each of the folders and passed these across the desk. "These photos are a couple of years old but are the latest available."

Charlie pulled both photos to him and studied each for several minutes, Eileen's first. He was surprised he remembered her as well as he did. Robert Maldone's picture, also a mug shot, sent a chill down the back of his neck. He turned and looked at the FBI agent. "What the Hell…Fred, this guy is nearly a dead ringer for that Claude Bell character Eileen was hooked up with when she first came through here."

"I know, right? I thought that would grab you. Eileen seems to have certain criteria in mind when it comes to men." He gave the Inspector a wry smile. "Harley Ponyboy being the exception, of course. These folders are copies by the way. I'll leave them with you, should you want to better acquaint yourself with Maldone...or reacquaint yourself with Eileen May, though I doubt you've forgotten much about her."

"Not hardly..."

"In any case, I thought you might want to commit Maldone's photo to memory."

The Legal Services Investigator only nodded, still somewhat bewildered. "I guess what surprises me, Fred, is why you've decided to share this information outside the Bureau?"

"I thought you might ask that. The truth is, Charlie, due to your renewed connection to the case through Harley Ponyboy's involvement, I thought it only fair you be brought up to date on the Bureau's position." He looked the Investigator in the eye before adding, "You understand this is privileged information and confidential until advised otherwise. No one else will have any knowledge of what we talk about here today. It's been my personal decision to bring you in on this because I feel your help could be crucial to our success at this point."

Charlie smiled, *Privileged information again. No one in his own circle liked the term, and he was beginning to see why. His friends didn't care to be cut out of the loop...especially when they were the loop.*

"I know it's a lot to ask, Charlie, but we've come into some information I think you'll find interesting and it's imperative it doesn't get leaked. You and I both know that happens occasionally, but in this instance, it could cost lives." This last was said with enough emphasis to insure there would be no mistaking its meaning.

Again, Charlie waited, mind racing, as he wondered what could make him so critical to the Federal Government's determination to round these two up.

Fred Smith again proved his ability to guess what the Investigator was thinking, when he said, "Actually, Charlie, it was the information you passed along after your visit to Eileen's Aunt Mary that prompted us to get things moving down in Albuquerque. The office sent a team of investigators from Salt Lake to interview Mary Chano. It didn't take them long to convince the woman that withholding information would not be in her best interest. They brought back what proved to be valuable insight into the whereabouts of the pair, no smoking gun, but they think her information could lead to apprehending both Eileen and Robert Maldone."

Charlie sat up and took a deep breath. He'd no idea Mary Chano would be brought into this and instantly wondered what sort of *information* the FBI was referring to. He thought he'd been reasonably persuasive when questioning Eileen's aunt and he hadn't learned anything like what the Feds thought they had. It must have been something Mary Chano had discovered later.

"Well, Fred, you know I'd be happy to help anyway I can, but I would hate to see Harley Ponyboy or his son involved in anything dangerous…or that might harm, or threaten their relationship. Those two are just now getting to know each other and beginning to put their lives in some sort of order."

"I'm aware of that, Charlie, and believe me, that will be foremost in my mind as the Albuquerque office sets this thing up." Fred nodded reassuringly, "When you called to say there was a suspicious couple hanging out at Harley's place the other night, we decided to kick this thing up a notch. Additional agents are on their way up here and we should have surveillance in place by this evening. They'll keep their distance—not only is Maldone street savvy—he's cautious beyond anyone we've dealt with in the past. He seems to anticipate our every move. Eileen May is much the same in my opinion, and just as vicious."

"Where do I come in Fred?"

"I was just getting to that… You could be a huge help in our surveillance. Your property and Harley's share a common entrance off the highway. And, you're pretty much in sight of one another's houses. That's a big advantage—could, in fact, make a real difference in how we go about this. To be honest we are a bit short handed, even with the two agents coming in, by ourselves we can't possibly cover all the bases." The FBI man toyed with the file folders, finally pulling loose a page that he passed across to the Investigator. "I've mentioned Maldone's uncanny ability to avoid us over the years and this may be why." He reached over and tapped the paper with a finger. "Maldone was once a student at Arizona State where he eventually earned a Forensic Science degree, graduating top of his class. He's no dummy, Charlie. Not at all like Claude Bell, who was smart enough, but not so educated or as focused as Robert Maldone."

"Really, I wouldn't have guessed that... Forensic Science degree, huh?"

"Majored in Forensic Science, but with a minor in Law Enforcement."

Charlie held the mimeographed copy to the light and perused it with a whole different view of what they might be up against. "This Maldone guy has made quite a career change, hasn't he?"

"That's the thing, Charlie, he never actually worked in law enforcement. The Bureau's Psych team did an extensive work-up suggesting he may have been prepping for a different sort of career all along. He's been at this for a while now. It's time someone brought him down."

"Given what I know now, I can understand how he's been able to keep a jump ahead of you boys."

Fred didn't say anything for a moment and when he did, redirected the conversation. "As far as we know, Charlie, Maldone isn't aware who you are, where *you* live, or even what you look like. You'll be pretty much invisible as far as he's concerned. This is bigger than you might think. Both these people are subject to indictment... Murder One. Robert Maldone, as a serial offender is our primary target, but Eileen May has long been at the top of my own personal list. There's a lot at stake here and I needn't remind you, there is absolutely no room for error when dealing with this guy. There will be a lot of eyes on the Bureau with this one."

Later, after Agent Smith left his office, Charlie Yazzie again picked up the folder on Robert Maldone and sat staring at the file photo. The longer he studied it, the more evil he imagined he could see in the man. Maldone showed his Indian heritage albeit with a lighter complexion and more refined facial features than most. The high cheekbones were there, but the eyes appeared lighter colored than he expected but that, he thought, might be just the photo.

~~~~~~~

Later that evening at home Charlie mentioned to Sue that he had decided to take the remainder of his vacation time. To catch up on some projects around the house, he said. The four days he'd spent chasing after Harley Ponyboy had already taken a bite out of his accrued vacation time but even that, was due to expire soon. It would be a good opportunity for him and Thomas to finish putting in the new fence along the drive and possibly get in a load of hay before winter.

His wife took this in stride, hoping the pair might also find time to work on a few of the things she had on her wish list. Little did Sue know that Charlie's real aim was something quite different. Even Thomas Begay would have no idea of the Investigator's hidden motives, at least until he figured them out for himself.

Sue had smiled at the mention of Harley Ponyboy and his son. They'd been there earlier for supper but hurried home afterward to watch a television series Harley said his son enjoyed. Sue was quick to invite them to stay and watch it on their set, knowing full well he wouldn't. It was a cartoon series and the two of them were equally captivated. She knew there was no way Harley would give up watching it on his new mega-sized television delivered only the day before. Though his new house had come well furnished, Harley still had gone on a major buying spree for those things which previously had been only a dream. He'd bought a new dishwasher and spent an afternoon hooking it up while reading the directions to the baby in his highchair who seemed to be paying attention and even giving advice from time to time—should Harley been able to understand it. He'd also found time to have the phone hooked up and made sure Harley Jr. had everything a coming two-year old could possibly hope for.

Sue smiled again; she would have to have a little chat with him about the amount of television they were watching. She doubted Harley knew how harmful that could be for a child his son's age...or for a father his age.

"Charlie, did you hear Harley say he has some people scheduled to install some sort of security system up at his place tomorrow?"

With tongue in cheek her husband smiled back. "Yes, he mentioned it, and said he didn't think we would be needing one." Charlie's tone turned slightly grim, "He already has those dang guineas running around everywhere; they'll make for a better alarm system than anything else. Putting in a security system can only mean one thing. Harley's probably keeping a good chunk of money right there at his house. He's really gotten into having *cash on hand*, as he puts it. Well, it's something he's never had before, I guess." Charlie frowned before saying, "I wouldn't talk any of this around though—security system, or not."

"I guess I'd know better than that." Sue pursed her lips in thought. "I wouldn't mind having a little cash on hand myself…that must be nice."

Charlie nodded. "I'm sure we all wish we had more of that. Harley's now one of the lucky ones who does, that's all."

"So, I don't suppose he'll be hiring on to help you and Thomas with your fencing project?"

Charlie grinned. "Oh, no, he says his working days are over, but I'd almost bet he'll drop by to tell us how we should do it."

"Well, I like having Harley living close by. We can at least keep an eye on the baby until he gets that under control. But I think you should have a little talk with him about how fast he's burning though his money. At the party the other night he told Lucy Tallwoman he was thinking of making some investments, for Little Harley's future and so on."

"He's a grown man, Sue…he's just acting like a little boy right now…he'll come around when he settles down and sees how fast that money is evaporating. Harley's a lot smarter than most give him credit for. Thank God, his house is paid for. He'll always have that, at least."

"You don't think he'd ever do anything to risk his house do you?"

"That…I don't know, it's always been hard to say what Harley might do, even under ordinary circumstances. Now that he has this baby on his mind, he doesn't seem able to concentrate on much of anything else. He did tell me he's thinking of hiring a housekeeper, though, so he can spend more time with his son, and keep track of his investments."

"Did he say what those investments might be?"

Charlie chuckled. "Well, he did mention he's going to look at some mules next week, he probably thinks that's a good investment. He does at least know something about that line of investing, for what that's worth."

Sue shook her head. "I heard he didn't come out so well on his last mule deal."

"No, not unless you factor in how it led to winning the Lottery. Harley's on a roll right now and he's enjoying the Hell out of it. I say we all just let him be a kid for a while…he never got to be one growing up, you know."

Sue turned away smiling. "Whatever you say, Big Guy… you're the Harley expert."

"No, actually Thomas Begay is the Harley expert, I'm only a longtime friend and interested bystander." Both smiled at this.

The next day, before Thomas got there, Charlie fed the horses a light morning feed and then strolled down to the end of the lane to check the mailbox. Harley Ponyboy was just coming down his own drive dragging little Harley along by the hand—seeing Charlie, he picked the boy up and hurried down to say hello.

"Did you look and see if I had any mail?" He was joking, of course, but it struck Charlie off-key for some reason.

"No Harley, everyone in this neighborhood checks their own mailbox. You may not have had much mail where you used to live, but now that you are a man of means you might find things have picked up."

"How so...?"

"There'll be a good many more things to deal with now that you have this new house, and a baby. I expect there'll be things you didn't even think of before. These are things you'll have to stay on top of."

"Such as what?" Harley shifted the baby to his other arm and narrowed an eye at his friend.

"Oh, all sorts of responsibilities, Harley, like utility bills, tax notices, and bank statements. And that's just some of the issues you'll have to keep up with." Chuckling at the look on the man's face, Charlie went on. "What I'm saying is, you'll have obligations just like the rest of us. And a lot of that's going to come to you through this mailbox."

Harley grinned at this as though he welcomed the challenge, obviously thinking Charlie might be exaggerating. Once again, he shifted his son back to his other arm. "I swear it seems like this boy is twice as heavy as he was when I got him. Do you think that's possible?"

"I don't know, Harley, have you been weighing him? I think most people weigh their babies on a regular basis."

"Weigh him? No, I didn't have any idea I should be doing that. I been hefting him around everyday though… He sure seems heavier to me."

"Get a scale, Harley, it'll take the mystery out of it for you."

"Well, I been trying to get him to walk and run as much as I can. But he seems to like me packing him around…too much of that can't be good, huh?" He thought for a moment. "Then too, we been watching quite a bit of TV lately. That could be part of it, I suppose. I'll just have to put him down more…make him do his own walking." Harley scratched his chin with his free hand. "A scale, huh? I'll put that on my list, no sense in hauling a fat baby around all day."

Charlie glanced at Harley's round belly. "No, a person needs to look out for that sort of thing. I hear it can sneak up on you." There was something pecking at the Investigator and he finally remembered what it was.

"By the way, I hear you're having a security system put in today?"

"Yep, in fact they should be here anytime now, nice people, and it's a Helluva deal from what they tell me."

"Oh…and where did you run across this deal?"

"Right there in my mailbox, Charlie, you were right about that, there was a card in there yesterday morning saying their company was running a big special, with the first ninety days free. I didn't see how I could go wrong with something like that. So, I just called them up—told them to come on out."

Charlie looked down to double check his own mail. "That's funny, we didn't get a card like that in our mailbox. I wonder why that would be?"

Harley switched his son back to the other arm, and pursed his lips in thought as he glanced up the road to the Yazzie place and then said, "Maybe they didn't think you folks had need of any security up there; they probably thought my house ta be the more likely target of thieves and such."

Charlie's first impulse was to laugh, but knowing Harley didn't mean anything by it, he only sighed and agreed, that might well be it. It was Harley's shifting view of things he found amusing. He doubted his friend even realized how he was coming across.

"I better be getting back up to the house, Harley, Thomas is coming by later—we'll be fixing up that fence coming down the lane."

"Ah, trying to spruce the old place up a bit, eh? Good for you, Charlie. You have to keep up with those older properties or they'll get away from you before you know it." Harley was grinning when he said this, but it caught the Investigator off guard. These days Charlie could never be sure what the man was getting at; he seemed to be developing quite a sense of humor...or something.

The Investigator looked down at the ground and almost said what was on his mind, then decided it probably wasn't worth the time it would take. He needed to get to work. He turned toward home, raising a hand to the pair in goodbye, and from the corner of his eye caught Little Harley waving back...that made him smile. He was still chuckling to himself when he came up on his front porch. He made a mental note to tell Sue why they wouldn't be needing a security system. And as he stood thinking of Harley and the baby, he couldn't help seeing how quickly the two were adjusting to their new life and the affluence that had come with it. It was only natural it should get away with Harley, he couldn't fault the man for that.

Just then, the clatter of a diesel truck caught his attention as it came rattling up the drive. He watched as Thomas stopped to have a word with the two Harleys. Later, when the tall Navajo pulled up to the house and unwound himself from the cab, he too was grinning.

"Harley's worried you might be biting off more than you can chew with your home improvement plan. He seems to think you folks might be trying to keep up with the "Ponyboys" and asked if I thought you needed any help…moneywise. I told him I didn't believe so, but I would check." Thomas put on his serious face. "Do you need any money, Charlie?" Breaking into a laugh he threw his hands in the air. "Harley just can't get it through his head that he won't be able to help everyone. He seems to think that money of his is going to last forever."

Charlie looked off across the river. "Well, God love him, his intentions are good, but he can only do so much. We both know that, I'm just afraid he's eventually going to run into someone who might take advantage of his generous nature."

Thomas pulled a few fencing tools from the bed of his truck before answering, "I can see that happening all right…speaking of which, have you seen any more of those people who were parked down by the highway the other night? I haven't been able to get that out of my head for some reason."

"No, I haven't seen anything I'd call suspicious, but I'm keeping an eye out. I did tell Fred Smith about them and he said he'd look into it." Charlie wished he could say more about what he and Fred had discussed but at this point couldn't quite bring himself to go into it. He knew Thomas to be of a perceptive nature and thought he probably would guess, sooner or later that there was more to all this than he'd been led to believe.

Thirty minutes into their work the two friends were already sweating as they took turns manhandling the posthole digger breaking into ground hard as adobe brick. Thomas straightened up to push back his hat, then wiped his forehead with the back of a hand. Hearing an engine, he looked to see a utility van going up the drive to Harley Ponyboy's house. The van had a magnetic sign panel on the door that Thomas had to squint to read. "Safety Services…well I wonder what it will be this time. Looks like our friend is about to get another new 'service' of some kind." Thomas chuckled, "I can't imagine what he's missed so far. He told me he already has cable TV."

Both men grinned at this as Thomas cocked his head to one side. "Did you hear about the TV he got talked into at the appliance store in Farmington? Biggest one they had. He told me it was just like going to a drive-in movie."

Charlie shook his head at this and he, too, turned to watch the men getting their tools from the service van. "Yep, those boys are right on time. I suppose he didn't mention he's getting a security system installed today." The Investigator smiled to himself noting the two clean-cut young installers in their crisp new uniforms. Fred hadn't mentioned this twist, but Charlie knew Federal Agents when he saw them.

Leaning on his shovel, Thomas studied the men for a few minutes. "Does Harley know the FBI is doing the installing?"

Charlie burst out laughing, "I didn't think that would get past you, *Hastiin.*"

Thomas Begay's ability to spot any kind of law was legendary and as he took up his shovel, he paused to stare up the road a final time, and then declared. "I'd lay a hundred to one Harley won't know the difference."

"Probably not, but if that's who they are, it's for his own good…" Charlie didn't see any point in denying it now. It was what it was. "Fred Smith must have thought, sooner or later, Eileen would try to get in touch with him."

Thomas spat on the ground. "Putting a tap on someone's phone is pretty heavy stuff. Fred must be serious about reopening that case against Eileen, huh?"

"Uh, I guess that could be it…" Charlie wanted to say it wasn't Eileen that Fred was worried about but thought Thomas would probably figure that out, too, eventually.

"Is that what we're doing out here with this fence? Keeping an eye on Harley Ponyboy, I mean?"

Charlie slammed the digger into the hole and frowned. "Maybe…" He lifted out a large clump of crumbling red clay before saying, "Keep it to yourself though, Thomas, that's the way Fred wants it."

"He must have some reason to suspect Harley might be in for some kind of trouble?"

"I expect he does…"

Thomas jammed his shovel into the growing pile of dirt and frowned when he asked, "Are you saying this is more of that damn *privileged information* you're always using as an excuse?"

"That's exactly what I'm saying."

"Well, in that case…you've already said too much, haven't you?" Thomas's grim smile said it all.

Charlie glanced at the man once or twice but remained silent. He hated not coming clean with Thomas, about anything, but this just wasn't the time. Fred had been adamant, and as Thomas just mentioned, he probably had already said too much.

Chewing at his upper lip, Thomas glanced toward the sky and thought there was some weather making up to the north but decided he wasn't there to make small talk and kept it to himself. In the back of his mind he was thinking, *the next time I talk to Harley Ponyboy on the telephone, I will have to be more careful what I say.*

As Charlie handed him the water jug, he saw Thomas was grinning to himself and knew the man was likely plotting mischief of some sort.

Thomas narrowed an eye at the service truck nodding thoughtfully to himself. "You wouldn't happen to have any potatoes, would you?"

Charlie frowned. "You mean on me?" But he knew exactly what the man was thinking.

Thomas said, "No, what the Hell… I mean up at the house…do you have any potatoes up at the house?"

Charlie laid down the 'diggers" and looked him square in the eye. "We're not stuffing a potato up the FBI's exhaust pipe, if that's what you're thinking." He was almost sure this was exactly what he had in mind. He couldn't count the times he's seen Thomas pull this back when they were young, and out to stir things up. He recalled the prank had never once failed to cause them more trouble than the fun they had doing it.

Thomas went back to his shovel thinking, *Charlie's getting old.* There was a time when he would have been up for it. But this was his neighborhood and then, too, he was the law himself now. He chuckled thinking, *if Harley knew what was going on, he'd be all for it. He's three years younger than Charlie though, maybe that's the difference.* It occurred to him then that he and the Investigator were about the same age, and couldn't help wondering…*why don't I feel that old?*

14

Suspicion

Eileen writhed beneath the sheet, twisting and turning—throwing her head from side to side, as a cold sweat dampened the pillow. Her skin crawling and itching like a bad case of lice. And just when she thought it couldn't get any worse, the cramping began, and every cell in her body raced to the ragged edge of rebellion. Had she not so strong a will she might have given up then …cried, screamed and ultimately begged. But that was not Eileen. She did none of these things, certain she would be gagged should she make the slightest sound. And as though this wasn't enough, she was bound hand and foot to the bed. Despite all this she was careful not to so much as glance at the man sitting at her side.

Maldone, not daring to leave the woman for a moment sat back in his chair, dozing now and again, through the long night. He had given fair warning how it would be. Not so bad, really, thanks to his supervision of the drug. Robert had seen worse than this, but was surprised, nonetheless, at how well she was taking it. He was beginning to think she might be back at herself by evening, or at the very least some functional form of herself. A lot depended on her recovery—they had things to do and people to call.

Leaning in slightly, he asked softly, "How are you doing, Eileen?" While he spoke in a low and comforting tone, it grated on the woman's every nerve.

Finally, she forced herself to focus on the sound of his voice, and only when she had located him, did she attempt to make visual contact. She blinked several times but found it hard to bear even a blurred sight of him. Her voice was barely a croak as she attempted to answer. Robert hurried to pour a glass of water which he held almost tenderly to her cracked lips.

"There now, that's better, isn't it?" Holding his head closer to catch what she was mumbling, he at first could make nothing of it. When he spoke again it was almost in a whisper, "Now what was that you said, Dear?"

Eileen turned and, without considering the consequences, spit in his face. Realizing what she'd done, she instantly drew back and braced herself.

Robert took an edge of the sheet and calmly wiped away the spittle. A benign smile spread across his face as he raised a fist to viciously backhand her across the mouth. He canted his head, looking down at her almost quizzically. He asked, "Well, then, does that make you feel better, Dear? Probably not, huh? Still it might help you clear your head and understand who you're talking to." He sat back in his chair with a sigh and asked softly, "Would you like an aspirin? How about a nice cup of soup, you haven't eaten in a while now you know...maybe just a little chicken broth? We have some little packets I picked up yesterday—I can mix one up for you, only takes a minute—there's hot water in the coffee maker. These really are quite good. I had one last night and found it tastier than I'd thought possible." Robert rose and peered down at Eileen, standing back some as though gauging the possibility she might be so foolish as to try it again. There was a tiny trickle of blood at the corner of her mouth…he somehow doubted she had it in her to make a second effort.

But she did, then opened her mouth as though to scream but couldn't quite force it out.

Grabbing up a pillow Robert clamped it across her face with both hands, pressing down hard until she stopped struggling, not overly long, of course, he was a man who knew what he was about…a man of experience…you might say. When he took the pillow away Eileen lurched forward gasping, coughed a time or two, and then fell back drained, and this time…remained silent.

"You know, Eileen, I'm doing my best to be reasonable here. I'm aware how hard this must be for you, but by tomorrow, I'm guessing you'll be in a much better frame of mind. This will all be behind us then and perhaps we can have a rational conversation—move forward with our little plan for your Mr. Ponyboy. Time's running out, Eileen…and I'm running out of patience."

~~~~~~~

The next morning, she woke from a fitful sleep to find herself no longer tied. Robert, seeing she had calmed down and might have regained her senses, had not only released her hands and feet but had covered her with an extra blanket. Now, by the sound of it, he appeared to be in the bathroom shaving, possibly thinking the worst had passed.

Eileen's first wild thought was to run, but understood rather quickly she likely wouldn't succeed, and even if she did it would be only a temporary solution. The next thing that came to mind was *where did Robert put his gun?* She couldn't imagine he'd have it with him in the bathroom. She realized now she was going to need some sort of equalizer. His knife might work. She hadn't seen that since the incident on the North Rim. Still she couldn't imagine him throwing it away.

When he came out drying his face, Robert had the look of an entirely different person. More relaxed, cheerful even. He wasn't one to let a little unpleasantness get in the way of so lucrative a project as this. He was quite willing to let bygones be bygones, should it suit the purpose of a greater good. Oh, there would be a reckoning...but not just yet...time aplenty for that should things go as planned. He would, however, make certain there were no loose ends left to trip a person up.

He sighed as he thought through this and turned to Eileen with a hesitant smile. "All better?"

Eileen, though unwilling to muster a smile in return, nodded amiably enough and rose to move to the bathroom. Her face still hurt from Robert's slap and was beginning to swell. She noticed he had already picked out fresh clothes for her and took them along without question. She was thinking much more clearly this morning and while there was no guarantee the craving wouldn't return to cloud her thinking later, she thought now she might at least make it. Looking in the mirror she put a hand to the side of her face, already bruised and spreading toward the eye. She turned her head slightly, wondering if makeup would cover the worst of it. Probably not. But it wasn't the first time the man had slapped her...and worse. She'd deal with it as best she could.

From the other room she heard the television and wondered idly if she and Robert would be on the news this morning. But, no, it was all about the Navajo Nation Tribal Fair, right there in Window Rock.

The announcer was cataloging the events as he introduced a previous year's clip of the "Fancy Dancers" segment. The sound of drums and jangling ankle bells were unmistakable. Eileen leaned out around the bathroom door to have a peek. The dancers were always one of her favorite events. Never a traditionalist, it had been a long time since she'd attended any such events. She could see the dances had changed considerably over the years, showing more of the hoopla of other tribes; the more intricate steps and spectacular costuming. The tourists wouldn't know the difference and be just as enthusiastic, cheering them all on. In truth, this new generation was more colorful and far more extravagantly costumed than the old traditional dances of the *Diné*. Those were more religious in nature and never meant for the eyes of the general public.

She'd heard somewhere the Intertribal Ceremonials, held in Gallup each year, were now drawing contestants from across the west, with some of the intermountain and plains tribes sending spectacular teams, often dressed in regalia costing thousands of dollars. It was a far cry from what she remembered as a young girl, yet it rekindled vague memories of those times, and temporarily she became lost in the remembering...

"Hey! Are you about ready in there?"

Robert's voice held none of its previous good humor. There was little doubt his patience was wearing thin; there could be yet another price to pay should she make him wait. When she came out, he looked her over with a critical eye, then reached into her open bag for a headscarf.

"Wear this. The town's already filling for the fair, but it won't hurt to have a little additional cover. We need to do whatever it takes to avoid attention." Then with a grim smile he went on, "There are more phone calls to make. It's time to get this thing moving." He gave her a sharp look. "Are you feeling all right? Take an aspirin. The fresh air will help—we'll get you some strong coffee and something to eat. You'll be better in no time."

Robert's last statement sounded more like an order than an encouragement. Eileen moved to the window and grimaced at her reflection in the glass thinking, *an aspirin...yes, that should make it all better.*

"It's cool outside, wear your coat and sunglasses, the big ones I bought you in Tucson." He himself donned a wool watch cap pulled low to meet his sunglasses and was bundled up as well. They should blend right in with the rest of the fairgoers and were highly unlikely to be recognized. The local law would have other things to worry about for the next few days.

"Oh, by the way, the operator was able to pull up Ponyboy's new phone number—we'll deal with him first."

Eileen was careful to do exactly as Robert said, yet was nonetheless determined at this point to find a way out. Her chances of getting through this ordeal in one piece were growing less as time went on; she could see now where the man's priorities lay and was certain she was no longer one of them. He had explained his plan in exquisite detail, which in the process, made her realize once again that she probably didn't need Robert Maldone. She was quite capable of pulling this thing off by herself. The right time would present itself, and when it did, she would be ready. She was not without her own resources, after all.

She would need a car, and some help with some of the more intricate details. There was one person left she could count on. Her aunt, Mary Chano, was only a few hours away. Eileen felt certain the woman would feel moved to help when she learned of her desperate situation. Mary owned a gun and knew how to use it, too. Yes, if there was one person, she could depend on it was her clan mother. Mary would never leave her adrift at a time like this. All it would take is a phone call;

it wouldn't matter now if it was made from the motel room or not. By the time Robert found out she'd broken this most inviolate rule, she would be long gone.

15

The Call

Harley Ponyboy was still somewhat leery of his new telephone. It had not, so far, been the great instrument of convenience he'd thought it would be. His experience with it had not so far been all that useful. That he had only two numbers on the list of people he might need to call probably had something to do with it. Thomas Begay and Charlie Yazzie were the only ones he had occasion to talk to, and in Charlie's case all he need do was walk the few yards to their house and say in person what he had to say. He, himself had received not a single call of any consequence.

When the phone finally did ring that morning, the baby was in his highchair with egg on his face, and he was busy at the sink cleaning up. Cursing under his breath so the baby couldn't hear, Harley wiped his hands on the dishtowel around his neck and then went to the new wall phone with a frown.

"Hello!" Harley spoke up, thinking the louder he talked, the more likely he would be understood.

"Harley? Is that you… This is Eileen, can you hear me all right?"

The stunned silence from Harley's end was about what she expected...she waited him out.

"Uh... Eileen? I been trying ta find you... Where are you? You sound close by."

Ignoring the question, Eileen stuck to the script, Robert Maldone, hovering at her shoulder, listened as he held up a finger, a clear warning not to stray.

"How is Little Harley? I really miss him...is he all right?"

Harley was beside himself, nervous and now unsure what to say. He moved to the table, wiped the egg off the baby's face and held the phone to his little ear, "Talk Harley...it's your momma."

The child stared at the phone a moment and then, head to one side, parroted the word, "mom- ma," he said it clear as could be, taking both parents by surprise. The boy was learning new words every day, and his father was doing his best to talk to him as much as possible. Sue told him that's how babies eventually learned to talk.

"Did you hear that, Eileen? This baby's coming along fine. He's already talking up a storm as you just heard."

Eileen didn't answer right away, and Harley thought he heard a catch in her breath. Giving the woman a little time to gather herself Harley Ponyboy found he was equally affected.

Finally, taking an audibly deep breath, Eileen spoke in a more controlled tone, sticking to the guidelines "Harley, we need to talk— I made a mistake. I need to have Little Harley back. I miss him." Gaining momentum, she toughened her stance. "I have a lawyer," she lied. "We can go that route if we have to, but I would rather come to some more personal agreement, between just the two of us." Her voice steadied and she spoke with more conviction, "Give this some thought, Harley, I'll call you back later after you decide what you want to do. I understand he's your son too… I'm sure we can come to some sort of an arrangement. If not, I mean to have that baby back, one way or another." There was a clatter of sound, as though she'd dropped the phone and several minutes passed with only static.

"Eileen? Are you there?"

Her voice, when he could hear her again, sounded muffled as though she had turned her head and partially covered her mouth. "Harley, I'll call you later…there's been a change of plans."

He remained listening for nearly a minute, Eileen's words echoing in his mind. He gave the handset a good shake thinking something might have come loose inside. Putting the receiver back to his ear he listened again and more intently this time. There was a very light static which hadn't been there before. He gave the phone a last questioning glance as he hung it up, not knowing if it would ever work properly again.

He turned to his son and said in a whisper, "Who do they think they're dealing with here?" Then reached over to tousle little Harley's unruly shock of hair. An icy calm settled over the man then as he took the baby's hand and shook it gently. "It will be a cold day in Hell when I give *you* back to *anyone*."

The baby slammed his spoon down on the tray and mirrored the determined look on his father's face, then unaccountably, began to sniffle and then cry. Harley put his head to one side gazing thoughtfully at his son and in a single illuminating moment realized one of the great truisms of parenthood. Babies are among the last honest people on the planet…you always know where you stand with a baby…when they are happy, they smile, and when they are not happy, they let you know that, too. There was not an ounce of subterfuge in them, nor a speck of deceit. Everything was up front and uncomplicated with a baby. He patted his son's head, reassuring him in a soft voice—letting the child know he was safe and in his rightful place in the universe.

Harley stood gazing out the window a few moments watching as the eternally vigilant guinea hens began flying up to their roosts. They were early this evening, possibly warned off by some imagined peril; the threat of a horned owl on his migration south perhaps. Harley took this as a sign he might want to heed his own internal indicators.

It was time to Lawyer Up.

Eileen's call was still running through his mind as he picked up his son and washed his frowning face and little hands. "A clean baby is a happy baby," he told him as enthusiastically as possible. The Health Services woman told him this and like everything she said, he had taken it to heart. He put Little Harley in his playpen in front of the television watching as the boy smiled—instantly caught up in one of their favorite adventures of the Road Runner and the Coyote. Harley was honestly trying to cut down on the toddler's television watching. It was just so easy a pattern to fall back into. He was working on it now, adamant they would start tapering off 'next week'.

His mind returned to Eileen's call. This time he picked it apart for some hidden meaning in her words. She had started off predictably enough, quickly working her way through the greater part of her obviously coached message—when there was a clattering sound as though she might have dropped the receiver. For several minutes he'd heard nothing, then traffic and passers by talking again. Then nothing... *What else had she said?* She had obviously been outside at a phone booth. Her last recognizable words were said as she bent over to retrieve the phone.

So, yet another change of plans—clearly more urgent this time and without the slightest clue as to her intentions. Nonetheless, there still was the promise of the long awaited, face to face meeting. Fruitless though it might prove to be, it should at least provide closure of some sort.

It was getting late and he'd already put the baby to bed by the time Eileen called again. When the phone rang, he picked it up with a certain trepidation.

Eileen didn't wait for him to say hello, her voice was little more than a whisper. "Harley, meet me at your old trailer at nine tomorrow morning. Come alone...and bring the baby...I want to see that he's been taken care of and is all right before this goes any further."

This time there was the muted voice of a television news anchor in the background and under that, Harley thought he perceived the sound of running water. She was in a room somewhere this time but still trying to avoid being overheard. The tone of her voice was crisp, business like and with a new confidence. "Someone will be watching, Harley, so no tricks." And then she hung up leaving a dull buzzing in his ear…then nothing. *Dead as a hammer!* He glared at the receiver and then gave it a good whack against the edge of the table hoping to revive it. The only thing to come of that was for the mouthpiece to come apart, which in turn, sent a puck-like device rolling across the hardwood floor. He retrieved the errant part and worked several minutes securing it back inside the instrument which it did with a reassuring click. He then screwed the mouthpiece back on with a hard twist and was rewarded with a clearly audible dial-tone. He looked at the phone a moment then broke into a smile, *I fixed it! This thing sounds like it used too.*

Now even more wary of Eileen's motives, Harley still could not totally abandon the thought of some sort of reconciliation, even if it were only a friendly relationship…unlikely though that might be. He found it odd Eileen hadn't mentioned this Robert Maldone she was traveling with and, while he knew it to be foolish, even this small suspicion offered some illusion of hope. But who else could be the *'someone'* who would be watching?

Harley went to the next room and directly to the bookcases left by the previous owner. He had promised the preacher he could have these books back should he return someday yet somehow doubted the man would ever be back.

Stretching to his full height, Harley felt around on top of the casing to take down his revolver. *One way or another, I will be keeping this baby.*

16

Surveillance

Thomas Begay slapped the dust off his trousers, gave the fence post a final shake and decided it would do. It was only the second day of fence building and already he regretted signing on. Glancing from under the brim of his hat, he studied Harley Ponyboy's distant house. A very nice house, he conceded. There had been no activity up there all morning, unusual according to Charlie Yazzie, who had mentioned their friend generally took his son for a little walk each morning about this time. And said Harley was encouraging the boy to run a little further each day...to greet the sun. Harley, himself came from a long line of strong runners and could only surmise the boy would someday be equally as good.

Charlie went for more drinking water—the ground was rocky, and the work hard. He left Thomas there at the fencing and to keep watch.

Agent Smith had called the night before and cautioned Charlie not to interfere beyond a watchful waiting. Should anything out of the ordinary happen he was to let him know at once. The FBI man still said nothing about the phone tap. Charlie finally conceded the man must have a good reason not to mention it, but nonetheless remained a little put out.

When the Investigator came back with the water, he checked out Harley's house before sitting down the jugs. Thomas was leaning on his shovel contemplating his current effort with a grim smile. It took twice as long to dig a post hole here as on his own place.

Charlie watched a moment before asking, "Nothing doing up at the Ponyboy place, huh?"

"Not a peep."

"Hmm, well, I've been warned not to make needless contact, for fear of scaring off anyone who might be watching, I suppose."

Thomas snorted, "No one warned me—how about I ease around the back way and see what's up with those two little men up there?"

Charlie chewed at his lower lip and considered what repercussions might come from Thomas being discovered. Still, he was curious himself thinking it over, finally agreed, "Just be sure no one sees you. Fred Smith likely has a spotter up there somewhere."

Thomas grinned. "The irrigation ditch is dry now; I can use that to get up to the hedge row." Grinning sarcastically Thomas whispered, "I'll be *really, really* careful,"

Charlie was doubtful, but nodded, nonetheless, and waved him off.

The tall Navajo slipped through Sue's little field of corn, then into the empty but still muddy mother ditch which would take him up and around the hill. Thomas was good at this sort of thing, as was Harley Ponyboy, the two continually making a contest of sneaking up on one another. It was a traditional game the two had practiced for years.

Despite his long legs, Thomas managed to stay out of sight as far as the hedgerow and safe from prying eyes. Spending several minutes in reconnaissance and without seeing anything suspicious, he took to his hands and knees and crawled under cover of the hedgerow to Harley's screened-in porch. Inside and out of sight he inched along the wall to the back door and twisting the knob, found it open, and silently eased his way into the kitchen. There was the sound of a television and Thomas smiled to himself as he turned toward it.

The cold barrel against the back of his neck stopped him midstride. His knees went weak and he automatically raised his hands.

"Don't shoot, I'm unarmed…"

"This is your lucky day, Pilgrim—I just made some popcorn—come on in."

Thomas could hear the smile in Harley's voice and exhaled with a whoosh as he put his hands down, turning to see his friend already turned and peering back out the window.

"Charlie didn't come with you?"

"No, Harley, he said he was getting too old to crawl down irrigation ditches."

"I wondered about that…" Harley was laughing as they entered the living room. "Me and Little Harley here was just having a snack before the Three Stooges come on." There was a large bowl of popcorn on the coffee table. "Have a seat there on the other side of Harley and help yourself to that popcorn."

Thomas sat down, and taking the bowl, grinned at the huge television set before saying, "Don't mind if I do, Charlie's had me digging postholes again this morning. I'm ready for a little break." Looking around the room he remarked, "Uh…why are all the blinds pulled, *Hastiin*?" Stuffing his mouth with popcorn, he looked over at Little Harley—who was eyeing him, and the popcorn.

Ignoring his question Harley Ponyboy raised a finger and shook it at the little fellow. "No, no, Harley, no popcorn for you."

The boy's answer was to throw down the 'special-for- babies rice cracker' he'd been gnawing on and make a defiant grab for the popcorn. Thomas whisked it away smiling while raising his eyebrows at the child, "Daddy said no, no!"

The boy clouded up and with a grim determination again struggled to reach the bowl.

"Why no popcorn for this boy, Harley?"

Harley sighed at the man's ignorance. "Babies can't have popcorn until they're a certain age. You didn't give your kids popcorn this young, did you?"

"No, if you'll recall, I was drunk most of the time my kids were babies. I wasn't around much. You're a lucky man, coming onto this boy so young, and you sober."

Harley first thought his friend was making a joke, but then saw the look on his face and knew he wasn't.

They both grew pensive for a moment and then suddenly sad for those long lost opportunities.

"So, what happens if this little porker gets ahold of this popcorn?"

"It'll either get caught in his throat or he'll stuff it up his nose."

"No! Really?"

"Well, I don't know that for a fact, but that's what the lady at Health Services told me." He studied his son. "No Sir, Little Harley, here, won't be getting any popcorn for quite a while yet. Give me that bowl and scooch over. Thomas, you don't know a dang thing about babies, do you?"

Their talk was interrupted by a light tapping at the back door, and Harley, around a mouthful, said, "Thomas, go let Charlie in." Then he indicated the television with a buttery forefinger. "This is our favorite part and I don't want to miss it."

"How do you know it's Charlie at the door?"

"Neither lawman nor outlaw are known ta knock on a person's door in this country, they either break it down or try to sneak in like you did...you should know that better than anyone." He smiled and blinked at the man. "I don't want to pull a gun on Charlie anyway—him being my lawyer, and all."

Thomas eased out of the room and was back in moments; the Investigator pushed through the door ahead of him. Charlie stood surveying the gathering with a dubious grin. "How's everything going this morning, boys? Popcorn for breakfast, I see." Then frowning, "You're not letting the baby have any of that are you?"

Harley turned down the sound on the Three Stooges, knowing it was a show that let the characters actions speak for themselves. He shook his head to the question about the popcorn, asking instead, "So, why are you two spying on us this morning?"

Thomas grinned behind Charlie's back. "The question is, Harley, why were you ready for us?"

All three were laughing now in the way old friends will do when they've come to a mutual understanding.

Without further preamble Harley said, "I had a call from Eileen this morning. She threatened to take my son." He pursed his lips in thought before saying. "You know I'm not going ta let that happen. Right?"

Charlie, having called Fred Smith only minutes before leaving his house, knew what was going on with Eileen, that's why he was there. He didn't dare say so, however, it wouldn't do for Harley to know his phone was tapped.

There had been no doubt in Agent Smith's mind: Robert Maldone's intent was to extort money from Harley and he was equally sure this had been the man's aim from the beginning. Fred doubted he would go much beyond these empty threats and was confident Robert was unaware the FBI was closing in.

While Charlie Yazzie partially agreed with the Agent, he was thinking Eileen might have finally realized she was in over her head with Robert Maldone and was now looking for a way out. The Investigator was determined it would not be at the expense of Harley Ponyboy and his son.

Only Charlie knew what Fred Smith had in mind, and the plan was not without its risks. Everything would depend on Eileen's next call.

~~~~~~~

At Charlie's insistence, Sue had again invited the two Harleys over for dinner, she had wondered about this, as they'd just been over the night before. She didn't mind. She'd taken an interest in the baby and his progress and found watching the interaction between the new father and his son appealing in a way she couldn't quite explain. Harley's parenting skills had continued to develop, and though she'd warned about too much television, she had so far been pleasantly surprised at how the two were adapting to their extremely different lifestyle.

Thomas Begay had left earlier in the afternoon, saying there was some work on his father-in-law's *hogan* he needed to catch up on, but that he would be available the next day if they needed him.

After dinner the Yazzie children, Sasha and Joseph Wiley, took the baby to the other room while the adults had their coffee. The sounds of the three at play made everyone smile.

As Sue began clearing the table and worked on the dishes, Charlie scooted his chair a little closer to Harley and asked casually, "So, has Eileen called back like she promised?"

"Yes, about an hour after you left this afternoon." He went on fixing his coffee…

"Oh, and how did that go?" Charlie hadn't heard from Fred since earlier that morning and was now a little surprised to hear Eileen had indeed made contact again. He'd expected the Agent to give him a call when that happened.

Harley appeared a little more upbeat during dinner, more so than he had in several days. Something was going on…there was no doubt of that. Charlie waited for Harley to answer the question about Eileen's call, when the phone rang. Charlie excused himself and went into the other room to answer.

Fred Smith sounded a little perturbed. "Charlie…is Harley Ponyboy and his son over at your house? Our guy saw them leave as though they were going for a walk and then some sort of birds got after him and began causing a ruckus—rather than give himself away, he had to back off."

Charlie started laughing… "Guinea hens, Fred, those were guineas. The neighborhood's infested with them. They belong to Harley now…came with the house…he's been feeding them recently because his son thinks they're hilarious. They're very territorial from what I hear. They apparently consider Harley's place as being under their protection or something."

There was a long silence on the other end and the Investigator waited, trying hard not to chuckle. When Fred next spoke, Charlie wasn't sure if he thought the guineas were a joke or what, but he didn't allude to it again.

"Harley brought his son over here to have dinner with us, Fred; everything's fine." Still he couldn't help wondering *you'd think an FBI agent would know what a guinea hen was.*

There was an audible sigh of relief when Fred heard Harley and his son were safe with the Yazzies. "Did he say anything about a second call he got from Eileen last night?"

"No, and it doesn't sound like intends to, either."

"I'm not surprised, Charlie. He let that woman sweet talk him into thinking she wanted to get back together—all about how Little Harley needed a real family...and on and on." The Agent raised his voice in frustration, "It was crazy, Harley was eating it up, too. Does he not have good sense or what?"

Charlie had to stop and think about that one. "He has good sense, Fred, except when it comes to Eileen May. When she gets in his head it's like he tunes out the real world and lives his dream."

The FBI man hesitated, sounding a little sheepish when he admitted, "Unfortunately, we had a glitch in our equipment toward the end of the call, it was mostly unintelligible. The boys are working on the recording right now but I'm doubtful they can pull any further information off it...other than what we already know. That's the reason I didn't call earlier. I was hoping for a miracle, I guess, but that hasn't happened. That said, we should already have all we need concerning their meet-up—I've given my people the go-ahead for tomorrow morning."

"So, you did put a bug on Harley's phone."

"We had no choice, Charlie." Fred sounded surprised the Investigator knew but remained unapologetic. "Eileen wants to meet him tomorrow at the Fair in Window Rock. It's opening day, and from what I'm told, there'll be a big crowd. Of course, there's no guarantee Maldone will even show up. And even if he does, we still might not know it. He's cagey, and cautious to a fault." Fred went on, but on another tack. "Then, too, there's always the off-chance Eileen is acting on her own and set up this meeting with Harley in secret." The agent sounded irritated but determined to follow through on what he was now convinced might be a rare chance to apprehend Robert Maldone. "Charlie, I'm afraid this is only one of the unknowns." The FBI agent wanted to make sure his next statement was clear beyond any shadow of a doubt, and raised his voice slightly when he said, "It's Maldone we want, Charlie—as far as Eileen goes…well, that can wait as far as the Bureau is concerned. That's not the way I would have played it, but that's the way the Agency says it has to go down."

Charlie's question was, "Did you get a locate on the phone they called from?"

"No, they're too smart for that, they know better than to give us enough time for a trace. Our people did, however, get a fix on the general area; it was a public phone right here in Farmington."

"Well, they do get around, don't they?"

"Yes, they do, at this point they could be right under our noses and we wouldn't know it."

Charlie hesitated to ask, but knew he needed to get something straight from the start. "Tell me, Fred...am I in on this?"

"That's up to you, Charlie. The Bureau won't know. Nor would they condone it if they did. This is strictly between you and me." The Agent let this sink in before going on in a more congenial tone, "There's nothing to stop you from dropping by Window Rock and taking in that fair tomorrow. Half the Navajo Nation will be there on this first day...just don't think we can help you in any way if things go south on us."

Charlie understood perfectly, was in fact, glad these were the parameters. "Fine, I'll have Thomas with me. It can't hurt to have a couple of undercover Indians in the crowd. We'll try not to raise any eyebrows and might even prove useful should things fall our way."

"What if Harley spots you?'

"I doubt it would surprise him... he won't give us away even if he does."

Fred thought a moment longer before a final warning, "Charlie, I know your first concern will be Harley and the baby. But let me reiterate, the Bureau will not cover for you and Thomas, or help you should they think it might endanger the operation's main objective. My Agents won't even know who you are. That means you'll be strictly on your own should things come apart. I won't be able to do a thing for you...before or after...is that clear?"

"I understand that, Fred, we'll do our best to stay out of your way."

"Good. Charlie, the woman is supposed to meet Harley in the livestock pavilion during the shearing exhibition. That's 10:30 tomorrow morning… Our guys will be in street clothes and look as Indian as we could find on short notice."

Charlie seriously doubted those agents would get past Robert Maldone's radar, and he could tell Fred Smith wasn't entirely convinced, either. The Investigator was now glad he and Thomas would be there, if only to keep an eye on Harley and the baby.

~~~~~~

The next morning Charlie left while it was still dark. Dawn would break clear and calm, with only a hint of winter on its breath—the sort of morning that often marked autumn's short run through that country. It was Charlie's favorite time of year. Idling quietly down the lane with his lights off he hoped to avoid waking the Ponyboys. He was almost sure the man wouldn't be up yet. Harley and the baby were becoming addicted to their huge new television, often watching late into the night, and thus had become leisurely risers. Harley often remarking to the baby that the big-screen TV was "just like being there." Easing past the house all was dark, even the guineas were still on their roost as the Investigator slipped by. Only the dim glow of a night light in Harley's bedroom gave evidence of life in the home.

He was to meet Thomas in Shiprock and go on to Window Rock from there. Charlie would leave his official truck at his office and ride with Thomas in his old Dodge, hoping to attract less attention to themselves should anyone be watching.

When Thomas Begay pulled up to the still dark offices of Legal Services, it was after stopping at the service station to top up the tank and for coffee, along with an eight-pack of his favorite chocolate encased doughnuts.

Charlie climbed into the truck without speaking. The two had known each other since their schooldays; neither felt need of idle banter, preferring to begin the trip in silence. Thomas pushed the doughnuts his way, and Charlie took one for the sake of not hearing him argue how good they were. There would be plenty of food at the fair and depending on the source, some of it would be quite good. Thomas drove nearly thirty miles without saying a word but had eaten half the doughnuts during that time. They were well down Highway 491 and making good time, as they generally did when Thomas was driving.

With only one eye open, Thomas seemed to be catching a few winks now and then, something he was known for. He was quite good at it and so far, without reason to regret it.

Charlie, after watching him for a mile or so, broke the silence, ostensibly, to ask if he was going to take the 134 cutoff. Not wanting to ruffle any feathers he said he only asked, knowing how easy it was to miss the turnoff.

Briefly opening the other eye at this, the driver nodded, but gave no other indication this was his intention.

"Would you like me to drive for a while, I'm coffeed up now."

An easily discernable frown made it clear, no help was needed.

"Well, I guess we're almost there, anyhow..."

The country was relatively flat through there, and eventually Charlie could pick out the top of the carnival's Ferris Wheel though still a good distance off. A carnival was integral, it seemed, to all fairs and major celebrations on the reservation. They were hugely popular and none of the larger gatherings were thought complete without one.

By the time the Tilt-a-Whirl came into view, Thomas was fully awake and taking a notable interest in the going's on. The trash-strewn parking lot was already beginning to fill with people out for a good time. Thomas was dressed to the nines. After his participation in Lucy Tallwoman's recent political campaign he had become more particular about his appearance. His Black Stetson was the same one the Japanese tourists had been so taken with on his recent visit to the North Rim. He also wore the turquoise set Concho belt he was so proud of, and again, his hair was in a traditional bun. The new black shirt and pants, along with tall boots with riding heels, completed the outfit. This time however he was just one of the many so dressed, and hardly turned a head.

Charlie, for his part, wore what he always wore, ironed Levi's jeans, white pearl-button shirt, and no extra jewelry of any sort. This day, Charlie favored a Silverbelly Stetson but with a lower crown than

Thomas's more traditional model. Factor in the low-heel ropers and his more modern appearance was regarded as the new norm.

Though still early, the wide fairways were already thronged with people. The livestock barns were plainly evident at the back of spacious fairgrounds.

Thomas often commented. "If there's one thing the *Diné* can say…it's that we're not short of dirt out here."

There was still more than an hour left before Harley's scheduled meeting with Eileen, and Thomas felt that left them plenty of time to eat. He wasn't one to miss a meal when it could be helped and stopped at the first likely vendor to look over the menu. It was a family run affair, featuring a limited and more traditional selection of dishes—things one might be served at a family's home table. Navajo tacos were the predominate menu item and both men agreed that was the more reliable choice. There was little difference from vendor to vendor in this nearly universal offering. The Navajo Taco was still king among Indian diners. Consisting of a large round of golden frybread hot from the oil, and with a depression in the center for the customary beef and red chili filling, it was the perennial favorite on the reservation, and one found on most any restaurant menu in this part of the country.

Frybread vendors were everywhere, as were barbeque stands featuring beef and mutton…and lamb for the harder to please tourists. Some off-rez people didn't care for mutton, finding its stronger flavor off-putting— should one not be raised eating it. The now ubiquitous Corn Dog took the eye of passing children as it does everywhere, and those vendors, too, were kept busy supplying the never-ending demand.

The two men took their loaded plates and drinks to a large tent set up with long tables and folding chairs, all filling at a rapid pace. They chose a place in a far back corner against a canvas wall—more in the shadows, yet with a good view of the midway as people streamed in from the main gate.

Thomas gave his full attention to the food, glancing up only once or twice until he'd had his fill. Charlie, on the other hand, ever watchful, only picked at his plate, though he also agreed it was quite good. He scanned the crowd constantly, thinking he might accidently catch sight of someone he thought could be connected to the upcoming meeting. He'd so far seen nothing of the sort.

Thomas Begay didn't appear surprised at this. Wiping up his leftover sauce with his last piece of frybread he declared himself done. Now on his mettle, the tall *Diné* rose to his full height and carefully searched the mass of people in the tent, and over their heads to those passing outside.

"I don't know why we're bothering with this, anyone not wanting to be seen won't be coming in the front gate anyway. And Harley won't drag the little guy past those carnival booths when he has an appointment to keep. He knows better than that."

Though Charlie hadn't thought about it he couldn't argue with the obvious truth of it and figured the same would hold for Maldone and Eileen. As far as the FBI were concerned, he guessed Fred would have his people already stationed at strategic points near the sheep sheds.

The pair began making their way toward the livestock pavilion, Thomas saying he knew where the shearing exhibition was held.

The demonstration had started slightly early, but a good crowd was already assembled around the raised platform. The man doing the shearing knew his business and kept his helpers busy supplying select ewes—good heavy fleeced ewes, that made him look better at his job. All the while, he kept up a running commentary of how the thing should be done so as not to cut or otherwise injure the animal. There was an art to it, no doubt, and a skilled person could make very good money for as long as the season lasted.

Charlie and Thomas stood across the shed, pretending interest in a display of the latest equipment for the up and coming sheep man. They were still a good distance from the crowd but close enough, they figured, to recognize anyone familiar…or maybe someone overly suspicious. Thomas eventually spotted Fred Smith at the far end of the enclosure, he had already passed the man over once, having never seen the agent in anything but a suit. He nudged Charlie. "There's Smith over by that pen of rams. He don't look very happy, does he?"

Fred had grown up in that part of the country and knew how to dress the part should need be, but he wasn't smiling and did seem out of sorts.

Charlie quickly located him, watching with amusement from the corner of an eye. "No, he certainly doesn't look happy."

"Well, it's early, maybe Harley and the woman just haven't shown up as yet."

"Maybe so, but I don't like it." Charlie gave the crowd another worried look. "At least Fred's agents seem to blend in, unless they're not here yet either."

Thomas grunted, "They're here all right, that's one of them there behind the shearing platform, and another just inside the door on the opposite side, the one looking at those wool bags, and vaccinating guns."

"I see them now—actually, they fit in pretty well."

"Not for me they don't…they've got law written all over them."

Charlie knew better than to dispute this accessment.

Another twenty minutes passed with all three FBI men appearing more nervous as the clock ran out on the supposed meeting. Fred Smith began circulating, slowly working his way around to the equipment display. He stopped and inspected a row of feeders and waited for Charlie to edge his way closer.

The Inspector reached down to read a price tag. "No-shows?" he ventured.

Fred nodded as though to himself and murmured, "Looks like it. It makes no sense. I don't know how they could have changed plans without someone getting wind of it. We still have a guy on the phone tap but haven't heard anything new from him—if the thing's still even working." Fred cursed under his breath. "Maldone seems to have a sixth sense when it comes to a trap…and he's lucky to boot."

"Anyone keeping an eye on Harley's house?" Thomas had edged up to the big poster on supply prices. He appeared to be running a finger down the list as he whispered as though talking to himself.

Fred didn't turn around, "Harley left his place well over two hours ago. He should have been here by now."

"Didn't anyone follow him?"

Fred was watching one of his guys headed their way and didn't answer for a moment. "We did have someone in charge of that… But he ran into car trouble."

"His car broke down?"

"Not exactly. It seems someone disabled it during the night. Put boards with nails in them in front of every tire."

"Any idea who would do that? Sounds like a pretty bold move to me…I mean, it being the FBI and all. Surely Robert Maldone wouldn't be foolish enough to risk something like that?"

"No, that wouldn't be Maldone's style. The agent did find a few tracks…possibly a small man…he thought."

After a long and uncomfortable silence Charlie was able to answer, "So. Where do we go from here?"

Fred looked out across the midway and shrugged. "I'll leave a couple of my guys here at the shearing shed on the off chance someone might still show up." The Senior Agent was clearly frustrated at the prospect of losing this chance at Maldone. "My sneaker unit is parked out by the rodeo arena, near the ticket booth; it's a brown Ford Bronco with New Mexico plates." Fred gritted his teeth and shook his head. "The Saddle Bronc event should be about to kick things off, and I expect there'll be a crowd headed that way. You and Thomas might want to mix in and keep your eyes open, Maldone could still be lurking about somewhere... I'll meet you out there in fifteen minutes."

Charlie studied the Agent for a moment before saying what was really on his mind, "You don't suppose this whole thing was a set-up, do you, Fred?" He hated to think Maldone was that far ahead of them.

"I can't imagine it, but stranger things have happened with this guy." He looked down at the ground... "Let me get back up with my people then maybe I'll know something more when we meet up out there."

Charlie nodded as he and Thomas moved toward the rodeo grounds, both now worried, knowing there wasn't much time to figure out what had gone wrong, and where Harley Ponyboy and his son were.

Halfway to the arena, Thomas stopped with an expletive loud enough to cause the old couple behind them to pull up short. The couple looked around suspiciously, wondering if maybe the tall man had stepped in something. Thomas half-turned and shrugged an apology to the couple, then lowered his voice as he came back in step with the Investigator.

"What you said back there hadn't even entered my mind, but now that it has, it pisses me off... I'm talking about this being a set-up... I'm thinking now it might well have been."

"Well, it's beginning to look like a real possibility, all right. And, too, I guess Eileen, or more likely Robert, could have spotted one of the agents and got scared off... Who the Hell knows what might have happened?" Catching sight of Fred's Ford Bronco Charlie nudged Thomas and indicated the sneaker unit with a push of his chin. Both smiled at the CB antenna, knowing it wasn't that at all.

"What's bothering me more than anything else is that Harley didn't show up either." Thomas swore again, this time under his breath. His immediate thought being *Harley Ponyboy is either a lot smarter than I thought...or he's a lot dumber.*

Charlie glanced around the parking area and then diverted Thomas Begay's attention to the arena just as a cheer went up from the crowd. "Fred won't be out here for a while yet. Let's me and you take a peek at the bronc riding. No point in hanging around Fred's unit and maybe being spotted. That is, if anyone's left out that cares." He didn't have to mention saddle broncs twice Thomas was a pretty good hand with a bucking horse himself and most likely would know a few of the riders from there on the *Dinétah*.

The pair took up a spot next to the chutes and watched the last contestant brush the dirt and manure off his clothes as he made his way back to the gates.

Thomas smiled as he recognized Slim Man Nez grinning up at his crew on the top rail of the chute. They were giving Slim Man Hell for not raking his pony up high enough. It didn't matter he'd come unglued a good three seconds before he'd made a ride. They were just joshing him. When Slim Man looked past the crew and spotted Thomas he grinned and abandoned his tormentors altogether and came to say hello to Thomas.

Thomas introduced the man, saying, "We didn't get to see your ride but I'm guessing we didn't miss much." Thomas knew the man well enough he felt comfortable making light of his effort.

Slim man shook his head as he beat the dust off his hat, "No, you didn't miss much, I guess I should'a wore some longer-shank spurs," He grinned, "They say I wasn't reaching him. Could just be I'm getting old."

"Is that why you fell off?" Thomas wasn't one to pass up a friendly dig at an old buddy. He knew Slim Man would doubtless do the same should their positions be reversed. …it's how cowboys sometimes console one another.

"Naa… he was a good horse and doing his best out there. He don't owe me nothin." Slim Man put a boot on the bottom rail and looking Thomas up and down smiled through the fence. "Uh… I don't see you with a number on your back do I, Big Man?"

Thomas chuckled, "No, *Hastiin*, I had to give it up. They couldn't find any broncs I couldn't ride to the horn."

Even Charlie laughed at this.

Slim Man shook his head and turned to go. "I have to help Bobby Joe get his shit together, he's up next… I'll be seeing you boys around."

Thomas watched the bronc rider go, and Charlie could see he missed the old crowd. His father had been a top saddle bronc contender when he was young and

Thomas himself was a pretty good bronc-snapper back in his younger days.

"That's what happens when you get old," Thomas mused, watching Slim Man limp back to the chute. "It takes away every damn thing you were good at."

Charlie sighed and looked at his wristwatch then nodded toward the parking lot. "Fred ought to be at his 'Sneaker' by now, I suppose we'd better head back that way."

17

Deception

Harley Ponyboy woke as the first hint of light greyed the bluffs along the San Juan. Looking first to little Harley's crib he peered through the slats to see a twist of blankets. He had several times come awake to check and found the baby sleeping quietly each time. Though a light sleeper Harley hadn't heard a sound from the boy all night. Bleary-eyed now at first light, he blinked at the crib, and then blinked again—nothing but empty blankets. His son was nowhere to be seen.

Jumping out of bed, Harley's feet found the floor only to trip over his boots which sent him flat on his face and almost under the crib. When he was able to focus, he found himself eye to eye with his son, now wide awake and trying to figure out how he'd come to be there. The two stared at one another for nearly a minute before Harley whispered "Dang it, Harley, what are you doing under here? You scared me half ta death!"

The boy smiled then and whispered, "Da-da…" and crawled over to touch noses with his father.

Harley pulled the boy out and sat holding and hugging him close, making certain he was all right. He studied the crib for some sign of how he'd escaped; eventually it dawned on him that the window curtain at the end of the crib hung twisted and out of place. The boy had been climbing everything he could reach and was not afraid to take a chance. Apparently, he'd used the drapery to pull himself up and over the edge of the crib—then instinctively clutching on to the fabric, slid the few feet to the floor. Not knowing what else to do, he had then crawled under his bed and fallen asleep. Once more Harley had misjudged how quickly the boy was developing a sense of independence. Old Paul T'Sosi had been right; he was learning fast…maybe someday he would even be a *long talker* like Paul.

As Harley dressed the boy and bundled him into his new hooded down coat with the fur trim, he couldn't help thinking how much he looked like the little Eskimo on his favorite ice cream bar. The pair stood grinning at one another a moment before Harley picked him up and went to the window to check outside. Everything appeared quiet and as the sun edged over a distant rim there was the added assurance of guineas alighting from the trees. Through the window Harley could hear the fowl's liquid chirruping as they talked quietly among themselves. There could be no better assurance that all was well. The baby clapped his hands at the birds and tried to imitate their calls. Looking toward the Yazzie house Harley saw Charlie's company truck was gone and smiled to himself—he'd felt certain that had been the Investigator's pickup slipping by his place earlier that morning. *Charlie was up to something and he was pretty sure he knew what it was.*

He thought he would give Sue time to get the kids off to school before calling, thinking maybe she would be willing to watch his son for a couple of hours. He knew he'd been imposing of late but silently swore he would make it up to the entire family when things settled down.

At this point he didn't figure he could ask Charlie or Thomas Begay for help. Both had been against him and Eileen getting together from the start. So, it was all on him now. Whatever might come of this, good or bad...he knew he would own it going forward.

Harley sat watching his son, still in his hooded coat, having a quick bowl of oatmeal. He had tucked a tea towel down his front and adjusted it to ward off the inevitable splashes and spills, all the while, keeping an eye on the kitchen clock.

When he heard the air brakes on the school bus, he knew it was time. Asking Sue for yet another favor bothered him. She had often said she would watch the baby any time...any time he needed her is what she'd said. Well, this was the time. Thomas had filled him in on Eileen's companion and what Maldone was capable of. First thinking his friend must be exaggerating, he had made light of it. But when Charlie Yazzie also weighed in and verified the claims, he took a more serious view of the man. He was not going to take little Harley to any sort of meeting Robert Maldone might be a part of—he had a good idea now what he was dealing with—and became even more determined to stay ahead of the game.

Sue came to the door smiling to see Harley with his diaper bag on one shoulder and the little Eskimo in the other arm.

Apologizing, he said something had come up and hoped she could watch the baby for a few hours.

Sue unable to hide her surprise had to think a moment before answering… "Harley, this is pretty short notice." Then seeing the look on his face, sighed and motioned him in. "Okay Harley, I'm sure you wouldn't ask if you didn't have a good reason."

"I do have a good reason, Sue. I had a phone call late last night about an important meeting…it just come up. I looked up here and didn't see any lights on, so I decided to wait till morning to ask." His face fell as he declared, "I won't be making a habit of this sort of thing Sue, honest, I won't. It will only be for a couple of hours, at the most, I can promise you that."

"Well, I do have to go out this morning, but not for long. Will it be all right if I take him along with me?"

"Uh…sure, that would be fine, he likes going places, he won't be any trouble." *I hope,* he thought to himself. "And…you won't be gone long, right?"

"No, no, I have to make a bank deposit is all, you know how Charlie is. I'm right on the edge with this one and need to get it in there as soon as the bank opens. Then I'll pick up a few things for dinner and we'll be right back out here." She silently calculated her list… "I imagine we'll be back before you are."

~~~~~~~

By the time Harley filled the tank in Shiprock he figured he still had almost an hour before he was due at the trailer—enough time to circle in the back way and check things out before anyone else showed up. He would leave his pickup well off the other side of the hogback and hike the rest of the way to the top. He'd have a clear view of the old place from there. It wasn't all that far to the valley floor on this side of the ridge.

Taking his time, he worked his way to the top of the narrow ridge, stopping every few minutes to make sure he hadn't been followed. Harley took the precaution of crawling the last few yards on his belly. He was in his element now—on home ground and with a lifetime of experience to back him up. He settled himself in a sprinkle of sage and greasewood and was nearly invisible. He had a clear view of the old trailer—still his trailer, in fact. He had already decided he would eventually give it away; the place wasn't much, but there would be someone who needed it as badly as he once had.

Harley settled in to watch. He hadn't forgotten his revolver and patted the jacket pocket a second time. The short barreled .38 would do him no good at this distance, but once down below it might come in handy. He pulled out the tail of his shirt and slowly polished the lens of his new mail-order binoculars; they had come in just the day before and he hadn't had time to familiarize himself with the adjustments. He played with the focus for a few moments and soon was able to zero in well beyond the trailer and even to the highway and beyond. The wind had come up out of the north and was already starting to whistle its way through the sage at the edge of the hogback. There was a storm coming.

He was ready.

18

The Devil

As Thomas and Charlie sauntered back toward Fred's sneaker unit, they could see he was already on the two-way and obviously involved in an animated conversation. Though still a good distance off, they could hear the Senior Agent curse, not something the man was known for.

The FBI man finished his business on the radio and looked up in time to see two coming. Getting out of the vehicle he slammed the door shut and with a grim last look at the unit, turned toward the two Navajo with a scowl.

The pair met him halfway and, indicating the Bronco, Charlie said, "I'm guessing that wasn't good news?"

Fred, obviously still angry, couldn't keep his voice from cracking, "No, it wasn't. Robert Maldone and the woman were living in a local motel right here in Window Rock and apparently, only checked out early this morning. We released a bulletin on the brother-in-law's missing car two days ago—local law spotted it in the back lot of the motel and verified the vin number.

The New Mexico plates, stolen about the same time, had just hit the list yesterday. One of the local Tribal cops notified our office." Fred hesitated before going on as though still trying to put it all together himself. "After our Agents talked to the desk clerk it didn't take them long to figure things out." The FBI man paused again but obviously wasn't through. "That's not all, I'm afraid... This morning a local waitress turned up dead outside town, at first glance she appeared to have burned to death in a car that later turned out to be stolen. A trucker happened by and spotted the flames in a wash just off the highway. He said he thought he saw a man standing in the light of the flames, just watching. It looked like the devil standing there, he said—but only for a second—then he was gone. The trucker came running with his fire extinguisher, too late, as it turns out, to save the woman's life, unfortunately, but he did prevent a total incineration of the evidence. Local authorities had a line on her within an hour, a thirty-two-year-old waitress for a local eatery; turns out she was well-acquainted here in Window Rock...it's a small town."

"Are you thinking Robert Maldone was involved?" Knowing what he did of Maldone Charlie thought it strange he would be guilty of something so unsophisticated.

"I know it doesn't sound like Maldone, but the motel he and Eileen were staying in was only blocks from the cafe where the dead woman worked. We have people there right now, questioning the owner and running down leads. Maldone has to be under a lot of pressure. Who knows...maybe it's starting to tell. One thing I do know is that we aren't letting up or giving up. Robert Maldone's time has come!" Fred said this with the conviction of one on a mission that wouldn't fail...couldn't fail.

Charlie Yazzie wasn't so sure. "So, now we don't know where these two are...or what they're driving?"

"We know virtually nothing, beyond what I've outlined here. We're letting the local authorities handle the official press releases but without making mention of any FBI involvement. We're hoping Maldone won't realize just how close we are. We have already cast a wide net. It's going to be hard for the man to get away this time."

As his horn alarm went off, Fred turned to his unit and stared in frustration...then shaking his head, he shrugged, and returned to the Bronco.

Watching him go, Thomas whispered in Charlie's ear, "It don't sound to me like they're *that* close. In fact, it don't sound to me like they know any more than we do. I can see now why Maldone and Eileen might have been scared off from the meeting this morning. But where was Harley Ponyboy—why didn't he show up?"

"Well, I can only guess that at some point someone must have called him to warn him off...or rearrange the meeting place?" Charlie grimaced, "That wiretap isn't doing Fred a whole lot of good now, is it?"

Thomas shook his head again and looked back north with a frown. "I'm thinking we ought to be getting back to Shiprock, maybe find out what's going on with Harley and that baby."

Charlie smiled. "Fred believes it was Harley who disabled his Agent's car up there last night and, that he may have found the phone bug they installed and tossed that too."

Thomas smirked, "I think Fred Smith is giving our little friend way too much credit. Harley's no Sergeant Joe Friday, you know."

"Maybe not, but it's possible we've never given him *enough* credit, that's all I'm saying. He's come a long way these last few years since Anita died. And this new baby has kicked things up a notch. Now that he has money, there's no telling what kind of changes are in the wind for Harley and his son." Charlie turned thoughtful as he replayed his last statement. This time when he spoke, it was with a qualifier. "I'm just afraid Harley's biggest lessons may be yet to come!"

When Agent Smith returned, it was with a wry smile. "While your Harley Ponyboy may have found the bug we had on his phone, a check of company records show he did receive a final and very brief call late last night. We know it was from right here in Window Rock, but not what was said. Whatever that was…it seems to have changed everything…we just don't know how or why yet."

It was when watching Charlie and his friend Thomas maneuver their way down the midway toward their truck that the FBI man felt a twinge of conscience. He should have mentioned what else his men had uncovered. Still, it was for these fellows' own good. He couldn't have them blundering into something they weren't prepared to deal with or that would jeopardize the Bureau's chance of intercepting Eileen May—and through her, Robert Maldone.

Fred stood for a few moments pondering this latest turn of events while subconsciously still aware of his surroundings, something instilled in him by years of training. Nothing seemed out of the ordinary, and certainly he didn't see anything he might consider suspicious. He opened the door of the Bronco with a final look around, and then with a sigh, got in and started the engine. Headed toward the highway and the long drive back to his office, Fred became totally immersed in his own thoughts and nearly oblivious to anything else.

At the other end of the arena, an old man in a beat-up stock truck lowered his rodeo program to look after the unmarked car with only the barest hint of a smile. Robert Maldone was not a man to be intimidated by the FBI or any other authorities. His greatest concern was the early morning disappearance of Eileen May, without a trace, or so it would seem. It had been instantly apparent to him this could mean the end of his carefully devised plan for Harley Ponyboy. His first thought was to check with his friend the desk clerk, see if Eileen had made any long-distance calls from the room—she had...several in fact. The one to Shiprock was to Harley Ponyboy no doubt, that was a no-brainer. She'd obviously intended making her own and very different arrangement with Harley, probably just before skipping out this morning. The other call had been made the night before and to the little town in Utah where her aunt Mary Chano, lived. Most likely crying on her aunt's shoulder…or had there been some more urgent reason for the call? In retrospect it was hard to believe Eileen could just disappear without some sort of help or support from someone. He might have to rethink this one.

There was only one thing that could have deterred Eileen from sticking to their original plan…and that was of his own doing. The television news story about the waitress had obviously struck a chord with the already distraught woman. She must have finally put him together on this one and realized what she may have let herself in for. He'd seen it in her eyes, an almost imperceptible change. Clearly, Eileen was more insightful than he'd thought. Even then, he felt she would hold to the plan, at least until they had the money in hand.

He did not at all discount the fact he'd brought this entire thing upon himself. He knew even before he called the waitress at her work and arranged the meeting…that it couldn't end well. And still, he was compelled to do it. He'd somehow convinced himself he was in a strong enough state of mind to maintain control of the situation…and of himself. That was just the sort of thinking that had nearly been his undoing in the past.

By late morning, Robert had donned a rudimentary disguise and showed up at the fairgrounds to sort things out for himself, something he had not intended to do under any circumstances—too risky. But he had done a lot of risky things in his life and gotten away with it. He quickly spotted several of the Federal Agents and had known immediately who was involved. It was plain to see the FBI had been working his trail for some time now. But obviously had no idea where Eileen was...or where he was, for that matter. This was when Robert realized he once again had control of the situation. Who, after all, knew Eileen best and whose plan had this been in the first place? In the final analysis, he was the only one with a workable backup plan already figured out. It would have to be some version of *this* plan that Eileen would adopt; nothing else could even come close to success in his opinion. After Eileen's first call to Harley, it was clear enough to him that the man didn't intend to submit to the kind of coercive tactics they first thought might work. To be fair, that had been his own initial assessment—he'd been the one to convince her it would be the way to go—on the off chance her hold on Ponyboy was strong enough to pull the man in without all the drama that would surely come with Plan B. What it now boiled down to, was this: someone would have to snatch the child. Only that would provide the sort of leverage necessary to separate this Harley Ponyboy from a respectable amount of cash. Only he knew how that should be played if there was to be any chance of succeeding.

In Robert's mind, there was always a right way and a wrong way to proceed in things of this sort, and he doubted Eileen had the skill or resources to pull it off the right way. It had been his reasoning all along that the surest way to go about this would involve a quick grab of Eileen's brat, and then a meetup in some isolated location where things could be sorted out, somewhere everyone, including Harley Ponyboy, would feel more secure—his new house wouldn't work, there were too many people around, not to mention the ever-present guinea hens who couldn't be bought off or out-maneuvered…or even be counted upon to be in the same place twice in a row.

No, the best place would be Harley's old trailer-house, isolated and out of sight of any neighbors. The real beauty of this was: he knew how to get there, and already had a basic lay of the land stashed away in his head. This was a well laid and evolving plan he was sure couldn't fail. Let Eileen and her Aunt do the heavy lifting on this one and then at the appropriate time, he need only step in and deal with Eileen and this Ponyboy character himself, making sure only he walked away with the spoils. There would, of course, be a final reckoning between Eileen and himself, he owed her that…and she deserved it…unpleasant though it might be. As far as the others went, that would have to be determined by fate, and a more fickle determination would be hard to imagine.

19

The Storm

On their way back into Shiprock, Thomas's thoughts on the matter were that Maldone would try to put as much distance between himself and Window Rock, Arizona as he possibly could, and as quickly, too. He doubted there was much chance the man would stick around for any further attempt on Harley Ponyboy and his son.

Charlie, having studied Maldone's file, didn't agree, and went on to explain why, "He's been counting on that money too heavily to even think of giving it up. The other thing is…he's probably still under the impression he's dealing with only local Tribal authorities. He's not counting on a full-blown FBI investigation which takes time to ramp up. He has no idea how long the Bureau has had him in their sights. I'm sure he knows they will take a hand eventually, but like Fred, I don't think he has the slightest inkling that the Bureau has already zeroed in on him and Eileen." It was several more miles down the road before another thought occurred to the Investigator. "And speaking of Eileen, I'm wondering how she's taking all this—so far, it's been business as usual for her. I'm sure this local woman's murder last night takes things to a whole new level, one that may cause Eileen to rethink her part in any further dealings with Maldone."

Thomas snorted, "Going on what we suspect happened to old man Benny Klee, I expect she's handling it just fine and is still capable of anything."

Charlie couldn't disagree with this and noted, "In which case Robert Maldone himself had best keep his guard up. I get the impression Eileen is not a woman to be toyed with."

They blew into Shiprock with a tailwind, in the vanguard of a serious dirt storm, Thomas's truck sent skeins of dust and grit scuttling along before it. They turned off at the Legal Services parking area to pick up Charlie's Tribal unit, still parked in front of his office. The Investigator was just getting in his truck when he noticed Arlene standing at an upstairs window waving. He waved back, and though she seemed to be mouthing some sort of message, he didn't figure he needed to go up there to find exactly what it might be. He and Arlene often had vastly different views of what was important. The woman could reach him on the radio should it be a real emergency. Right now, time was getting away from them. The two Navajo decided they would continue on to Charlie's place with both trucks—Thomas Begay following along behind so the Investigator wouldn't have to bring him back to Shiprock later on. Thomas had been adamant that he go along in the event, as he put it, "Harley has got himself into some sort of fix." He said this in the manner of someone certain to be proven right.

The two agreed they would first run by Harley's place on the off chance he might have made it back home by now. But they also intended to check in with Sue and see if she might know anything that would be helpful. Beyond that, their only other option was to wait for further info from Fred Smith and his agents—or they could just wing it from here on out. Neither of the two men thought they should wait.

~~~~~~~~

Up on the hogback above his old trailer house, Harley Ponyboy was about ready to call it quits and leave his hidden lookout before the storm hit. But when he noticed an old flatbed truck pull off the road at the far edge of his viewing range he waited and watched. Even with the high-powered binoculars he had trouble making the vehicle out through the wind and dust—only that it was a dark color. The truck eventually pulled in behind an old abandoned *hogan* where it would have been completely out of sight should Harley not have had the vantage of an elevated lookout and a powerful set of glasses.

No one had lived in that old *hogan* for years and though Harley knew most everyone's vehicle for miles around he had no idea who this flatbed belonged to. Possibly it was only a traveler pulling over to catch a few winks or wait out the fast building storm before continuing north into Utah. *That's probably what it is,* he thought, *it's only good sense for a person to stay out of sight when sleeping along these lonely roads.* These were different times and more dangerous than it once had been there on the *Dinétah*. Harley watched for a few more minutes but eventually decided to call it good and return to his truck. But just as he was about to leave yet another vehicle came into view, their lights barely visible at first, but obviously traveling fast. So, once again he waited. This sedan, like the flatbed truck, had a front license plate but unlike the truck this car was clearly not from Arizona…Utah maybe. That wouldn't be unusual close as they were to the Utah border.

Of the Four Corners states, Arizona and New Mexico are the only two not requiring a front plate. Utah and Colorado do require one. Harley concentrated on the bumper of this lighter colored car and soon saw that it was indeed, from Utah. Slowly refocusing the binoculars as the vehicle drew ever closer, the sedan seemed to be slowing down. Nearly to the trailer's turnoff, the vehicle came into better focus as it pulled over for a minute, possibly waiting for someone, he thought. He could see quite plainly now that it was an older silver or grey Pontiac. Thomas Begay would know the year exactly…but he himself had no clue.

The sedan seemed somehow familiar but only in that vague way which leaves a person uncertain and still wondering. The car was almost to the trailer before it finally dawned on him. *That's the old Pontiac I saw in Mary Chano's side yard when I was in Utah asking about Eileen.* He thought he would never see the woman again, let alone see her car driving up in his yard.

The driver pulled up directly in front of the trailer and then just sat there—not getting out or even honking the horn, obviously assuming the lack of other vehicles meant he wasn't home—possibly leaving them undecided if they should wait or not.

Up on the ridge Harley was catching the full brunt of the stormfront—sand lifting from the crest of the ridge in waves, stinging his eyes whenever he lowered the glasses. The wind was beginning to howl, sending curtains of red dust so thick he could barely make out the distant and abandoned *hogan,* let alone whoever was parked behind it. They were totally hidden in the fury of the storm, the blacktop itself, now and again disappearing in the dirt laden gusts.

Down at the trailer nothing stirred, no indication of who, or what, awaited him there. Harley had not anticipated two adversaries if that's what he was up against now.

Backing off the ridge, he worked his way back down the far side of the hogback to his truck, almost certain he could access the sand wash that ran behind the trailer and then four-wheel down the arroyo unseen. This shortcut should make it only a few minutes to the rear, of the trailer. Those people parked down there might decide not to wait, but if they were, who he thought they were…they would still be there.

Edging his way down the deep and narrow head of the wash was a bit precarious but eventually things began to open up; the walls turning more to clay than layered sandstone. He had often hauled firewood home this way, but that was with his old truck, already beaten all to Hell. As the near vertical walls grew higher, he felt safer from prying eyes yet knew it would now be impossible to turn around or get out of the rugged defile without going all the way on to the highway, and then only by way of the culvert that ran underneath. A highway crew had long ago cut a rough track down from the paved road in order to clear flood debris, rare though that was. There would be no other way to get his truck out now. Just before the trailer he idled up next to the bank—almost touching the wall itself—and just behind his back deck. He shut off the engine, waiting and watching a few moments before scooting over to the passenger side door to get out, closing it softly behind him. He doubted anyone heard the truck over the keening of the wind. His gun, still in the pocket of his Levi's jacket, bumped his hip at every step bolstering his confidence. Going to the back of the truck he climbed up into the bed and from there found it an easy reach to the top of the wash, and only yards from the back door of the trailer. All completely hidden from the front of the house and the silver Pontiac…should it still be there.

He climbed the rickety old steps leaning sideways into the wind to keep his balance, then with one hand holding tight to the brim of his hat, he edged cautiously toward the back door. Crossing the old deck, mindful of the bad planks, he opened the screen door not allowing it to bang against the wall as it was prone to do in a blow.

Figuring people knew he had nothing worth stealing Harley never locked his doors. And now he first took the precaution of peering through the little glass pane before opening the door. Once inside he kept low to the floor and inched himself across the narrow kitchen to a window with a closed blind. He had the eerie feeling someone had been there before him yet with no premonition of their being there now.

Harley was expert at lifting the edge of a blind, just that miniscule amount needed to see without being seen. He had picked this up watching Eileen's covert vigilance in those days she'd spent hiding out here…how long ago that seemed now.

The faded silver sedan was pulled up close to the porch and even through the tiny slit, Harley could see quite plainly who was sitting in the front seat…his heart missed a beat as he recognized Eileen at the wheel. She had her head turned, watching her side mirror as though afraid someone might have followed her. Her Aunt Mary sat next to her and it was a moment before he realized Harley Junior was the bundle on her lap. This brought a catch to his throat making it hard to breathe. In the back seat, he could discern only the outline of a shadowy form and was unable to make out who it was. Was that Sue, or was it Robert Maldone? Deciding finally that they wouldn't have left Sue behind to raise an alarm, it had to be her. Little Harley, on the other hand, was clearly fine, waving his arms now and again as he jabbered away at his aunt.

Harley let the venetian blind slip back into place, sighing deeply, as an icy calm fell over him, something he'd only experienced a few times in his life. It was the realization of what was at stake—how critical it would be to approach this thing exactly right—it would take nerves of steel, and even then, things might end badly. The wrong move, even the wrong word, could prove disastrous, not only to his son, but to Sue Yazzie, as well. That he himself might go down didn't enter his mind, nor would it have mattered. Every wild scenario imaginable flitted through his head as he studied what he might be up against.

It only made sense that it was Sue in the back seat. The person wasn't big enough to be Robert Maldone, not from what he had heard of the man. There was no doubt in his mind they would have had to take the baby by force. Eileen would have understood that well enough, he suspected she must have used a gun to pull off so bold a move. One thing he did know, Sue Yazzie would never have given up his son without a fight and that meant she might already be hurt or incapacitated. He doubted Eileen, even with her aunt's help, could have taken Sue down without some sort of weapon.

As he reached in his pocket for the Colt and thumbed back the cylinder release, he made sure every hole was filled and each of those cartridges showed a live primer. He had checked this before leaving home, of course, but this was his way of thinking when stressed; the easy things first, leaving his subconscious to sort out the rest. When the time came, he would react with the deadly decisiveness that comes only from the primordial cortex of one's brain.

All the while, and at the outer edge of his thinking: *Who, was in the flatbed truck hiding up the road...and where is that person?* Given what he knew now, could the answer be more obvious?

Harley took a deep breath and held it as he flung open the door, gun poised to confront Eileen May—she was the dangerous one—and despite all, she was the one he might have to shoot. She had crossed the line when she took his son, and he would deal with her now on that basis alone—and in terms she could understand. The safety of Sue and the baby would depend on how quickly he settled with Eileen May.

"He has a gun!" Mary Chano's warning could be heard even through the windshield.

Probably what saved Eileen's life in those last seconds, was her instinctive reaction. Still gazing back down the road and caught by surprise, she instantly threw up her hands. Seeing it was Harley Ponyboy she did—for just an instant—consider going for the gun lying next to her on the seat. She was immobilized by Harley instantly leaning into his revolver; sights centered in the middle of her forehead. It was Harley's face that stopped her—there was not the slightest sign of recognition in his eyes. This was a person she didn't know and one who felt absolutely nothing for her. It was a look she would never forget and one that left her knowing for certain the game was finished. That the man was on the verge of killing her was so obvious everyone in the car flinched and drew back...except for Little Harley who, raising his chubby hands to his father, laughed and called out in his own language.

Mary Chano let a hand flutter to her mouth, the other already raised to shield the baby. Then clenching both eyes shut the older woman began to pray.

Eileen, at first nearly paralyzed, became hypnotized by the black hole staring back at her, and came to the realization she was at last looking through a porthole to eternity. She, too, then shut her eyes and gritted her teeth. Only peeking as Harley Ponyboy jerked open the door—grabbing her arm he pulled her from the car. As she was dragged across the seat a pistol clattered to the ground and went skittering just under the edge of the car. Still holding Eileen by the arm, Harley scooped up the fallen gun and slipped the weapon into his back pocket before motioning Mary Chano to give him the boy— which in her terror she did, and so abruptly the boy almost slid past him. With Little Harley now in hand he pushed Eileen to the ground and nudged her away from the car, telling her if she moved, he meant to kill her before she could take another breath. Never had Harley Ponyboy addressed another human in such a way.

Gathering up his son he ordered Eileen's aunt out of the car, warning her with his eyes not to move. Opening the rear door, Harley saw Sue Yazzie bound and gagged, still looking a little dazed and unsure. She had never seen Harley in so deadly a rage and not sure he wouldn't lay a portion of the blame on her.

Seeing Sue apparently unharmed but for a large purple bruise above her left eye, Harley asked her to lean his way and removed the gag.

She shifted closer, whispering how sorry she was for letting someone take Little Harley from her. "I was outside the grocery and putting the baby in the truck when this woman, acting like she wanted directions or something, walked up and slammed me across the face with a gun. I went down not knowing what happened, and when I came around, I was already shoved into the back seat of this car and tied up."

Now confident Mary Chano was no longer a threat, yet keeping an eye on Eileen, Harley Ponyboy whispered back, "Everything is gonna' be all right now, Sue, none of this is your fault. I know you did your best."

Glaring down at Eileen, Sue Yazzie flipped her hair to one side. "I told her she wouldn't get away with this." Seeing the woman was silently crying, she looked away but without a trace of pity. With a grim smile Sue offered her hands to be untied. Rubbing her wrists for a moment, she held out her arms for the baby and was both gratified and reassured when the still frazzled Harley Ponyboy passed his son over without the slightest hesitation.

He then motioned the other two women up to the trailer door. Sue followed behind, hugging the baby to her, and when everyone was inside, watched as Harley ordered Eileen and her aunt to take a seat at each end of the long couch.

Harley and Sue Yazzie took chairs at the kitchen table directly across from the women. Little Harley was unusually quiet, subdued by the somber look of the adults. The baby put his head on Sue's shoulder and hid his eyes as she rocked him back and forth, wishing she knew where her husband was, but knowing Charlie was by now, likely wondering the same about her.

Eileen's aunt spoke, finally, cautiously and in a tired voice, "I only come down here to help Eileen with the baby. She told me she left Robert for good but didn't have a car or anyplace to go. She told me she was feeling better now and well enough she wanted Little Harley back." Mary looked at her niece…more sad than angry. "She didn't tell me I'd be helping to kidnap this baby, or that she was going to demand money for some 'permanent custody papers' as she called it. She didn't say any of that until it was too late. I had no choice but to go along with it then." Mary didn't look directly at Eileen when she said these things, and her niece remained silent, not disputing any part of it.

Eileen raised her head to glare at Sue Yazzie and then glanced disdainfully at Harley as though *he'd* betrayed *her*. Finally, she blurted out, "I didn't want any harm to come to our baby, Harley. I only wanted to make an agreement that would be in his best interest…for his future, you know."

Nodding, Harley said in a low voice. "You already did that when you left him out there at your cousins' in Kaibito. I could see then how interested you were in his future." Harley's words cut like a knife even for someone as hardened as Eileen May. The woman looked away and pretended not to notice as Sue Yazzie cuddled the baby, whispering and comforting him and when Harley wasn't looking, she sent Sue a dark glance which promised reprisal.

Still holding the gun on the two women, Harley wasn't sure he believed Mary Chano's confession—but, definitely did not believe Eileen, not that it mattered much anymore. He watched the pair like a hawk, unsure yet what to do with them. Mary's little confession hadn't made things any easier. Thankfully, in the end, her fate wouldn't be up to him.

Harley's greatest fear now was that Robert Maldone was out there somewhere. He was convinced of it and could almost feel the man taking his time, waiting his chance to swoop down on them. Maldone wouldn't be coming just for the money now, he would be bent on revenge against everyone there, maybe even the boy.

The wind, gusting to a fevered pitch fairly whistled down the wash, sandblasting the old trailer down to the aluminum and rattling the tin roof panels as it howled its way across the sage flats to the highway now drifted in furrows of sand.

Harley Ponyboy had seen a lot of windstorms in his years there but none so powerful as this. He thought of the anchor cables securing the old trailer in place and couldn't help wondering... *would they hold*? He had set those anchors deep, looped them around the frame and clamped them tight. Still the trailer swayed in the gusts and occasionally, he thought he could feel it lift slightly on the windward side as though on the verge of going over. He looked at Sue and saw she felt it, too, and worried for the baby who clung to her, wide awake now, but again hiding his face in her shoulder. The boy's eyes, when he peeked out, were round with fear.

Harley shifted in his chair and realized he still had the small-frame semi-auto in his back pocket—the one Eileen dropped getting out of the car. He brought it out and blew the dust from the action. Having no experience with a pistol of this type he wasn't sure how to check if it was even loaded. He could see it had a clip and pushed and prodded its release until finally it ejected, and he could see it had cartridges in it. Still, he was uncertain if there was one in the chamber. He caught Mary Chano eyeing him as he shoved the clip back into place.

Mary said, "That's my pistol, my husband bought it and gave it to me for my protection only a few years before he died. I don't know if bullets get old or not, but that gun hasn't been messed with for a long time. He taught me how to shoot it back then, but I never needed to so far." Mary watched Harley study the gun and, becoming impatient, she said, "You have to push down that little latch on the slide to put one in the chamber. Pull the slide back hard and let it go quick to load one in."

Harley considered this…figuring it out finally, then returned to her question. "No, I never heard of bullets getting old. I have myself shot .22 shells I knew were ten, or even twenty years old, and they would kill a rabbit as good as any." Pointing the pistol at the floor, he pulled back the slide and then released it to see a round slapped into the chamber. He looked doubtfully at the gun. "I hope we don't need this thing, but if we do, I guess we'll find out if it works or not."

Eileen was watching, too, and realized now she wouldn't have known it wasn't ready to fire and was lucky she didn't throw down on Harley with it. She wondered if Mary had neglected to tell her this part on purpose. She didn't bother looking at the woman, deciding it didn't matter at this point.

Harley caught Eileen looking his way and asked calmly, "Where's Maldone? What sort of rig is he driving?"

Eileen stared a moment it was clear the question would require an answer. "I don't know. I don't think I was followed. He was driving an old black Ford flatbed, last I saw…it had a stock-rack on it, but they are easy to take off, it may not have one now. Robert comes by his rides easy and doesn't keep them long."

Harley nodded at this and said, "You were followed, all right." And with a sweep of his hand to the south declared, "He's out there somewhere, right now." Then he turned and leaned across the table to whisper to Sue Yazzie, "I'm going to have to go looking for this guy before *he* comes to us. I can maybe keep you and little Harley out of it that way." He slid the pistol over to her. "That little button under the trigger guard is the safety, just push it in and hold tight to the grips when you pull the trigger." He looked her in the eye and murmured apologetically, "I don't expect you'll have ta use this, but if have to, don't hesitate…shoot." Throwing a quick glance at the other two women, he asked her, "Can you keep an eye on those two over there, Sue…can you do that for me, do you think?"

Sue had gone with Charlie a few times to shoot his revolver. She knew the basics, and at point blank range had every confidence she could do what had to be done. "I'll watch them, Harley, you don't have to worry about that."

Chewing at his bottom lip, Harley hesitated a moment before going on, "If it happens that I don't come back, do not unlock this door for anyone else. Shoot right through the door if you have to. It looks like there's five, maybe six, rounds left in that clip so try to count your shots. That can be important."

As Sue realized what he was saying her eyes widened. Swallowing hard, she nodded firmly, not quite trusting herself to speak.

Harley tousled the sleeping baby's hair, then moving over to the back door he buttoned his jacket as he gave the two women on the couch a warning look. Locking the door behind him he let himself out in so strong a gust he nearly lost his balance and had to raise a hand to shield his face from wind driven grit. It felt like the temperature had dropped another twenty degrees.

Holding tight to the railing he made his way off the deck and stood a full minute listening to the wind, trying to find some rhythm to the gusts. He knew exactly where everything on the place was located…that should be a big advantage. He had left his hat behind knowing it would require one hand just to keep it on his head. His handkerchief was around his neck and he now pulled this up and over his nose to just below his eyes.

Looking in the direction of his old mule shed, which he knew to be less than forty yards away, he could not make out so much as an outline of the structure. It was hard for him to believe a man like Maldone would be out there in these miserable conditions…not when he could hole up in a nice warm truck until he was ready to make his move.

The man could be anywhere between here and the old *hogan* nearly a mile down the highway. By now the blowing dirt and sand would have covered any sign of his passing. Maldone, not knowing the country and with no better option, would probably opt to drive as near the trailer as he dared, then slip in afoot to catch them unaware. *Charlie Yazzie said this Indian was tough, and smarter than most people, too.* Harley didn't doubt any of this but in his current frame of mind no longer cared. He slipped out to the far end of the old trailer to peer off down the one-lane track to the highway, thinking he might at least be warned by a chance glow of headlights given that Maldone would almost certainly have to use them at some point.

After a few minutes watching, and not seeing or hearing anything in that direction, Harley returned to the edge of the wash and again used the bed of his truck to climb down into the arroyo. Turning in the direction of the highway he figured he'd better circle around and come in behind Maldone, rather than meet him head on and be caught in the open during a lull and possibly spotted. There was a feeder gully only a hundred yards away—too steep and narrow to get a truck up—yet it might allow a man on foot to climb his way out and surprise the man where he least expected it then settle with him once and for all.

It didn't take long to reach the gully, but only half-way to the top he came upon a place where a large rock had recently been dislodged and that stopped him cold; it was a big rock and would have taken something big to kick it loose. It suddenly occurred to him he might already be too late—Robert Maldone might have somehow found his way down into the wash ahead of him, slipped past in the darkening storm.

That was the other thing Charlie had said about the man. "Fred says he's blessed with an inordinate amount of luck in everything he does." Maldone could already be on his way to the trailer. Harley was sure of it now and the thought was so overpowering he was convinced to whirl and make his way back down the cut. Half-way down his haste got the better of him; he slipped and lost his footing, clutching and sliding his way to the bottom where he hit his head on a sandstone outcrop.

Harley came to his senses not knowing how long he had lain there in the dirt, stunned and trying to gather his wits.

Finally, taking a deep breath, he rose and managed to take off in an unsteady dogtrot. Head pounding, he pushed directly into the storm, with only the fear in his gut to keep him on his feet. *What a fool I been ta let the threat of this man rattle me like this.*

It had seemed the right thing to do, meeting this danger head on and out here where he held every advantage—thinking it was the surest way to protect his child and Sue.

There in the wash the howling, dirt-filled wind made for a gloomy and treacherous passage. Remaining staunch even in the face of a growing dread he couldn't help wondering *Am I too late?*

He had underestimated the man.

20

Retribution

Robert Maldone came without warning, fierce and filled with rage, hitting the back door with the full weight of his shoulder splintering the casing and sending debris across the room and up against the kitchen table.

In terror, Sue instinctively turned away, shielding the baby from flying glass even as she thought of the loaded pistol on the table.

Maldone, his own pistol in his right hand, saw the threat immediately and made a dive for the gun only a split second ahead of Sue Yazzie's desperate bid for the weapon.

Seeing the weapon was lost to her, Sue instinctively dropped to the floor, shutting her eyes and shielding little Harley with her body, she shuddered at the thought of how close to death they were.

Seeing this, Eileen leaped from the couch with an oath, tackled Robert from behind, taking him to his knees and causing Sue's pistol to be thrown from his tenuous grip.

Mary Chano though nearly paralyzed with fear, came alive then and driven by concern for her niece and the child, rolled off the couch to scoop up the gun. Clicking off the safety she hesitated, fearful she might hit her niece—yet in the line of fire.

Robert, struggling to get up, drove an elbow into Eileen's ribs, knocking her behind him and against the couch. He then half-turned to deal with Mary Chano—but too late. Mary, merely feet away, had only to point and shoot and this time did not hesitate. Firing twice in quick succession she saw the first shot was a solid hit, but the second barely grazed his ribs. Trembling and stunned by her own action, Mary let the pistol dangle uselessly as though in disbelief of what she'd done yet hoping it would be enough.

Maldone had taken a smashing hit to the right shoulder, the bullet shattering both bone and nerves. He was now bleeding a steady stream and appeared stunned, unable bring his weapon to bear. Struggling to overcome an overpowering wave of nausea, he attempted to transfer the gun to his good hand.

Eileen reached over and wrested the pistol from her aunt's hand just as Robert finally managed to switch hands and raised his pistol in a frenzy of determination. Eileen and Robert fired at virtually the same instant, each taking a grievous hit in the process.

Eileen, trying to stand, fell back on the couch, the pistol still clutched tightly in one hand, she looked silently down at her shirt front and watched as bright and frothy blood bubbled from the little hole above her diaphragm.

Robert, weaving unsteadily on his feet, looked down to feel a vicious burning pain, as digestive acid, and worse…began leaking into his body cavity feeling like shards of glass in his intestines. In a red haze he seemed to remember an old Apache relative once saying that back before the whites came, his ancestors—be it with lance or arrow, or knife—tried always to aim for the gut. Nothing was more painfully debilitating. And, though an enemy so injured might linger on for days, such a wound was nearly always fatal. If the trauma itself didn't kill them the sepsis or infection eventually would.

Robert lowered himself to the floor and with his back to the wall, looked across at Eileen and could make out a curious little half-smile as she watched him struggle to remain conscious. She seemed almost at peace then, and somehow even satisfied with the fate she'd brought upon herself. Neither attempted to speak, nor did anyone else in the room, there wasn't a sound, even from the baby.

The thud of footsteps running up the back stairs caused Sue to look up just as Harley Ponyboy bolted through the shattered door. He assessed the situation at a glance, instantly drawing down on Robert Maldone, who had already dropped his weapon, and bent over in pain grappled with the sickness of death.

Harley looked then to Sue and saw her nod that she and the baby were all right. Turning his gun to Eileen he watched her open her eyes to peer, as through a mist, smiling weakly up at him. It was a different smile from that she'd given Maldone. There was no malice in it and she only shrugged slightly as her eyes began glaze, no longer able to stay open she slowly closed them for the last time.

Mary Chano moved next to her niece and sat cradling Eileen in her arms, staring past everyone else as though it were just the two of them there alone.

Sue Yazzie half-rose as she took the baby into her arms. Keeping him turned from the room, she sat rocking him there on the floor murmuring a little song in Navajo. The child had neither cried nor called out during the ordeal, and Sue thought this must have been the way it was back in the times her people were at war and was glad he'd seen nothing of what happened. She could only hope there would be no lasting effect from the ordeal.

Harley hadn't taken his eyes off Maldone even as the color drained from the man's face....he watched grimly as he breathed his last without ever opening his eyes. And only then was Harley able to take a full and calming breath.

21

Requiem

Charlie pushed back his hat and took a deep breath as he led everyone from the hearing room.

Mary Chano being the only survivor to have done any actual shooting had, with the testimony of Harley and Sue—and surprisingly even a good word from Agent Fred Smith—been exonerated. The woman left for home with the hope, she said, that her being duped into Eileen's scheme, would not prevent Harley from letting her see her nephew from time to time.

Harley, knowing that without the woman's quick action in firing that first round they might all be dead, agreed to think it over—knowing in his heart, he couldn't refuse Mary this last link to Eileen.

Charlie, as much surprised as anyone by Fred's support of the woman, wondered if it might not have something to do with the information Eileen's Aunt had afforded the Bureau Agents when first they called on her in Utah.

Fred had never revealed what that information was and had skirted any questions on the subject. Charlie had to believe the Agent might himself be under some

'Privileged Information' mandate and unable to say anything.

He and Thomas had discussed the situation several times over the past week. Charlie recalled Fred had seemingly been on the verge of divulging something on that fateful day they'd parted company at the Fair Grounds in Window Rock. In any case, he intended to ask again when the two met later with Tribal Officer Billy Red Clay, "For an interagency evaluation of the case," he'd said.

Having Robert Maldone off their priority list would lift a heavy burden from everyone's mind. Eileen May no longer being a threat to the Ponyboy family would also be a welcome relief.

Fred Smith's only regret was that Eileen's part in the long-ago Benny Klee murder would now most likely never be known.

Rather than wait around for her husband's meeting to be over Sue decided to ride home with Harley and the baby. Thomas was to meet them at Harley's for dinner later. Lucy Tallwoman and her father, along with Thomas's children, would be there as well.

Sue and Lucy Tallwoman would be preparing the food at Harley's due to his more spacious accommodations.

Harley himself was getting into the swing of entertaining and enjoyed showing his appreciation for his friend's past favors with his own brand of hospitality, which often included a small gift at each place setting.

~~~~~~

Charlie ran by his office to again look over the files on Robert Maldone and Eileen May. He wanted to have it all straight in his mind before the meeting. Driving the short distance over to Tribal, he was surprised to see Fred's government car already there and checking his watch saw he was a little early. Not wanting to interrupt, he stopped a moment for a word with the duty officer whom he had not previously met. After introducing themselves the two chatted a minute as a matter of courtesy after which the man directed him back to Billy's new office. *Everyone seems to be moving up in the world these days, and all of them so young, too.* He sighed then, smiling, as he remembered Billy's converted-stockroom office of only the year before. The young Liaison Officer had come a long way from his days as a patrolman. Charlie was proud to have had a part in that, pleased he could contribute a little mentoring to Thomas's nephew along the way.

The door was open, and the other two lawmen grinned and looked up as he came in. Billy pointed to a seat as Fred scooted his chair over a smidge to make room. The office was twice the size of his old one, but so were the desk and the overstuffed chairs handed down from the Captain's office, which made the room seem not as spacious as it might have been.

Billy was first to speak, "Agent Smith was just filling me in on more backstory in the double homicide out at Harley's old place last week. Uncle Thomas said you two only missed out on it by less than thirty minutes."

"That's about right, we were only guessing when we decided Harley might be out there. As it turns out we were a little late with that thought." The Investigator smiled ruefully. "Harley had things pretty much in hand by the time we arrived. We'd have been even later if that storm hadn't laid down when it did. I don't know that I've ever seen a worse dirt-storm."

"That's what my uncle said, too." Billy wasn't smiling when he continued. "I'd have gone out there with you boys...if I'd known. I called over to your office not two hours before...left a message with Arlene for you to call me. I never heard back."

"Things were happening pretty quick that day, Billy, I guess I dropped the ball."

The Policeman's face broke into a grin, "Well, it sounds like it was a long dirty ride for nothing anyhow...so probably just as well."

Fred Smith spoke for the first time. "Do Harley and the boy seem to be doing all right, would you say?"

"Yes, they are. That baby's a lot like his father. Nothing seems to bother either one of them for long." Charlie waited hoping Fred would mention Mary Chano. Which might allow him to bring up a few of his own questions. But he didn't and changed the subject without giving Charlie an opportunity to ask.

Fred, leafing through some papers, said, "I did get the reports back from the lab on that waitress that was killed over in Window Rock—that had to be Maldone. The coroner seemed certain she was killed with the same knife Forensics later found in that flatbed Ford down the road from Harley's old place. That, and because the restaurant owner, identified Maldone as the man he'd seen chatting the woman up only the day before, it's pretty much a lock it was his work—despite the sloppy job. And, too, there's always the chance he did it that way on purpose, to throw us off. In any case the man's a done deal now."

Charlie nodded and looked down at his fingernails a moment, adding, "The sad thing is we'll probably never know what he did with those other women...or where they are now."

"No, but we know a lot more about him than we did before and have a pretty good timeline of where he's been these last few years. Our people think some of those times and places coincide with a number of disappearances. It will all be archived as a cold case file. Someday there may be a way to match him up to some of those murders. Technology is a wonderful thing and developing at an amazing rate. I just hope we're still around to see how it all plays out." The Agent sounded so sure of this Billy Red Clay sat wide-eyed as he listened. Charlie happy to see the young Policeman was a believer in a brighter future for his work and secretly hoped Fred Smith was right. Maybe Billy, at least, would someday see all these things come to pass.

Tribal Police, in conjunction with the FBI, had been working up a list of women on the reservation who'd gone missing over the last few years, and had become convinced each of these cases should remain open and not forgotten. Billy wanted to have a hand in in these cases even if he had to work them on his own time. He felt he could go about it in a way the FBI couldn't— Navajo to Navajo and in their own language. He swore to himself he would continue those investigations even if it took the rest of his life. And like Charlie and his Uncle Thomas, Billy wasn't one to give up once he had his teeth in a thing.

The men talked a while longer, going over various and probable scenarios in the two cases, and were finally beginning to wind down when Billy received a 'priority' call. The Policeman shrugged at the pair, indicating he would be tied up for a while. The other two, nodding to each other in agreement, mouthed a goodbye and with a wave, headed for the door.

Out in the parking lot Fred followed the Investigator over to his truck and Charlie knew this was the time to ask those questions that had gone unanswered in the meeting.

Charlie didn't get more than a couple of sentences out of his mouth before the FBI man raised a finger. "That's what I'm here to tell you, Charlie. That file was sealed until today, but I'm at liberty now to fill you in on a few things our Agents up in Utah uncovered regarding Mary Chano and her niece. The information is still considered confidential as far as the Bureau is concerned, but I am at least now able to divulge some of it at my own discretion."

Pointing to the passenger door, Charlie grinned, "Step into my mobile office, Fred, it's getting damned cold out here in the wind."

Chuckling to himself, the FBI man, went around the front of the truck; settling himself in the passenger seat, he wasted no time in presenting his case. "First off, Charlie, I want you to know I wasn't happy about withholding any of this from you, but it's the way the Bureau wanted it, and at the time I had very little say in the matter. Now, however, you can feel free to let Harley Ponyboy in on as much of this as you think wise." Then taking a deep breath the Agent began. "Charlie, Mary Chano wasn't Eileen's aunt… She was her mother." The Agent paused to let this sink in. "The father was her sister's husband from when Mary went to live with them, several years before Eileen was born. That's why the sister wanted nothing to do with Mary, or Eileen. Mary Chano raised the girl, ostensibly as her aunt and clan mother. It not only fit the traditional pattern of Navajo clan duty, but also protected her and the child from being further ostracized." Fred paused and watched to make sure Charlie was taking all this in.

"So, you're saying Mary Chano is actually Little Harley's grandmother…?

Fred took his time replying. "Yes, that's the way it is according to Mary, and our investigation, including hospital records, birth certificate, and so on, all confirm that to be the case." The FBI man picked a piece of lint from his jacket and held it up to the light for a moment before flicking it away. "I'm hoping none of this information will be a problem for Harley, or his son, and in time, might even help put things in a better perspective." The FBI man paused before going on as though wanting his next words to be clearly understood.

"In fact, the only caveat, as far as I can see, would be if something should happen to Harley. The boy's next of kin would then be Mary Chano, who as his grandmother would be in line to inherit custodial right of the boy—and possibly even become executor of his father's estate. I'm not saying Mary couldn't handle it, but when I questioned her about this, she told me she's having health problems herself and should it come down to it, wasn't sure she would be able to care for the boy." Fred was obviously troubled by the thought of this and watched for some sign of how Charlie felt. "Of course, should some other arrangement be made by Harley beforehand—that would be a different story altogether.

Charlie agreed as he looked out toward the power plant on the banks of the San Juan. Dense grey smoke flowed almost horizontally from the tall stacks sending the nostalgic odor of coal as far as the town itself. The Investigator took a breath reminiscent of his childhood, knowing someday this would all be replaced by something cleaner and better for the children growing up here on the *Dinétah*. He didn't know what would take the place of coal, but there would be something.

He turned back to the conversation with a simple statement, "Harley mentioned to my wife, that should anything happen to him, he would like for us to have the boy. I may as well tell you now, Fred, Harley already has me listed as executor of his estate and should it ever come to that…he wants us to take the boy and raise him as our own. We signed the papers only yesterday. Harley's been a part of our family for years now, and Sue grows fonder of his son each day. I don't expect any of this will ever come about, but if it's a comfort for him to think he's safeguarded the boy in this way, then we are happy to oblige."

Fred nodded at this, as though he himself felt easier now about the boy's future.

The two men smiled as they shook hands and parted company.

Addendum

These stories hearken back to a slightly more traditional time on the reservation, and while the places and culture are real, the characters and their names are fictitious. Any resemblance to actual persons living or dead is purely coincidental.

~~~~~~~

Though this book is a work of fiction, a concerted effort was made to maintain the accuracy of the culture and characters of that time and place. There are many scholarly tomes written by anthropologists, ethnologists, and learned laymen regarding the Navajo culture. On the subject of language and spelling, they often do not agree. When no consensus was apparent, we have relied upon "local knowledge."

Many changes have come to the *Dinè*—some of them good—some, not so much. These are the Navajo I remember. I think you may like them.

ABOUT THE AUTHOR

R. Allen Chappell is the author of ten novels and a collection of short stories. Growing up in New Mexico he spent a good portion of his life at the edge of the *Diné Bikeyah*, went to school with the Navajo, and later worked alongside them. He lives in Western Colorado where he continues to pursue a lifelong interest in the prehistory of the Four Corners region and its people, and still spends a good bit of his time there.

For the curious, the author's random thoughts on each book of the series are listed below in the order of their release.

Navajo Autumn

It was not my original intent to write a series, but this first book was so well received, and with many readers asking for another, I felt compelled to write a sequel—after that there was no turning back. And, while I must admit this first one was fun to write, I'm sure I made every mistake a writer can possibly make in a first novel. I did, however, have the advantage of a dedicated little group of detractors quick to point out its deficiencies…and I thank them. Without their help, this first book would doubtless have languished and eventually fallen into the morass…and there would be no series.

Navajo Autumn was the first in the genre to include a glossary of Navajo words and terms. Readers liked this feature so well I've made certain each subsequent book had one. This book has, over the years, been through many editions and updates. No book is perfect and this one keeps me grounded.

Boy Made of Dawn

A sequel I very much enjoyed writing and one that drew many new fans to the series. So many, in fact, I quit my day job to pursue writing these stories full-time—not a course I would ordinarily recommend to an author new to the process. In this instance, however, it proved to be the right move. As I learn, I endeavor to make each new book a little better...and to keep their prices low enough that people like me can afford to read them. That's important.

Ancient Blood

The third book in the series and the initial flight into the realm of the Southwestern archaeology I grew up with. This book introduces Harley Ponyboy: a character that quickly carved out a major niche for himself in the stories that followed. Harley remains the favorite of reservation readers to this day. Also debuting in this novel was Professor George Armstrong Custer, noted archaeologist and Charlie Yazzie's professor at UNM. George, too, has a pivotal role in some of the later books.

Mojado

This book was a departure in subject matter; cover art, and the move to thriller status. A fictional story built around a local tale heard in Mexico many years ago. In the first three months following its release, this book sold more copies, and faster, than any of my previous books. It's still a favorite.

Magpie Speaks

A mystery/thriller that goes back to the beginning of the series and exposes the past of several major characters—some of whom play key roles in later books and are favorites of Navajo friends who follow these stories.

Wolves of Winter

As our readership attained a solid position in the genre, I determined to tell the story I had, for many years, envisioned. I am pleased with this book's success on several levels, and in very different genres. I hope one day to revisit this story in one form or another.

The Bible Seller

Yet another cultural departure for the series; Harley Ponyboy again wrests away the starring role. A story of attraction and deceit against a backdrop of wanton murder and reservation intrigue—it has fulfilled its promise to become a Canyonland's favorite.

Day of the Dead

Book Eight in the series, and promised follow-up to #1 bestseller, Mojado. Luca Tarango's wife returns to take Luca's remains back to Mexico and inveigles Legal Services Investigator Charlie Yazzie to see that she and Luca's ashes get there for the Mexican holy day.

The Collector

Book Nine in the series brings most of the original characters into play, but centers around Lucy Tallwoman. The murder of her agent causes her life to spiral out of control as unseen forces seek to take over the lucrative Native Arts trade.

Falling Girl

This book was somewhat of a milestone for the series, both as the tenth book, and as a story generated by thoughts and emails from long time followers of the series. The redoubtable Harley Ponyboy once again comes front and center, as he seeks to renew a lost infatuation with a woman so reviled by his fellow characters...and by our readers, apparently, that they have called for another shot at the woman. Who can say what lies in store for poor Harley this time around...

From the Author

Readers may be pleased to know they can preview selected audio editions of the series on their book pages. Our Audio books can also be found featured in public libraries, on Audible, and Tantor Audio Books and, of course, in many retail outlets. There are more to come. Kaipo Schwab, an accomplished actor and storyteller, narrates the first five audio books. I am pleased Kaipo felt these books worthy of his considerable talent. I hope you like these reservation adventures as much as we enjoy bringing them to you.

~~~~~~

The author calls Western Colorado home where he continues to pursue a lifelong interest in the prehistory of the Four Corners region and its people. We remain available to answer questions, and welcome your comments at: rachappell@yahoo.com

If you've enjoyed this latest story, please consider going to its Amazon book page to leave a short review. It takes only a moment and would be most appreciated.

Glossary

1. *Adááníí* — undesirable, alcoholic etc.

2. *Acheii* — Grandfather *

3. *Ashki Ana'dlohi* — Laughing boy

4. *A-hah-la'nih* — affectionate greeting*

5. *Billigaana* — white people

6. *Ch'ihónit't* — a spirit path flaw in art.

7. *Chindi* — (or *chinde*) Spirit of the dead *

8. *Diné* — Navajo people

9. *Diné Bikeyah* — Navajo country

10. *Diyin dine'é* —Holy people

11. *Hataalii* — Shaman (Singer)*

12. *Hastiin* — (Hosteen) Man or Mr. *

13. *Hogan* — (Hoogahn) dwelling or house

14. *Hozo* — To walk in beauty *

15. *Ma'ii* — Coyote

16. *Shimásáni* — Grandmother

17. Shizhé'é — Father *

18. *Tsé Bii' Ndzisgaii* — Monument Valley

19. *Yaa' eh t'eeh* — Common Greeting—Hello

20. *Yeenaaldiooshii* — Skinwalker, witch*

21. *Yóó'a'háaskahh* —One who is lost

Notes

1. *Acheii* — Grandfather. There are several words for Grandfather depending on how formal the intent and the gender of the speaker.

2. *Aa'a'ii* — Long known as a trickster or "thief of little things." It is thought Magpie can speak and sometimes brings messages from the beyond.

4. *A-hah-la'nih* — A greeting: affectionate version of *Yaa' eh t'eeh*, generally only used among family and close friends.

7. *Chindi* — When a person dies inside a *hogan*, it is said that his *chindi* or spirit could remain there forever, causing the *hogan* to be abandoned. *Chindi* are not considered benevolent entities. For the traditional Navajo, just speaking a dead person's name may call up his *chindi* and cause harm to the speaker or others.

11. *Hataalii* — Generally known as a "Singer" among the *Diné*, they are considered "Holy Men" and have apprenticed to older practitioners sometimes for many years—to learn the ceremonies. They make the sand paintings that are an integral part of the healing and know the many songs that must be sung in the correct order.

12. *Hastiin* — The literal translation is "man" but is often considered the word for "Mr." as well. "Hosteen" is the usual version Anglos use.

14. *Hozo* — For the Navajo, "*hozo*" (sometimes *hozoji*) is a general state of well-being, both physical and spiritual, that indicates a certain "state of grace," which is referred to as "walking in beauty." Illness or depression is the usual cause of loss of *Hozo,* which could put one out of sync with the people as a whole. There are ceremonies to restore *Hozo* and return the ailing person to a oneness with the people.

15. *Ma'ii* — The Coyote is yet another reference to one of several Navajo tricksters. The word is sometimes used in a derogatory sense or as a curse word.

18. *Shizhé'é* — (or *Shih-chai)* There are several words for "Father," depending on the degree of formality intended and sometimes even the gender of the speaker.

20. *Yeenaaldiooshii* — These witches, as they are often referred to, are the chief source of evil or fear in traditional Navajo superstitions. They are thought to be capable of many unnatural acts, such as flying or turning themselves into werewolves and other ethereal creatures; hence the term Skinwalkers, referring to their ability to change forms or skins.